Would a man who could be so gentle and patient *hurt* her?

Rowan stole a sidelong look at Niall. He hadn't seemed interested in her that way at all, although a few times she'd seen flickers of expression that had made her wonder.

"What if I come with you Friday?" he asked.

"You're serious."

"I'm serious."

Probably, she should make some polite disclaimer, but…he wouldn't have offered if he hadn't meant it, would he? "I would love it if you could come."

"We'll leave by 7:00 a.m.?"

"Ugh. Yes."

He laughed. "Sleep tight."

How wonderful it was to be smiling when she slipped back into the house. Feeling relief and joy and, yes, trepidation, because why *was* he being so nice? But, oh, she was so grateful that he was.

He was the kind of man she could—

No! Don't even think it. Not happening.

But she still felt happy. And yes, Niall MacLachlan was the reason why.

Dear Reader,

When I first imagined a hero who played the bagpipe, I envisioned him in a kilt, the dagger thrust in his kneesock. I was influenced, I think, by the commonly known and melancholy history of the pipers stirring the Scots to fight and die at the Battle of Culloden in 1748.

What I didn't know until I started doing some research was that the bagpipes have a far more ancient lineage than the eighteenth century. Ancient Greek writings dating to fifth century B.C. mention bagpipes. Emperor Nero of Rome may have played a form of bagpipe.

But maybe more significant, I hadn't given a lot of thought to what the music sounds like. Or perhaps I had, and just didn't know it. Because Niall MacLachlan was made to play the bagpipe. He mentions at one point playing the lament at a policeman's funeral. The music he plays fits this man, expresses the hurt he's held inside his whole life. He's never admitted to himself how lonely he is, but he chooses to play music that will haunt the listener long after the bagpipe has fallen silent. He turns out to be an extraordinary man who has never dealt with childhood grief. This is one way he can express it while also holding on to one of his few good memories: his father teaching him to play the bagpipes.

Oh, I love heroes like Niall! And I love to torment them, too. I asked myself what kind of woman would be his worst nightmare, and there was Rowan—a young, single mother who is suddenly his landlady living in close proximity. A woman who has a good deal of pride but clearly needs help. Who brings with her two annoying kids and an even more annoying dog. Who steals his peace, and threatens the life he's chosen for himself.

I hope you fall as deeply in love with Niall as I did.

Janice Kay Johnson

PS—I enjoy hearing from readers! Please contact me c/o Harlequin Books, 225 Duncan Mill Road, Don Mills, ON M3B 3K9, Canada.

From Father to Son
Janice Kay Johnson

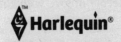

TORONTO NEW YORK LONDON
AMSTERDAM PARIS SYDNEY HAMBURG
STOCKHOLM ATHENS TOKYO MILAN MADRID
PRAGUE WARSAW BUDAPEST AUCKLAND

Recycling programs
for this product may
not exist in your area.

ISBN-13: 978-0-373-60688-7

FROM FATHER TO SON

ABOUT THE AUTHOR

The author of more than sixty books for children and adults, Janice Kay Johnson writes Harlequin Superromance novels about love and family—about the way generations connect and the power our earliest experiences have on us throughout life. Her 2007 novel *Snowbound* won a RITA® Award from Romance Writers of America for Best Contemporary Series Romance. A former librarian, Janice raised two daughters in a small rural town north of Seattle, Washington. She loves to read and is an active volunteer and board member for Purrfect Pals, a no-kill cat shelter.

Books by Janice Kay Johnson

HARLEQUIN SUPERROMANCE

HARLEQUIN ANTHOLOGIES

SIGNATURE SELECT SAGA

*Lost…But Not Forgotten
†The Russell Twins
**A Brother's Word

Other titles by this author available in ebook format.

PROLOGUE

NIALL MACLACHLAN LAY on the narrow, hard bunk in his cell in the juvenile detention center and stared at the ceiling. This place was a shit hole. He was bored. He should've taken a book from the library cart in the rec room earlier. He hadn't wanted to look like some kind of nerd, though, so he'd played ping pong and watched part of a Mariners game even though he thought baseball was a stupid sport. But now he was alone, even though there were two bunks. Eventually, if he stuck around, they'd throw someone else in with him. Other times he'd been in juvie, he'd had a roommate.

He couldn't believe he was still here. He'd spent the past two days trying not to think about whether Mom really meant it when she'd told the cop that she was done with Niall and that he could rot in here as far as she was concerned. Other times, she or Dad had come and gotten him. Mom especially would rag on him, and he'd slump down in his seat and tune her out. Totally out. It wasn't as if she'd actually *do* anything she threatened, like grounding him or curfews or forbidding him from seeing Tyler or Beck, who she said were bad influences on him. Niall smirked every time she said that. If anyone was the bad influence, it was *him*.

"And proud of it," he said to the ceiling.

The words sounded braver than he felt. Truthfully, the two days of silence from his mother alarmed him a little. Okay, he could see why she was mad. This wasn't the best time for him to get caught smoking a joint. Not when yesterday was Dad's sentencing. Mom was already freaked about that. But hey—anybody know what the word *hypocrite* means?

He laughed out loud. *My dad the drug dealer.* And Mom—who planned to go sit in the front row at his sentencing hearing to make some big fake showing of how Dad is a great family man—is pissed because her son was smoking a joint.

Except... Wow. Mom yelled a lot, but she came and got him anyway when the police called. Only, this time she hadn't.

Tomorrow, he told himself, pretending the anxiety balled in a greasy lump in his belly was really his stomach rebelling against the crappy food. Mom was trying to scare him, and he was mad at himself that it was working. Some.

A guy down the row started yelling and

pounding on the wall. Footsteps echoed in the corridor as a guard went to see what was happening. Eventually, the yelling escalated and there were grunts and thumps. Niall didn't pay that much attention. There were fights in here all the time, or guys flipped out because they were addicts going cold or they were afraid their mommies would be mad or who knew.

My *mom will be mad.*

So?

He rolled over to face the wall, knowing lights-out would come anytime. Someone would come and get him tomorrow for sure. All that talk about sending him to a juvenile lockup was bull. For one joint? Yeah, right. *They* were only trying to scare him, too.

Not working.

NIALL WAS EATING BREAKFAST when a guard called his name. He took another bite to show he wasn't in any hurry then lazily swung his legs over the bench seat—screwed to the ground so it couldn't be used as a weapon—and sauntered toward the impatiently waiting guard.

He was ushered to one of the small visitor rooms. It was about damn time she got here. He'd be a good little boy until she got him out, and then he'd tell her what he really thought. Niall was forming the words in his head when he saw who was sitting in one of the two chairs at the small table.

Duncan. Niall's eighteen-year-old brother, who had graduated from high school in May and was to leave for college in six weeks. A few times, Niall had thought that Duncan was already gone in every way that mattered. Spirit, heart, dreams. Only his body was left to catch up.

But now Duncan sat looking at him, his face so somber Niall felt a weird hitch of fear.

"Where's Mom?" he demanded.

"She's...gone."

Behind them, the guard left and closed the door, although he stood outside where he could watch them through the window.

Niall dropped into the other chair. "What do you mean, *gone?*"

"Dad got ten years."

Niall whispered an expletive.

"Yesterday, Mom said she's done. When I got home from work, she was already packed. She waited only long enough to talk to me. She said she can't do anything for you or Conall." Conall was the youngest MacLachlan brother, only twelve to Niall's fifteen. Con was already a major screwup.

"Gone." Niall couldn't look away from Duncan's eyes, the same shade of gray as his own. "But...we're her kids. You mean... She can't just

ditch us." His voice had been rising. At the end
it cracked.

Duncan had the strangest expression on his
face. What he said was a flat "She did."

Panic swelled in him until he could hardly
breathe.

Mommy? Daddy? I didn't mean it!

If he didn't have a parent to come and get him,
he would get locked up for a couple of months,
maybe. And then sent to a group home. And
Conall, he'd go to a foster home. Except he was
so angry, he'd get in trouble right away and then
nobody would want him. Niall could imagine
him running away, ending up a street kid.

Niall clutched his stomach and bent forward
until he was bowed over the table. "How could
she do that?"

"I don't know. I think she's been leaving for a
long time. She hasn't even tried with Conall."

Niall nodded. He'd wanted her to get mad because he had gotten thrown into juvie again, but
the truth was, Mom hadn't bothered in a long
time. Lately, when he was in trouble all she
would do was look at him with this blank expression, as if... As if she was already gone. He
hadn't known how to identify that expression,
but now he did. It was just like Duncan's. Both
of them were so out of there, they hadn't waited
until their official departure dates.

Niall struggled to speak. To sound as if this didn't matter. He didn't realize that he was rocking himself until he bumped the table with his belly. Holding himself still, he said, "So…what? You came to give me the official notification?"

"I came to take you home."

Dazed, Niall looked up. For the first time he noticed that Duncan looked older. Harder.

"What?"

His brother repeated, "I'm here to get you."

"They're releasing me to *you?*" Niall's head swiveled and he stared at the guard through the window, as if that would tell him anything.

"Yes. Here's the thing, though." Duncan paused, then snapped, "Look at me."

Niall straightened in the chair to stare in disbelief at the stranger his brother had become.

"Things are going to be different from now on. I won't put up with any of the shit Mom and Dad did. Most of your friends are history. You won't drink, you won't do drugs, you won't party. You will get your grades up to a minimum B average. You'll mow the lawn, wash dishes, cook your fair share of meals. When I tell you to do something, you will do it. Do you hear me?"

His brother's face held no compassion, no kindness, no regret. Only implacable determination.

Niall's lips formed the word, "Yes."

"If you defy me in any way, I will become your worst nightmare. Do you understand that?"

Niall nodded. He understood something wonderful and terrible at the same time. Duncan had given up his chance to leave for college. He'd given up everything, because his brothers needed him.

Niall understood something else, too. In making the decision not to abandon them, this big brother of his had changed. The frighteningly intense focus that had made Duncan valedictorian of his class and star athlete all while holding jobs and saving money for the future that had meant everything to him, that focus would now be turned on Conall and Niall. He would demand of them what he'd always demanded of himself. Perfection.

I can't do it.

Duncan's eyes had acquired a film of ice, like a winter pond. There was no love in them, only resignation and resolution so cold Niall had to repress a shiver.

He thought, *I'm going to hate him,* and then, with agony and shock, *This* is *love.* Hard as bedrock. The real deal.

The kind neither of their parents had ever given them.

CHAPTER ONE

MAYBE IF I WENT BACK to bed and started over.

Detective Niall MacLachlan looked down at the dead body sprawled on the kitchen floor and knew that no do-over was possible.

The body was not a murder victim. It was the corporeal shell of his landlady.

He attempted no resuscitation. He knew dead when he saw dead. Rigor mortis had set in. The old lady must have gotten up during the night. Niall knew she hadn't been sleeping well. Heartburn, she'd told him, but she kept nitroglycerin at hand.

This wasn't what you'd call a tragedy. Enid Cooper had turned eighty-eight in April. She'd lost two inches in height from crumbling bones and had confessed to Niall that she hurt all the time. Her worst fear had been ending up in a nursing home.

Maybe, he thought, her last emotion had been relief. He'd like to think so.

She had family who would mourn, he guessed. He didn't know them, had been careful to avoid any introductions, but he'd seen a young woman with two little kids come and go. She'd mowed the lawn this spring and summer. Niall had kept his distance, but had paused a couple of times to admire her. She was a small, curvy package with fabulous legs. She was also, however, a mother and likely a wife. He suspected she would be Enid's heir, too.

Which made Enid's decision to kick the bucket very bad news for him. He was a selfish son of a bitch to be thinking about himself right now, but he had time to kill while he waited for the appropriate authority to take over. Beyond tugging down the hem of Enid's nightgown so that her birdlike, liver-spotted legs were decently covered, there wasn't anything he could do for her.

He'd signed a new one-year lease not six weeks ago. This would be his second year living in the tiny cottage tucked on the back of the large lot, behind Enid's 1940s-era bungalow. Living here had worked out fine for him. Enid ignored him and didn't mind that he ignored her. She was deaf as a post and didn't like to be bothered with her hearing aid, which she said whined. Niall played the bagpipe. Your average landlord or landlady did not consider him an ideal tenant. Enid and he were a match made in heaven. He didn't like to think what was going to happen now.

A uniformed officer arrived and Niall explained that he'd come to check on Enid because the kitchen light wasn't on. This time of the morning, she would have long since had breakfast and tea. Enid tended to linger over her tea. He'd knocked on the back door, gotten no response and felt enough alarm he'd gone back to his cottage to get the key she had given him in case of emergency.

"I'd hate to die and not be found for so long I shrivelled up like a mummy," she'd told him. "I don't much like that idea. So if you don't see me around, feel free to check."

He could do that. She'd asked little enough of him. Rental payment once a month—which he deposited directly into her bank account as getting out was hard for her—and the understanding that he'd keep an eye on her from a distance.

Enid had been dead for a few hours, but the mortician would get his hands on her before she began serious decomposition. Niall hadn't told her that in the incessantly damp climate of the Pacific Northwest, corpses didn't dry up leatherlike. He didn't tell her that what did happen to them was a whole lot more unpleasant than mummification.

He hoped that if she was opposed to being embalmed she'd have discussed it with her family.

It was with relief that he escaped after a silent goodbye.

As luck would have it, the first person he saw when he arrived at the public safety building that housed the police department was his brother Duncan. Captain Duncan MacLachlan, only one rung below the police chief who was currently under fire for publicly making a racist remark and who was at risk for being fired. Even though Duncan was a hard-ass, he backed his officers and was known for being fair, smart and the soul of integrity. The general hope was that the city council would give the job to him, rather than hiring from outside the department.

Niall had very mixed feelings for his brother.

They were a hell of a lot closer than they'd been even a year ago, though. Duncan had mellowed when he'd fallen in love. Niall had watched the process with bemusement.

Duncan had pushed through the doors on his way out, and the two of them stepped aside so they weren't in the way of traffic. Although barely midmorning, it had to be eighty degrees already. A humid eighty degrees.

"You just getting here?"

"I found my landlady dead."

Duncan nodded without apparent surprise. "What'll that do to your lease?"

Niall grinned. Trust his big brother to hold no sentimental feelings whatsoever. Except where

Jane was concerned, of course. Niall shrugged. "I don't know. I guess I'll find out."

Rather than offering another brisk nod and continuing on his way, Duncan kept standing there. He was wearing one of the suits that made him appear more like a politician than a cop, and he had to be looking forward to the air-conditioning in that big SUV he drove. But instead of heading for it, he shifted his weight, hemmed and hawed.

"I was going to call you today," he finally said.

Niall was entertained by the unexpected and unnatural sight of Captain MacLachlan looking irresolute.

"Yeah?"

"Jane wants you to come to dinner. Tonight or tomorrow?"

"Is there an occasion?"

Expression strangely vulnerable, Duncan met his eyes. "Jane's pregnant."

Niall found himself momentarily speechless. "This a surprise?" he asked at last.

Duncan shook his head. "No. I'm thirty-seven, Jane's thirty-two. We didn't want to wait too long."

"My brother, a daddy." Niall smiled broadly. "Congratulations."

"Thanks."

"How far along is she?"

"Three months. She wanted to wait until she

was past the danger point before we let people know. You're, uh, the first."

Niall nodded, feeling honored even though—face it—there wasn't a whole lot of competition here. Jane was alienated entirely from her family, and Niall was the only member of Duncan's who had a relationship with him. Mom had made no effort to stay in touch with any of them, and Duncan had rebuffed Dad's one attempt to reconnect. Conall hadn't spoken to Duncan in close to ten years. That left—ta da!—Niall.

"I'll be an uncle," he said, disconcerted by the idea.

His brother shared one of his rare grins. "Yeah, you will."

"Huh."

Still smiling, Duncan clapped him on the back. "Dinner?"

"Tomorrow night."

"I'll tell Jane." With long strides, he headed across the parking lot.

Niall stood where he was, watching him go. Well, damn, he thought, and felt a funny ache inside. He might have labeled it as jealousy, except he didn't want any of what Duncan had.

Still, a baby MacLachlan. Who'd have thunk?

HOMICIDE AND MAJOR CRIMES detectives almost never fired a gun outside of the range, where they were required to keep their skills sharp. The telephone and the internet were their tools. They spent a lot of time on hold. They talked. They listened. They pretended to understand and sympathize with scumbags.

Which was probably why Niall was a little slower than he should have been reaching for his Glock.

During a belated lunch break, he had pulled into the bank parking lot with the intention of going in to deposit a check. Before he could get out of the car, his attention was caught by the sight of a guy hustling out of the bank gripping the arm of a woman who was walking really, really close to him. The incongruous part was that with both hands she clutched a black plastic trash bag, stuffed full. And—oh, hell—she looked scared out of her skull.

At the exact same moment Niall's brain clicked into gear, the guy looked at Niall's car which, while unmarked, shouted cop car. Plain maroon, but a big, powerful sedan. Grille behind the driver's seat. Serious radio antenna. Then his eyes met Niall's and he lifted a handgun.

Niall flung open the door and dove out at the exact moment the passenger window exploded.

He snatched his Glock from the holster and groped for his radio. "Shots being fired. Bank robbery in progress," he managed to spit out before stealing a peek over the trunk.

Another shot rang out. Brick chips flew from the wall a few feet from his head.

Damn, damn, damn. The guy had dragged the woman behind a minivan in the lot. He had a hostage, and he was seriously willing to do anything to get away. Including killing a cop.

Niall hadn't taken a shot yet. He wouldn't until he thought he had a good one. *God.* Even aside from the hostage, there were other people in the parking lot, businesses across the street, passing cars.

Niall swiveled on his heels and saw a woman who had gotten out of her RAV4 standing not fifteen feet away with the keys in her hand, her mouth forming a horrified O. He gestured vehemently, relieved when she gasped and threw herself out of sight around the front of the vehicle. Other people farther away were gaping, too freaking stupid to realize a stray bullet could catch them. A man came running out of the bank yelling, but ducked back when a bullet chipped more bricks inches from him.

Niall's car jumped when another burst of fire found metal. He dropped flat to the pavement so he could see the feet beneath the minivan. Black bag, too. He wondered if the teller had gotten a dye pack in it. He grunted. Man, this was going to be a mess no matter how it played out. The FBI would be all over it, and who wanted to deal with them? Although he wouldn't mind if they showed up right now.

The feet were moving. Toward the rear of the vehicle. So it wasn't the guy's minivan, or the woman's, either. The guy was figuring to bolt for cover behind another car. Make his way to his own, maybe. Time was his enemy. He had to get away before more cops arrived and he got surrounded.

Sirens sounded, but not close.

Niall rose to a crouch and crab-walked forward, rounding the hood of his car. He snatched a quick look, his finger tight on the trigger, and saw that the guy had pushed the woman out into view. She once again clutched the trash bag in front of her as if it were a shield. Niall had never seen such terror on anyone's face. Was she a teller? An unlucky customer?

Wait. Wait.

The guy appeared. Not enough of him— he was using the woman for cover. He took a wild shot to pin Niall down, but it was the back window of the car that imploded. Good. He'd miscalculated which direction Niall would move.

Wait.

Niall had never felt so steady, so cool. He was thinking, waiting with extraordinary patience, willing the instant to come when he could kill this bastard without unduly risking the woman.

There. The woman stumbled. Niall pulled the trigger and the Glock jerked in his hand exactly as it did at the gun range. *Bang, bang, bang.* Blood blossomed; glass on the minivan exploded; the woman fell forward, then, screaming, began to crawl away.

The bank robber was down, broken glass all around him. His handgun skittered away across the pavement from inert fingers. He lay sprawled, unmoving.

Glock held out in the firing position, Niall walked cautiously forward until he stood only feet from the man. There was one hell of a lot of blood. *Dead,* he thought coldly. His second dead body for the day. At least he'd only killed one of them.

This was also, however, his second shooting resulting in a fatality in the past year. The first was a crazy guy who'd intended to slit Jane's throat. Niall had gotten there ahead of Duncan, so he'd been the one to take the shot. He'd as soon this didn't become a habit, he reflected, in that weird way a mind worked at a moment like this.

Sirens rose to a crescendo. Police cars slammed to a halt blocking both exits from the bank parking lot. Officers leaped out and took cover. A lot of weapons were drawn on Niall.

Something made his glance slide sidelong to the broken windows of the minivan, and a monster of fear rose in him. There was a child car seat inside. A Mercedes-Benz of car seats, it occurred to him, even as he realized there was a kid in that seat, slumped forward. Blood was shockingly red against the dandelion-pale fluff of hair.

Please God, don't let me have killed that kid.

THERE WERE ONLY A FEW mourners at Enid Cooper's funeral. Her contemporaries were gone, or in assisted living. A couple of neighbors were there, and Rowan Staley and her father. Not Mom; she and Dad had separated and filed for divorce.

At least Rowan had persuaded her parents-in-law not to attend. She had been able to leave the kids with them. Maybe at six years old Desmond had been old enough to attend a funeral, but why should he have to? It wasn't an open casket; Rowan wouldn't have that. Gran had had a thing about dignity; she would have *hated* the idea of everyone filing past gazing at her wrinkled, dead face.

Gran's tenant, whose name escaped Rowan, was here, too. When she'd seen him coming and going at Gran's, he'd never stopped to introduce himself or anything like that. A couple of times he had given a distant nod before disappearing inside the tiny cottage. Despite his unfriendliness, Rowan had actually been glad to know he was there. After her divorce, she'd had the wistful thought that *she* could live in the cottage, but it wasn't big enough for her and the kids. And even though Gran had room in her house, she was too old and not patient enough to live with a rambunctious kindergartener and a wistful four-year-old. Never mind the dog. Gran didn't hold with animals being in the house. Rowan hadn't had any choice but to take the kids and move in with her in-laws, relieved that Gran would be safer having a law enforcement officer living right there behind her house.

She'd been told he was the one who'd found Gran. And he'd cared enough to come today to pay his respects. Rowan wondered if he would bother speaking to her or her father after the service was over. She was betting not.

The minister was talking, but it was like the sound of running water to Rowan. Pleasant but holding no meaning. He hadn't even known Gran. She hadn't attended a church service in at least ten years, maybe more. He was young, new. This was his standard spiel. His tone was filled with warmth and regret, which she appreciated even though he couldn't possibly feel either emotion. This was like a stage performance for him, she supposed.

I should be listening.

Dad's gaze was fixed somewhere in the vicinity of the pastor, but his expression was abstracted. He and his mother hadn't been close; as she'd gotten older and crankier, she'd also become increasingly disapproving. Gran had been one hundred percent disgusted with her son's recent conduct. But still. He must have good memories. Regrets that were way more genuine than the pastor's. As mad as Rowan often felt at her dad, what if he died and she had to sit at his funeral trying to remember the last time she'd said "I love you?" Remembering the angry words they'd exchanged?

She gave a shudder and stole a look sideways, to find that Gran's tenant had turned his head and was watching her. Goose bumps chased over her skin. He had a craggy face, dark red hair cut short and flint-gray eyes. Eyes that were— not cold, Rowan had decided the first time she'd seen him. Remote. As if he stood a thousand paces from the rest of humanity. Didn't know her, didn't want to know her. Or anybody else.

It had to be her imagination. Maybe it was a typical cop look, cynicism to the *n*th degree. Or maybe he didn't like *her.* Did he think she'd neglected Gran? The thought filled her with outrage. She glared at him, saw his eyebrows twitch, then he inclined his head the slightest amount to acknowledge her existence and turned his attention to the front.

Why had he been looking at her at all? Did he guess she was Gran's heir and therefore his new landlady? Or would he have assumed he would be dealing with Dad?

Dad had been a little put out when the will was read and he found out his mother hadn't left either her relatively modest savings nor her house to him, but to his credit he'd mostly been rueful.

"The two of you always were close," he had said, shrugging. "And you've been trying to take care of her."

Rowan wished now she had been able to do more.

Or maybe Gran had known. Guessed, anyway. Rowan hadn't talked even to Gran about her marriage, or her shame at feeling relieved when Drew died. She hadn't admitted how miserable she was living with his parents, who were entirely fixated on her children. Their Andrew, her husband, had been an only child.

"Desmond and Anna are all we have left," one or the other of them said, too often. The *hunger* in their gazes when they looked at their grandchildren unnerved Rowan. There was too much need, too much desperation, too many expectations being fastened on young children who didn't understand any of it.

The Staleys had been shocked when she informed them that she had inherited her grandmother's house and would be moving into it with Anna and Desmond. She couldn't cope without them, they declared, and they didn't like it when she insisted that she could. It was true that she *hadn't* been able to cope before this, not financially, anyway. She worked as a paraeducator—a teacher's aide—at the elementary school. She didn't make enough money to pay for daycare for Anna, as well as rent. But now she would be able to afford a preschool for Anna. She would own her very own home, and have rental income, as well, from the cottage.

Paid by the man with the russet hair and chilly gray eyes. She didn't know how she felt about the idea of him living so close. Perhaps she'd scarcely see him. It hadn't sounded as if he and Gran had much more than a nodding acquaintance.

Rowan hoped he liked dogs. She might be able to keep the kids away from him, but Super Sam the dog didn't grasp the concept of boundaries. Thank heavens Gran's backyard was fenced. The unfortunate part was, the cottage was *inside* the fence. The kids and tenant both would have to learn to close gates.

She stole another look at him to find that he appeared entirely expressionless. Somehow she felt quite sure he wasn't thinking about Gran any more than Dad was.

Any more than I *am.* Rowan felt a quick stab of guilt. *Oh, Gran. I did love you. I will be grateful for the rest of my life for this gift you've given me.*

Freedom.

STILL SWEATING OVER the bank parking-lot shooting, Niall hadn't gotten to sleep until nearly 3:00 a.m. This had been a hell of a few days. Only yesterday he'd had to face an Internal Affairs panel to justify his actions, as if he wasn't second-guessing himself already, the way any good cop would. Then his sleep wasn't restful, any more than it had been the past few nights. No surprise to wake filled with horror. The last images of the nightmare were extraordinarily vivid. In his dream he'd reached for the little kid with the pale fluff of hair, lifting the child's chin to see dead eyes that still accused him even now.

Damn it, he thought viciously, scrubbing his hands over his face. *Enough already.*

Niall got up to use the john, splashed cold water on his face and stared at himself in the mirror.

Bad enough he'd shot and killed a man. He'd

learned a lesson last year, when he'd killed for the first time: you paid a price for taking a life, even if taking it had been the right thing to do. Mostly, he thought it right and just he should suffer some doubts, be plagued by nightmares. Killing wasn't something anyone should take lightly.

The little girl, though, that was something else. She'd come within a hair's breadth of having her head blown off. *God. What if it had been my bullet?* As much as her face, that was the question driving him crazy.

Knowing sleep would be elusive, he went back to bed, where he lay staring up at the dark ceiling, hitting the replay button over and over and over until the tape should be wearing out. The gray of dawn was seeping between the slats of the window blinds before he fell asleep again.

The sound of slamming doors, shrill, excited voices and a barking dog jerked him from sleep. What the…? With a groan, he rolled his head on the pillow to peer blearily at the bedside clock. Eight-thirty. He was going to kill someone.

Even half-asleep with his head pounding, he winced at that. Now that he actually *had* killed two men, those words didn't come as lightly to him as they once had.

He sat up and put his feet to the floor. A woman was laughing, a low, delighted trill. A kid yelled something and the dog went into another frenzy of barking. There were other voices—several adults. The racket had to be at the next-door neighbor's. Enid was barely in the ground. Her estate couldn't possibly be settled.

He staggered from his bedroom into the combination living room/kitchen/dining room and separated the slats of the blinds on the front window enough to give him a view of Enid's house. Then he stared in disbelief.

Oh, crap. Oh, hell. Oh...

A U-Haul truck had been backed into the driveway. The cargo door was already rolled up. A couple of people were currently hauling a mattress out of the truck and down the metal ramp. A dog was running in crazed circles on the lawn, chased by a boy and, trailing well behind, a tiny girl in pink overalls and purple shoes that, to Niall's dazed eyes, seemed to be flashing sparkling lights. The back door of Enid's house stood open. A woman was carrying a lamp in. She'd no sooner disappeared inside than a different woman came out empty-handed. She called something to the kids, who were too busy running in frenetic circles to acknowledge her.

It was the granddaughter. The curvy package with the fabulous legs, exposed almost as effectively in snug jeans as when she wore short shorts.

Those were her two kids. The dog… Was it theirs? The husband was probably one of those men.

An expletive escaped Niall's lips. They were moving in. An entire family was moving into Enid's house, separated from his cottage by the width of a lawn and one old apple tree.

He kept staring, shock almost—but not quite—numbing him. There would be a swing hanging from the branch of that apple tree before he knew it. The dog would crap all over the lawn and set up an uproar every time Niall came and went. The kids would have friends over. Soon, there wouldn't be two of them, there would be half a dozen.

This was his worst nightmare.

He'd have to break the lease.

And pay massive penalties, unless Enid's granddaughter was as eager to see him gone as he was to go.

Uh-huh. And where would he be going *to?*

Maybe it was time he bought a house, he reflected. He could certainly afford to. But the idea had always filled him with uneasiness. It still did. A one-year lease was all the commitment he'd ever wanted to make. Actually owning his own house, his own piece of land, putting down roots… Making some kind of unspoken promise, if only to himself, to stay here, in his hometown….

He let the blinds spring back into place but stayed where he was, staring at them. Outside the pandemonium continued.

There had to be another rental somewhere that would be suitable. This was Sunday. Once everything settled down out there, he'd slip out and grab his newspaper. Maybe he'd spot an ad that said something like, Nice house, Privacy! No near neighbors!

Rural. That's what he needed, Niall decided grimly. So what if it took him longer to drive to work, if come spring he had to fight the traffic congestion caused by tourists out to view the tulip and daffodil fields?

God help me, he thought, and stumbled into the tiny kitchenette to put on a pot of coffee. Clearly, going back to bed wasn't happening.

AT FOUR-THIRTY IN THE afternoon, a firm *rat-a-tat-tat* on his door made Niall go on sharp alert. He'd been lying on his sofa brooding, feeling trapped. Would he never be able to come and go without risking the possibility of having to exchange neighborly greetings?

He swore under his breath and stood. It would be her, of course. No, maybe not. Maybe he'd get lucky and be able to deal with the husband. If there was one.

No such luck. Not only the woman stood on his doorstep, but her two children, the little girl latched on to her leg and gazing suspiciously at him, the boy's eyes filled with curiosity. The dog was trying to shove between them and get in the door. Niall automatically stuck out a foot to foil the break-in.

His gaze traveled up—although it didn't have to go very far—to meet the young woman's. She was sort of a blonde, with big brown eyes. Bangs were pushed to one side, and the rest of her baby-fine hair was in a ponytail. Maybe her hair was really brown and she'd had it highlighted.... But Niall shook off that conjecture immediately. She wore no makeup, the bangs looked like she trimmed them herself, and she had a big splotch of what could have been mustard on her faded T-shirt. Which, he couldn't help noticing, fit snugly over generous breasts. C cup for sure.

He became aware that, as he studied her, she was likewise inspecting him from his bare feet to his equally faded T-shirt. He thought she looked both wary and apprehensive. His mouth quirked slightly when he noticed that the little girl, who had moonlight-pale hair but Mommy's soft brown eyes, had an identical expression on her face. Her clutch on her mother's thigh tightened.

"I'm afraid I don't know your name," the woman said.

He actually did know hers, he'd realized yesterday even before being handed the program for the service. Enid had mentioned it a couple of times. It had caught in his memory only because Rowan was an unusual name.

"Niall MacLachlan," he said. "I assume you're Enid's granddaughter."

"Yes. Rowan Staley." She had a beautiful voice. The trill of laughter he'd heard earlier had to have been hers. "These are my children, Desmond and Anna."

The boy piped up, "Hi." The girl only stared, her eyes narrowing.

Niall had the thought that he could develop a soft spot for her.

"Hello," he said and then waited, meantime keeping a cautious eye on the dog who had made an enthusiastic, tail-wagging circuit of the yard and was now closing in again. The damn thing looked as if he'd been put together with spare parts. Niall had seen garden art in which rusting springs, trowels and what-not were welded together to form fantastical animals. The dog was even rust-colored.

"We've moved into the house," Rowan said.

No shit. He nodded then couldn't resist saying, "Pretty quick."

Her eyes narrowed, increasing the resemblance to her tiny daughter. "What's that supposed to mean?"

"Nothing. I was surprised, that's all."

"I'm Gran's sole heir. There's no one to object and no point in the house sitting empty while the will goes through probate."

His answering stare was deliberately bored. She flushed, giving her a rosy-cheeked look. No elegant cheekbones here. She wasn't plump, but she had a lot of curves packed onto a frame that couldn't possibly top five-foot-two or -three.

"I'm now your landlady," she said sharply.

The dog sprang forward, forcing woman and children to stagger aside, and flung himself happily at Niall.

"Sit!" he snapped. Apparently surprised, the animal dropped to its haunches. Equally surprised, his family stared at him. Niall said, "Have you looked into that ugly dog contest? There might be prize money."

"That's not nice!" the boy exclaimed. "Super Sam is…is…"

Something like a chuckle was welling up in Niall's chest. He suppressed it.

Rowan looked as indignant as her son. "How can you say that? Sam's…cute."

The *cute* came out kind of weak. Niall let his silence speak for itself.

The little girl said in a sweet, high voice, "We love Sam."

The dog leaped up, ran a wet pink tongue over

her face and bounded off. After a small sigh, Rowan said, "Speaking of Sam. One of the things I came by for was to ask that you keep the gate closed. He doesn't have an awful lot of common sense, and he, er, likes to dig holes, which some of the neighbors might not appreciate, so we really need to keep him confined."

That was a nuisance, but not unreasonable. Niall nodded. "I can do that."

"Thank you." She was trying for crisp sarcasm, but couldn't quite pull it off. Not her style, Niall thought.

"Anything else?" he asked.

"I haven't yet had a chance to study the rental agreement," Rowan said. "Once I have, perhaps we can talk about it."

"What's to talk about? Unless one of us doesn't intend to honor it?"

She didn't look away. "And which one of us would that be?"

"Depends on how things go, doesn't it?"

Her lips compressed. "Yes. It does." She backed up a step, taking her children with her. "Mr. MacLachlan…"

"Detective. I'm with Stimson P.D."

He saw the moment she made the connection. "I read about you in the paper." And, clearly, hadn't liked what she'd read. She opened her mouth to say more, glanced down at Desmond and changed her mind. "What a pleasure it's been to meet you," she said, and this time the sarcasm worked better. So well, in fact, that he couldn't help smiling.

His new landlady looked momentarily startled, then mad. She gave a nod that made her ponytail bob and her bangs swing, then steered her kids off the porch. Both their heads were turning to look back as she marched them across the lawn.

Still smiling, Niall closed the door. With luck, his all-too-close neighbors wouldn't come calling again in the near future. The kid—Desmond— was right. Niall *wasn't* very nice. He reflected that he'd been inspired by the hot pepper stuff orthodontists gave parents to apply to their kids' thumbs when they wouldn't quit sucking on them. A preventative measure.

His smile died, though, at the memory of overhearing his sergeant grumble about how his five-year-old had developed a taste for the damn pepper, and was sucking her thumb even more now.

Okay, not foolproof, but worth a try.

CHAPTER TWO

THE GUILT WAS GETTING him down.

He'd expected to struggle with some complex emotions regarding the shooting. Niall didn't question his decision to take down the bank robber, who'd been doing his damnedest to kill Niall and very possibly would have shot the poor teller once he didn't need her. The adrenaline kept surging, though, at unexpected moments. That was okay; he knew from experience that this was a problem time would cure.

It was the sight of the toddler in the car seat that was haunting him, waking and sleeping. Two days ago, Duncan had called to let him know that the bloody bullet embedded in the car door beside the little girl wasn't Niall's. Relief had dropped him into a chair with a thud. *Thank God,* was all he could think. He already knew she'd gone home after only a two-night stay in the hospital. The bullet had barely creased her skull.

Not my bullet.

But, damn, it had been a close call. He'd *known*

how high risk a shoot-out was in the middle of town with civilians all around. People often sat waiting in a parked car—although he was still infuriated at the father who had left a child that age alone while he went into the bank. Niall couldn't seem to stop asking himself whether he'd done the right thing. If he'd backed off somehow, given the guy space to make a getaway… But he couldn't figure how he could have done that. And then there was the hostage.

In the week since the incident, he'd gone around and around a million times, never arriving at any satisfactory conclusion. Unfortunately, Niall had had an abundance of time to brood, since he was on routine leave following the shooting. Instead of doing desk work, he had chosen to use vacation days. He had a hell of a lot of them saved to use.

And now he felt like crud over being so rude to a woman who was probably perfectly nice and had been well-intentioned. Two little kids, too, who'd stared at him with shocked eyes by the time Mom hastily bore them away. No, he wasn't the friendliest guy on earth, but he knew he'd have been more civil if he hadn't been sleep-deprived and on edge.

He finally ventured out two days after that initial meet-and-greet to ease his conscience. Rowan and the children were in the backyard.

She seemed to be happily setting pink flowering geraniums into pots on the porch. A green plastic sandbox shaped like a turtle had appeared yesterday, and the girl sat in it with a shovel and bucket. The boy and dog both had crawled beneath the giant rhododendrons that had grown dark limbs together along the fence line.

The girl—Anna—and Rowan both turned their heads at the sound of his door and watched him as he walked across the grass toward them. He half expected tiny Anna to bolt for her mom, but she didn't move.

Rowan eyed him without welcome. Damn, she was pretty, he thought, dismayed at his seemingly unstoppable physical reaction to her. She was more wholesome than his usual type, but that might be because he avoided the home-and-hearth kind of woman like the plague. This one had such a lush body, what man wouldn't notice?

"Hi," he said. "I, uh, thought maybe I could be a little more civil than I was the other day."

"That wouldn't be hard."

He grinned. "No. I guess it wouldn't."

"Did you get out of bed on the wrong side?"

"Something like that," he admitted. He glanced to be sure neither kid had gotten too close. "You read about the shooting, I gather."

Rowan nodded, expression cool.

"The aftermath of something like that is always…unsettling. I haven't been sleeping well."

"I read it wasn't you who shot the child."

"No. I was trying to be very conscious of how many people were in potential danger. Even so…" He sighed. "It was a relief to know it wasn't my gun."

"But it could have been."

"I actually only pulled the trigger a couple of times, when I was pretty certain I had a clean shot to take him down. He was the one spraying bullets all over the parking lot."

She looked down at the trowel in her gloved hands. "At least she's okay."

Niall made a sound of agreement even though he felt defensive. Maybe he still hadn't resolved in his own mind how much responsibility he bore for that little girl's near miss, but that was different than seeing judgment in some civilian's eyes.

"You did some nice things for Gran," Rowan said.

He shifted uncomfortably. Sure, he'd done a few repairs, rebuilt those back steps Rowan's feet rested on, picked up groceries and prescriptions a few times, but that was common decency, nothing above and beyond.

Those soft-as-a-pansy brown eyes met his. "*Do you intend to stay?*"

He hesitated. "I'm not a hundred percent sure."

How did he say, *It depends how noisy and intrusive your kids are?* "Do you have a husband in the picture?" He hadn't seen one, but could have missed him.

Her face tightened. "I'm a widow."

He said the polite thing. "I'm sorry."

She shrugged.

"Well," he said. "I was depositing the rent directly into Enid's account. Let me know how you want me to handle it now."

"All right."

The boy crawled back out from beneath the rhodies, followed by the dog. The boy had acquired a few scratches and quite a bit of dirt. The dog—well, his coarse, rusty coat probably never looked clean. Spotting Niall, the dog tore across the lawn, the boy following at a trot. Niall braced himself for possible impact.

"Sit!"

The dog sat.

"How *do* you do that?" Rowan asked, eyes wide with astonishment. "Super Sam and I went through an obedience course, and it didn't do a speck of good."

"I mean it, and he can tell."

She glowered at the dog, who was obviously desperate to leap up. His tail was swinging furiously, his butt waggling with it, and his big brown eyes, a deeper brown than his mistress's, were fixed on Niall's face.

With resignation, Niall said, "Okay, boy," and submitted to a fervent greeting. The boy hung back shyly, but looked as if he, too, would have liked to bound at Niall.

"I have a goldfish."

He looked down to see the girl had abandoned her sandbox to come stand beside him. Her head was tilted back to allow her to stare up at him.

He cleared his throat. "Do you?"

"Uh-huh. You wanna see?"

No. Hell, no! He was going to be so sorry if he let these kids think he wanted to be buddies. He shot a helpless look at Rowan, who was smiling softly at her daughter, apparently oblivious to his discomfiture.

"Uh…I've seen goldfish."

"*My* goldfish is named Goldie. 'Cuz he's gold."

"Goldfish are really orange," Desmond said importantly. "You should have named him Orangie." He cackled at his humor.

His sister ignored him. "I won Goldie."

"At the school carnival," the boy said. "She threw a quarter into a jar." His tone suggested it had been an accident. "She picked Goldie, 'stead of one of the stuffed animals." His gaze slid to Rowan. "Mom wasn't very happy. She tried to talk Anna into trading Goldie in for a panda bear, but she wouldn't."

"Goldie's alive," Anna informed him.

Niall's sense of humor was apparently alive and well, too, in defiance of his recent crappy mood. He was trying to hide his smile when he met Rowan's, rueful but beautiful.

A small hand crept into his and tugged. Niall started.

"Come see Goldie."

"Anna…" her mother began, but he shook his head.

"It's okay."

Desmond stuck close as they went in the house. Super Sam let out a pitiful whine when the screen door slammed shut in his face. As he allowed himself to be pulled through the house and upstairs, Niall heard Rowan talking to the dog.

The family was far from unpacked, but Anna's bed was covered by a pink-and-purple comforter imprinted with unicorns and princesses and a castle. Her white-painted dresser had pink ceramic drawer pulls. Goldie lived in a glass bowl atop the dresser. A very small castle sat on the bottom of the bowl, and a couple of strands of fake seagrass waved in the water as he swam hopeless circles around the perimeter.

Niall learned that Goldie liked being talked

to. Desmond fed the fish a few flakes; Mom wouldn't let Anna feed the fish, he said, because she dumped in too much food, which wasn't good for him.

"I get to feed Sam, too. He's my dog."

Anna's lower lip shot out. "Is not!"

"Is, too."

"Is not! He's *our* dog. Mommy said so."

"Well, I take care of him."

She wanted to argue about that, but evidently couldn't. She contented herself with a scowl, unnatural on her small, elfin face.

Niall took a look at Desmond's room, too, where a spaceship was under construction with Lego bricks. Plastic as well as stuffed dinosaurs seemed to be the dominant theme. He resisted their invitation to look at Mommy's bedroom, too. That was a picture he'd just as soon not have in his head.

Rowan studied him narrowly when the three of them came back outside.

"You've made some changes," he observed.

"I plan to make more. Gran hadn't painted or remodeled in forever."

Probably never, was his guess.

"We're keeping most of her furniture for now, though. I didn't keep most of ours when…" She didn't have to finish.

He nodded.

"We lived with our grandparents," Desmond said.

Niall turned his head to look at the boy. There had been something in his voice. Reserve. For a kid as outgoing as him, that was unusual. Rowan was watching her son, too, a few lines marring her forehead, but she didn't say anything. It seemed there was a good reason for her hasty move to Enid's house.

"Desmond having to change schools?" he asked casually.

Rowan shook her head. "My in-laws live only about a mile away. Walking distance, really."

She didn't sound altogether happy about that. Given his job, Niall was used to listening for undertones, and there were plenty here. But they weren't his problem, he reminded himself. In no way, shape or form.

"I need to be going. Grocery shopping," he decided, impromptu. He hesitated, his inner jerk doing battle with nice-guy Niall, who won the tussle. He said reluctantly, "If you need me to pick anything up for you…"

She beamed at him. "That's really nice of you. But not today, thanks."

Oh, this was going to come back to bite him in the ass. They all thought he wanted to be friends now. And he so didn't.

He did like that smile, though. It had something in common with the bright, cheerful flowers she was planting. It was a happy smile.

The realization that she hadn't looked happy the rest of the time gave him momentary pause. There were as many shadows in her eyes as he saw in his own every morning when he shaved in front of the mirror. He wondered when her husband had died and how. Why she'd moved in with the husband's parents instead of staying in whatever home she'd already had. Why she'd fled the in-laws' the instant the opportunity offered itself.

He was frowning when he let himself out the gate, rolled his motorcycle out of the detached garage and donned his helmet.

Not your business. You don't want to know.

No. He'd have to raise avoiding them to an art form, for his own self-preservation. He didn't get involved. Not with anybody, far less a sweet-faced young widow and her children.

It was a shame about the children, though, *and* the sweet face, given how sinfully sexy her petite body was. Shaking his head with regret, he kicked the Harley's engine to throaty life and steered out of the driveway.

THREE DAYS LATER, Rowan suddenly realized how quiet the house was. She stuck her head out of the kitchen. "Desmond?"

No answer.

She followed the sound of the television to the living room, where a Disney movie played. Anna lay curled up on the sofa, sound asleep.

Rowan smiled down at her. Anna had decided recently that she was too big a girl to nap, but long habits could be hard to break. She looked comfortable enough, so Rowan decided to leave her where she was rather than carry her up to bed.

Had Desmond gotten bored with the movie and gone upstairs to play? She went up and found his bedroom deserted. Ditto Anna's and her own.

Her heart sank. He must have gone outside without her noticing. She trusted him not to leave the yard, but she didn't trust him not to have gone knocking on her tenant's door.

Please don't let Niall have been home.

Desmond had become infatuated with the brooding police detective. She couldn't figure it out. Niall wasn't anything like Drew, who she knew Desmond missed dreadfully. She had hoped his grandfather would fill some of the void, but... No, she didn't want to think about that right now. She had to find her son.

The moment she opened the back door, she saw him. Niall had come out on his porch and was listening, head bent and arms crossed, as Desmond expostulated on some enthusiasm or other. He was bouncing on his toes in his excitement.

With a sigh, Rowan started across the yard. Niall saw her coming. His face was mostly expressionless, but she thought there might be a plea in his eyes.

"Desmond," she said, "what have I told you about bothering Detective MacLachlan? You cannot come over here every time you get bored."

"I'm not bothering him, Mom. Am I, Niall? He says I can call him Niall," he said as an aside to his mother, to forestall her reproof. "'Cuz we're friends, huh?"

Like ghosts, several emotions passed through her tenant's gray eyes, "I did tell him to call me by my first name. 'Detective' is for work."

"*He* never had a dog." Desmond sounded astonished at the concept. "Not even when he was my age. He said his mom didn't like dogs. I'm real glad you like dogs, Mom. 'Cuz then we wouldn't have Sam."

Thumping drew their attention. Sam might not be the brightest bulb, but he did know his name. She hadn't noticed him lying on the porch, although she should have; his head was all but resting on Niall's foot.

His bare foot.

He seemed often to go barefoot, she'd noticed in the slightly less than a week they had lived here. He had quite sexy feet, an observation which had taken her by surprise. Rowan did her very best not to notice men as sexual beings. And feet weren't supposed to be sexy anyway, were they? She didn't even know why the word had crossed her mind. His feet were long and bony, with a few copper-colored hairs curling on his toes. Even so, at the sight of them close up, she felt a funny, warm, melting sensation low in her belly.

Of course, if she concentrated on his hands, long-fingered but strong, she had something of the same sensation. And he was very well built, she could see that; broad-shouldered, lean, powerful in a streamlined way. His hair was a beautiful color, a deep, rich auburn that in sunlight revealed itself to be composed of strands of a dozen colors. She wouldn't have thought of him as a redhead at all, except that his jaw stubble was copper colored like the hairs on his forearms and toes. It made her wonder if he had much chest hair and whether it, too, was as bright....

Sternly, she slapped down any such speculation. She didn't actually *want* to see his chest, or to touch it. Definitely not to touch it.

In her marriage, Rowan had learned to dread the sexual act. She had no reason to think it would be different with any other man. No, she wasn't going there again, however much Desmond wanted a father. And she had to figure out how to keep him from bugging Niall, or she suspected she was going to lose her tenant. She hated the idea of having to find someone new. Niall might not be the friendliest man on earth, but he was *safe.* Plus, according to Gran he didn't hold parties—in fact, almost never had a visitor at all—was neat, occasionally helpful and quiet. Although how Gran knew about the quiet part was a mystery. Niall could have howled at the moon without Gran hearing.

Keeping a renter in the cottage was a financial necessity for Rowan, and she hated to imagine the possibilities if Niall left.

"Are you going back to work soon?" she asked, trying to keep the hopeful note from her voice. His ironic look told her she hadn't succeeded.

"Probably next week. You should know I don't always work regular shifts. Don't worry if you hear me coming and going at strange hours." When she nodded, he asked, "Do you work?"

"I'm a para-ed at the elementary school. A teacher's aide," she translated. "It lets me work the same hours as Des is in school. Before, her grandparents took care of Anna, but this year she's going to a preschool instead."

"Grandma is mad about that," Desmond said.

Rowan laid a hand on his head. "Disappointed, not mad."

"She *sounded* mad."

"Okay, upset."

Niall, she couldn't help noticing, was listening to the conversation closely. In their few interactions, she'd become aware of how much he took in while not, if he could help it, participating. She wondered what he thought about them.

Then she almost laughed. He thought they were a huge nuisance, that's what he thought.

"Please," she said, "let me know if any of us are bugging you. I mean it."

Eyes widening, Desmond looked up at her, then at Niall.

"I'll do that," he said with what she thought was a sigh, although she sensed more than heard it.

"But I haven't bugged him yet, have I, Detec— I mean, Niall? I've been real polite, haven't I?"

Niall was apparently not immune to the plea in her son's eyes."You have been polite. Which—" his gaze fell to Sam, whose tail thumped "—I can't say for your dog."

Desmond cackled. "Dogs aren't polite. 'Cuz they don't know they're supposed to be!"

"Is that so?"

"What has Sam done?" Rowan asked, apprehensive.

"Given half a chance, he shoots in the door and gallops through my place as if it's a rodeo arena.

I've fallen over him twice when I stepped out on the porch. He's been gnawing on my Adirondack chair." He nodded toward the bright blue chair, where the dog's teeth marks whittled into the wood. "He stares in the window."

The smudges along the lower panes of the front window were, evidently, nose prints. Rowan winced.

"He seems to be trying to dig a tunnel under the cottage. Take a look around the corner," he suggested. "He has something else in common with convict escapees. The middle of the night is his favorite time to work on his project." He paused. "The tunnel happens to be right underneath my bedroom window. Oh, and I ate out here one night and was stupid enough to set my sandwich down while I reached for my beer."

He didn't have to finish.

"I'm so sorry! I…" Her shoulders sagged. "Well, I don't know what to do about Sam. Maybe I could tie him up some of the time. And…and keep him in at night. Only, if I do that, he…"

He lifted one eyebrow in a masterpiece of sardonic inquiry.

"He chews things up," she admitted. "Mostly the kids' toys. It's hard to get them to put everything away."

"And if he couldn't find a toy, he'd start in on

the furniture." He leveled a significant glance at his porch chair.

"Possibly. Still."

His sudden grin took her breath away. "Don't worry about it. I can afford to replace the chair if he gets all the way through the leg. And it's better to have him digging by the foundation than under the fence."

"Yes, but sooner or later he'll happen to dig beside the fence," she muttered.

If anything, his grin widened. "Happen? Implying your dog is stupid, by any chance?"

"He's not!" Desmond declared, indignant.

Rowan finally had to laugh. "I can't blame it on overbreeding."

"No, you definitely can't do that. He must have a dozen breeds in him. His legs sure as—" his gaze briefly settled on her son "—heck don't come from the same ancestor as his body does, and then there's the head, and the ears, and…"

"Mommy, you said he was cute. Why are you laughing?"

"He is cute. In a, well, sort of ugly way." She bent to hug her six-year-old. "Looks don't matter anyway. It's his heart that really counts."

So why, she asked herself, was she so drawn to this man's looks? She had no idea what his heart held. Except he had been kind to the kids, after that first meeting. He did avoid them, but when either of them cornered him, he was nice. And that said something about his character, his heart, didn't it?

Probably, but it really didn't matter. This was as friendly as they were going to get.

"Excuse us," she said to Niall. "I don't want Anna to wake from her nap and find us missing." She firmly quelled Desmond's protest and marched him back to the house, feeling Niall MacLachlan's thoughtful gaze all the way.

"I HAVE TO REEXAMINE my whole life," Rowan's mother told her. "Did your father *ever* love me? I think back to conversations and get this jolt. Maybe he wasn't thinking and feeling anything like I believed he was. That vacation we'd planned where he suddenly had to stay behind and work. Remember? We went to Ocean Shores? Was it a woman? Were there other women all along? He completely refuses to talk to me. 'Think whatever you want,' he says, as if that's any answer!"

Rowan knew she was supposed to offer sympathy and understanding. Sitting on her back porch with the phone to her ear instead of mowing the lawn the way she'd intended, she was feeling low on sympathy and even lower on understanding. If only Mom didn't call every day or two, reiterating the same miseries.

Mom and Dad's separation had come as a huge shock to Rowan. Even worse was the way they both used her to bad-mouth the other one.

Dad had started to date from practically the moment Mom moved out, and that was the part that was infuriating her. Hurting her, too, probably, Rowan realized, but the whole subject had become an obsession.

Her best tactic would be to start dating, too. Dad might not want to be married to her anymore, but his pride would be stung by the sight of her seemingly enjoying herself with a succession of men. Rowan would have suggested it—her mother was an attractive woman who'd kept her figure at fifty-two—except Rowan could totally understand Mom never wanting anything to do with a man again. A desire she frequently proclaimed, and one Rowan shared.

"Mom, I really have to go," she said.

As if she hadn't spoken, her mother went on and on. Her father was making himself look ridiculous, dating women half his age—which Rowan thought was a slight exaggeration. Dad's latest was maybe mid-thirties, bad enough. "Why don't *you* talk to him?" Mom suggested. "He might listen to you."

A car was pulling into the driveway, and Rowan's heart sank when she recognized it. Glenn and Donna Staley, her parents-in-law, had come calling.

"I don't care who Dad dates," she told her mother, perhaps more brutally than she should have. "I don't want to meet them, I don't want to hear about them and, honestly, Mom, what difference does it make who he dates? You're getting a divorce."

"You blame me for feeling hurt by his foolishness?"

Rowan sighed. "No. Of course not, Mom. But I'd love to see you focus on yourself now. On finding what makes *you* happy." As long as it was something besides calling her daughter to bitch about Dad. "I'm sorry," she said. "I have to go. Glenn and Donna are here."

"Oh? You didn't mention that you were expecting them."

"That's because I wasn't," she said, possibly a little tersely. Not that she necessarily would have told her mother they were coming, but she wasn't thrilled to see them.

She ended the call to her mother as the couple reached the bottom of the porch steps.

"I don't see the children," Donna said, her disappointment obvious.

"Anna is napping, and Desmond is playing with a neighbor boy at his house." Rowan had

been pleased to find another boy exactly Desmond's age who lived less than a block away, and
delighted when the boy's mother suggested they
plan a few playdates.

Glenn frowned. "Do you know these people?"

"You left Anna alone in the house?" exclaimed
Donna. "Dear, is that a good idea?"

Rowan dug deep for patience. Donna loved the
kids, but worry also made her judgmental. "The
back door is open. I'll hear her the minute she
wakes up. And since she can't reach the lock on
the front door, she can't get out even if she'd do
something like that, which she wouldn't. And
yes, I went with Des the first time to Zeke's
house and had coffee with his mother. She's very
nice, a stay-at-home mom."

"You know we'd have happily taken him today
if you wanted to have time on your own," her
mother-in-law said.

Did she sound disapproving? She often did,
but Rowan wasn't sure this time. She knew
they weren't happy. Of course they were sorry
to miss seeing Desmond. They hadn't wanted
Rowan and their grandchildren to move out of
their home, and even though she had needed to
escape, Rowan understood how they felt. They'd
grieved terribly after Drew's death, and having
Anna and Des close had been a huge consola-
tion for them.

Rowan was proud of her smile. "I wasn't looking for time on my own. Desmond needs friends his age. A new one is welcome." She picked up the phone and stood. "Would you like a glass of lemonade? Why don't we sit out here so we don't wake Anna."

"I thought you told me she'd given up her naps," Donna said. "Are you sure you want her to sleep? Won't she fight bedtime tonight?"

"Some days she doesn't nap, but she's still in transition. I figure if she falls asleep on her own, she needs the rest." Rowan kept the smile fixed on her face. "Lemonade?"

"I suppose." Glenn snorted. He was eyeing the broken run-off pipe for the roof gutters. "Your grandmother didn't keep this place up, did she?"

Couldn't he pretend to be a little excited for her? Rowan didn't let herself sigh. No; Glenn took pride in being blunt. He'd made no secret of his opinion of her moving out on her own with two young children when she had the option of being taken care of.

They'd both become more critical since Drew died. Rowan had been reasonably sure they never quite approved of her. The first thing Donna had ever said to her was, "What kind of name is *Rowan?*"

Drew had insisted that Rowan was being too

sensitive when she told him she didn't think his parents liked her. "That's just Mom and Dad," he said, sounding resigned.

Rowan had clung to the fact that they did adore their grandchildren. And they had been generous in taking her and the kids in after Rowan realized she would have to sell the house to cover the debts Drew had left. They'd refused her offer to pay rent and rarely even let her buy groceries, which had allowed her to put some money away. How could she not be grateful, even if some days they'd made it hard? If only they'd respected her right to parent her own children the way she thought best, she wouldn't have felt so desperate to get away from them. Even so, Rowan had been ashamed of the fervor with which she'd seized the chance to move out.

Perhaps, she thought now, if she'd involved Donna in the redecorating plans that would have appeased her.

But rebellion immediately sparked in her. Was it so bad to want to make the house totally hers and Anna's and Desmond's?

Was it so bad to wish she could she could restrict their contact with the kids to an occasional outing and too many packages under the tree on Christmas morning?

Rowan didn't know whether to hope that Anna

would sleep for a long time and they would give up and go away, or that she'd wake up and give them a grandchild fix. She had a gift for softening them both. Rowan worried more about Des, who they seemed determined to correct and mold, chide and stifle. More than Anna, he was slated as the replacement for their son. In the last year, he'd gone from being happy to see Grandma and Grandpa to shutting down and getting quiet in their presence. It infuriated her that her confident, bright, happy kid had to feel that way. Even if she'd loved living with Donna and Glenn, she'd have moved out at the first opportunity for Desmond's sake.

"Why don't I come in and help pour that lemonade?" Donna said. "And I can take a peek to see what you've done to the house. I'll be quiet, but you know dear Anna wouldn't want to miss our visit!"

How could she say no, even though her mother-in-law didn't know how to keep her voice low? Even though it meant hearing again that Donna didn't understand how Rowan could possibly want to live in a place that was so dark and *dingy*. Why, it wasn't fair to the children, when they'd had such a nice room at Grandma and Grandpa's.

If only Drew and she hadn't both grown up in

Stimson. If only Gran had left her a house somewhere else, far, far away.

Minneapolis, she thought wistfully. *Florida.
Anywhere at all but here.*

CHAPTER THREE

NIALL GROANED AND PULLED his pillow over his head. It muffled the far-off wails, but didn't entirely mute them.

What the *hell* was wrong with that little girl, and why wasn't her mother fixing her? The kid had been squalling for half an hour or more, and it was three o'clock in the morning. She'd probably awakened the entire neighborhood. He knew exactly when she'd started, because her first screams had inserted themselves neatly into his recurring nightmare about the toddler with the dandelion puff of hair soaked with blood.

Okay, he hadn't minded that she'd woken him up. If only she hadn't kept crying and crying and crying.

He should get up and close the window. He could turn a fan on instead. Bonus: it would provide white noise to block those pitiful sobs.

With another groan, he cast aside the pillow, got up and pulled on the pair of jeans he'd discarded on a chair. Not bothering with a light, he chose a T-shirt by touch, then fumbled his way from the bedroom. Outside, he saw that several lights were on in the main house. Good to know. At least Mom wasn't such a heavy sleeper she'd been ignoring the poor kid.

He rapped lightly on Rowan's back door, bewildered by why he was doing so. What could *he* do?

Through the glass inset, he saw her approach, her expression wary until she snapped on the outside light and recognized him. Anna clung to her like a monkey, legs wrapped around her mother's waist, arms probably choking her.

As Rowan opened the door, Anna's sobs quieted to hiccuping breaths as she turned a wet, hectically flushed face to Niall.

"I'm so sorry." Rowan looked distraught. "I should have made up my mind sooner what to do, before she woke you up."

Anna's face crumpled. "What's wrong?" Niall said hastily.

"She has an ear infection. I'll have to get Desmond up…"

"He's sleeping?" he asked in disbelief.

She made a face. "Trying. We need to go to Emergency."

"You'd better get dressed." He was having to raise his voice to be heard above the renewed sobs.

"Yes." She looked hopeful. "I don't suppose you'd hold her?"

Oh, man. Why hadn't he stayed in bed?

He'd been trying not to notice that she wore only a T-shirt that reached midthigh. It had a cartoon character on the front, faded by frequent washings. The thin cotton knit fabric clung to her body. Her daughter's legs, clamped around her, had pulled the hem up almost high enough for him to see whether she wore panties beneath it or not. The speculation was enough for his body to harden despite the squalling kid.

"Uh...sure. If she'll come to me." He hesitated, cursing the common decency that had gotten him out of bed and over here in the first place. "Do you want me to stay with Desmond? Or..." He looked at the hysterical little girl. Despite deep reluctance, he said, "Maybe I should come with you. Drive, so you can concentrate on Anna."

"Do you mean that?" Rowan's eyes welled with tears.

Hell. Now she was crying, too.

"Of course I do. If it would help." He found himself holding out his arms and hoping the little girl would go into them, even though normally he would consider that a fate worse than death. "Go on. Get dressed."

With an especially piercing sob, Anna catapulted herself at Niall. She latched on tight, buried her face against his neck and cried. The rhythmic sobs reminded him unpleasantly of a siren he longed to turn off. Rowan gave him one fraught look, then fled.

Feeling way out of his depth, he bounced the girl a little. "Hey, hey. I know you hurt. We'll get you all better before you know it. Come on, honey." He began to walk. He'd heard new fathers talk about walking the baby endlessly. Maybe it would work here, too. "Crying doesn't help. I think it's making you feel worse."

She wasn't impressed by the argument. She continued to sob, he continued to walk and hold that small, hot body close. It seemed like forever but was probably less than five minutes before Rowan reappeared, dressed in a haphazard way, Desmond at her side. Niall had wondered where Sam the dog was; he hadn't showed himself when Niall crossed the yard or entered the house. Now he peered cautiously around the door frame but didn't come any closer.

Smarter than they'd given him credit for, maybe.

They took Rowan's car since the kids' safety seats were already in it. Niall drove while she sat in back between them. In his desperation, he exceeded a few speed limits and rocketed to the load/unload zone in front of the emergency entrance at the hospital.

"You take Anna," he suggested. *Please. Please*

take Anna. "Desmond and I'll follow you once I park."

"Thank you." Rowan clambered over her daughter, unbuckled her and carried her into the maws of the hospital. Niall and Desmond sat without moving or speaking for a moment in the absence of sound. Niall didn't know about the kid's eardrums, but his were ringing.

"She gets lots of ear infections," the boy finally said, matter-of-factly.

"Does she." Niall gave his head a shake and put the car back into Drive. Maybe he and Desmond could walk really slowly.

Would the doctor only give her antibiotics, or would they be able to do something to take her pain away? A shot of morphine, maybe?

Desmond was able to unbuckle his own seat belt. However, when Niall circled the car to him, he said, "Can you tie my shoes? I can't see."

"Sure." Did he know how to tie them? Niall didn't remember how old kids usually were when they learned. Sure enough, when he knelt on the pavement he found the laces straggling. He could feel a bony ankle, too; no socks.

Tying this little boy's shoelaces, Niall had a feeling of unreality. What was he doing here? How had this happened? Why hadn't he stayed in bed?

I don't get involved, he thought desperately, but

here he was. *No.* He wasn't involved, for God's sake, he was only giving an hour or two to help out a young mother. And it didn't hurt to stay on his landlady's good side, right?

A small hand tucked itself confidingly into his. "You'll be able to find Mom, right?"

"Yeah," he said, rising to his feet. "We'll find Mom." His smile came out of nowhere. "Hey, all we have to do is follow the sound of Anna crying. We could track her down in the deepest, darkest forest. Never mind a hospital. That's easy."

"Yeah." Desmond suddenly sounded cheerful. "She is kind of loud, isn't she?"

"Oh, yeah."

They walked across the parking lot, lit by sodium lamps. They seemed to be alone out here. The faint crunch of their footsteps was the only sound.

"I'm glad you came."

Niall looked down at the face turned up to his. Bizarrely enough, he realized that, in a way, he was glad, too. Rowan's kids could be pains in the butt, no question, but they were okay. Even sweet, in their own way. And Rowan had needed someone tonight. He'd seen it in her eyes.

This isn't personal, he told himself. *I'm a cop. Cops protect and serve. That's all I'm doing.*

All the same, he hoped like hell no other cops

happened to be lurking in the emergency room to see him. His reputation as the ultimate loner would be shot.

The glass doors slid open. Ahead he could see Rowan, turning away from the check-in counter, Anna clutching her and crying, but more quietly now. Sadly. Rowan saw him, and the weariness and distress on her face eased. Niall had the strangest sensation under his breastbone. He couldn't begin to identify it, and didn't try very hard, only led Desmond over to his mother.

"She's heavy. Do you want me to take her?" he offered.

He had the thought that this could be atonement for his part in what had happened to that other little girl, in the bank parking lot.

ROWAN WANTED TO CRY AGAIN, which was ridiculous. She hadn't cried in years, not even when Drew had died. For weeks her eyes had been so dry they burned, and she'd wondered if something was wrong with her. But now, Niall's kindness was doing something to her. Weakening her.

"I'm okay." There were only five other people in the waiting room, thank goodness. A man who was leaning over and clutching his stomach, the woman with him watching anxiously, her hand on his back. A scrawny, twitchy, tattooed girl with a bruised, puffy face. And a woman who

might be in her forties who was cradling a ten-
or twelve-year-old boy close, her tenderness and
worry palpable. Rowan went to the closest chairs
and sank gratefully down, holding Anna in her
lap. Desmond climbed onto the chair next to her,
and Niall sat on his other side.

"Did they say how long the wait would be?"

She shook her head. "It shouldn't be long,
though. Since there are so few people here."

She'd seen him assess every single person in
the room, from the receptionist to the ten-year-
old, the minute he walked through the sliding
doors. Now his gaze lingered on the tattooed
teenager who looked as if she'd been beaten up.

After a minute he said, "Desmond says Anna
gets these a lot."

"Yes. The antibiotics always work, but she has
a miserable day or so first. I keep hoping she'll
outgrow this." She rubbed her cheek against her
daughter's hair. "So far, no cigar."

"There must be a reason."

How like a man. There was a problem; there
ought to be a fix. And he wanted to know—
now—why no one had found it.

Obscurely, she found his attitude to be comforting. Maybe only because someone else cared.

Not fair, she reminded herself. Donna and
Glenn cared. Except she could tell they thought
she was somehow at fault. Because she'd passed

on some frailty that ran in her family—certainly not in theirs—or because she let the kids eat junk food too often, or should be cleaning wax out of Anna's ears, or in some unknowable way wasn't a good enough mother. The implication was always there.

Niall's quiet, reassuring presence, the way he was looking at Anna with worry, his implacable tone—as if the doctors were the ones to blame, not her—it was so different, she found herself feeling steadier and, at the same time, less self-reliant. *Weaker,* she thought again.

"I'm not sure they even look. I don't know. Desmond's never had a single ear infection."

A nurse appeared through the swinging doors and called a name. The man clutching his stomach and the woman with him stood and followed her into the back. Ten minutes passed. Desmond grew bored. Niall found him a *Ranger Rick* magazine with pictures of wild animals that entertained him for a while. Anna's cries dwindled into an occasional miserable whimper. She grew heavier as she relaxed. Rowan shifted to get more comfortable.

Niall suddenly stood, came to the chair on the other side of her. "I'll take her for a while. You need a break."

He meant it. Rowan didn't know why she was surprised. Drew had been a good father. He'd have insisted on taking a turn, too. But that was different. Nonetheless, she gratefully shifted Anna to his arms and watched as he settled her against him as if he'd done it a thousand times. After a minute, Rowan turned her attention to Desmond. She found a crayon in her purse and they did a simple word match puzzle in the magazine.

The teenage girl went back. Five or ten minutes later, so did the mother and boy. None of them reappeared. An ambulance raced into the bay, lights flashing, briefly exciting Desmond. Hospital personnel hurried out and helped unload a man onto a rolling gurney, hooking a bag of fluids above him and adjusting an oxygen mask. Everyone moved really fast. After a while, the two EMTs came back out and drove away. Desmond fell asleep against Rowan's shoulder. She peeked at Anna and saw that she was still awake, but barely, her eyes mere slits between puffy, red lids.

"Anna Staley."

Rowan started.

"You take Anna and I'll carry Desmond," said Niall, standing.

He seemed to assume he'd come back with her. The independent woman she usually was thought she ought to protest, but, oh, this was so nice to be able to lean, if only a little. Why not enjoy it while it lasted? So, without arguing, she accepted the transfer and they all traipsed after the nurse as if they were the family they appeared to be.

The nurse led them to a curtained cubicle, where she took Anna's temperature and pulse, made notes and went away. The wait after that was, thankfully, brief. Niall appeared completely patient. Beyond their small space, Rowan could hear voices; footsteps passed now and again. Then the curtain rattled on its rings and a woman her mother's age in a white coat appeared. She wore a stethoscope around her neck.

"I'm Dr. Ellis," she said briskly. "What seems to be the problem?"

Rowan told her, and with a lighted speculum Dr. Ellis looked into Anna's ears, shaking her head as she did so. "You poor thing. Flaming red. Hmm." She persuaded Anna to stick out her tongue and was able to look down her throat. She hmmed a bit more and said, "Her tonsils don't look awful, but they're a little ragged. You say she's had frequent infections?"

"Yes."

"I'm going to give you an antibiotic tonight, but also a referral to an ear, nose and throat specialist. She needs to have her adenoids checked, and it's possible those tonsils should come out. Worth a good look, anyway."

"Yes. Please."

She gave some suggestions for immediate relief, all of which Rowan had heard before and already tried, sent the prescription for the antibiotic winging off to the hospital pharmacy from the computer and breezed out.

"Let's take the kids to the car," Niall suggested. "Then I can go back in and pick up the prescription."

She'd already given her insurance information, so they didn't have to stop on the way out. Rowan had to hurry to keep up with Niall's long stride. Desmond's weight seemed to be nothing to him. She cringed to think what it would have been like without Niall. As much as she'd come to resent her parents-in-law, at least she hadn't had to drag Des along the last few times she'd brought Anna to Emergency in the middle of the night.

"I'll pay you back," she said to Niall, when he closed the door on Desmond's side and looked at her over the roof of the car.

"Looks like Anna's asleep at last. Close your eyes, too, if you can."

This time she sat in front. Once she'd locked the doors, she did put the seat back a bit. She couldn't doze, but she came close. Time had a dreamlike quality. She didn't know how long it was before he came back, handed her a bag and then started the car. They didn't talk during the short drive.

When they got home, Niall said quietly, "I'll carry him up to bed," and she could only nod. Anna stirred when she picked her up, but Desmond stayed limp and unresponsive. Rowan had forgotten to lock the back door, which earned her a glance from Niall, but all he did was carry her son upstairs and turn into his bedroom. She gave Anna a dose of the strawberry-flavored antibiotic and another dose of painkiller, tucked her in, and looked up to see Niall waiting in the bedroom doorway.

"She okay?" he murmured when Rowan joined him in the hall.

"Mostly worn-out, I think. But maybe she'll sleep for a few hours."

He looked down at her with those gray eyes that didn't reveal anything, however kind he'd been tonight. "You need to do the same."

"Yes." She smiled. "You, too."

"Yeah." His voice had dropped a notch, sounded husky. "I will."

"Thank you," Rowan whispered.

His hand lifted and he tucked a strand of hair behind her ear. His knuckles seemed to linger against her cheek, but that might have been her imagination. He backed a step away. "I'll lock up," he said, low and gentle, then turned and went downstairs.

Rowan stood where she was until the lights

downstairs went out and she heard the click of the back door. She was so tired she was swaying on her feet. It was hard to make herself turn out the hall light, too, and go into her bedroom. She stripped off her clothes and bothered with the T-shirt she wore as a nightgown only because she would probably have to get up again with Anna.

Sleep pulled her down. Just before she fell into it, she thought how lucky her grandmother had been to find Niall. How lucky *she* was.

Yes, but he didn't want *to be with us tonight.*

What a strange thought. He'd been wonderful. And yet…something told her that the whole while, a part of him had strained to escape.

He was really a stranger, so it shouldn't hurt to know that he'd helped because he felt he had to, not because of any tender feelings for her or the kids. Shouldn't hurt? Didn't. *Of course* it didn't hurt, she told herself, and fell into the thick velvet darkness of sleep.

ROWAN STOOD AT THE KITCHEN sink, her hands in soapy water, and watched her son through the window. She hadn't noticed in time to stop him from knocking on Niall's door. She'd first spotted him standing there staring at it as if it would surely open any minute. Sam was at his side, Desmond's hand gripping the dog's ruff. For once, Sam's tail wasn't wagging. She saw the minute Des gave up; his shoulders slumped, his head bowed and he turned away, disconsolate.

Rage rose in her, almost choking her. How could Niall *do* this to a little boy? He'd systematically avoided them since that night. Three days now, and he had managed to come and go when none of them were outside. He didn't answer knocks on his door, even though Rowan knew he was home. He was letting them know, bluntly and cruelly, that he had no intention of getting sucked into their lives.

If it was only her, she wouldn't have minded. Anna, she thought, had been getting attached, but she was less aware of his rejection. Desmond, though, had latched on to him with all of a little boy's need, and now Niall was knowingly hurting him.

What she wished she could do was find an excuse to evict the jerk. Maybe she could find a genuinely *nice* man to live in her small rental. No, not a man; a woman. She wouldn't set Des up for this again. She ached, watching him walk so slowly back across the lawn, scuffing his feet, never once raising his head. She hoped Niall was watching, too. She hoped he felt guilty.

Rowan snorted. Who was she kidding? If he was capable of guilt, he'd be letting Desmond down gently instead of cutting him off, *whack,* sorry, don't want to see you, kid.

Drying her hands, she went to the back door and opened it. "Hey," she said, "I was thinking about baking cookies. You want to help?"

"Not really." He sat on the bottom step. "Sam and me want to stay out here. That's okay, isn't it, Mom?"

No, she wanted to say. No, it isn't, not if you're going to stare at Niall's house and wait for something that isn't going to happen. But how could she?

"Maybe Zeke would like to come over," she suggested.

He shook his head. "He has swimming lessons today."

Now *she* felt a pang of guilt. She'd meant to sign Desmond up, too, but what with moving and starting work on the house, it had slipped her mind. "I'll bet I could get you in for the last session," she said. "I'll find out when it starts."

"Can Anna take lessons, too?"

"The doctors don't recommend she get water in her ears. You know how I put plugs in her ears even in the bathtub."

"Zeke says he's doing real good. He swam all the way across the pool." Desmond sounded impressed.

"You already know how to put your face in and float and kick. You'll be swimming across the pool, too, before you know it."

"But I'll be in Beginners, won't I? Zeke says *he's* gonna be in Advanced Beginners next time."

Lousy mother alert. Her shoulders sagged, too. Maybe Donna and Glenn were right. Maybe she *wasn't* a good mother.

"I can swim," she said. "What if we go to public swim sessions and I teach you? Maybe you could catch up before the next session of lessons starts."

His face brightened even as she was thinking, *Wait! What do I do with Anna?* She should have thought before she opened her mouth. But Anna's grandparents would be thrilled to have her. It could be a sort of…consolation for them. A chance to spend time with one of their grandkids, while Rowan had a good excuse for not leaving Desmond with them. *Yes. That might work.*

"Really?"

She smiled at her son. "Really."

"That would be cool," he decided. "I bet I can learn real fast."

"I bet you can, too."

"Do you think Niall knows how to swim?"

She aimed one brief laser-sharp glare at the cottage, wishing it could pass through walls and impale her tenant. "Who knows?" she said lightly. "He's just a guy who was renting from Gran, Des. I know he was nice to you, but he must be really busy. We were lucky he could help us out the other night, but let's not count on him, okay?"

The animation left her son's face. After a moment he bowed his head again. "I thought he liked me."

She hesitated. "I'm sure he does, but..."

"It doesn't matter," he mumbled. "I've got Super Sam. And I like living here better than Grandma and Grandpa's."

"Good." Rowan hugged him. "You sure you don't want to help with those cookies?"

For a moment she thought he was going to refuse again, but finally he shrugged and climbed to his feet. "I guess I might as well."

He trudged into the house after her, and right at that moment she hated Niall MacLachlan with all the passion in her heart.

HE'D MISSED HIS LITTLE hobby.

The man moved soundlessly across the lawn, loving the cloak of darkness. It had been over a year since he'd done this. He had to worry about being caught, even though he never had been. Still, he would indulge himself for a while, for a few weeks or months, then quit again before the police got involved. He could find what he needed on his computer. There was plenty available online to satisfy his craving.

Lately, though, he'd found himself noticing

who lived where. His excitement had sharpened, even before he'd made a conscious decision to start again.

Really he should wait until fall, when darkness came earlier. He'd noticed, though, that parents were letting their children stay up much later these days, perhaps because it was summer. Nine or ten o'clock, and there were still games of tag going on in the street. What were those parents thinking? Anything could happen to their children, out in the dark.

Of course, *he* wouldn't hurt them. He only allowed himself to look. Looking was enough.

This rambler didn't even have a fence, which meant no dog, either. Dogs were a nuisance, although fortunately their families often took them in at night. He moved quietly along the side of the house, staying out of the light cast through the kitchen window. The next window was dark; dining room, he thought. The one after that was dark, too; master bedroom, he hoped.

The two smaller windows were bathrooms. He heard water running, muffled voices. It was the next window that interested him. A light was on in the room; somebody had already pulled the curtains, which were blue cotton with spaceships rocketing between bright golden stars. The hand that had pulled them was careless, though. There was a crack on one side, enough for him to see into a little boy's bedroom.

To get close, he had to step into the flower bed, which he didn't like. He'd have to remember to scuff the dirt before he left, so no obvious footprints remained. The thorny cane of a rosebush snagged his pants, and he stifled a curse. But the boy was alone in the room, taking his pajamas from beneath his pillow. He was old enough to get undressed and dressed himself.

This close to the window, the man heard the mother call, "Chad? Did you brush your teeth?"

"Yes, Mom."

"I'll be there in a minute to tuck you in."

The boy took off his shirt and dropped it in an open hamper. His back to the man, he kicked off his sneakers, pulled off his socks and then his jeans and briefs. Filled with intense pleasure and the sharp arrow of anticipation—*turn around, turn around*—the man unzipped his pants. So quietly. He loved knowing he was invisible out here.

He reached down to touch himself.

CHAPTER FOUR

NIALL HAD HEARD THE VEHICLE pull into the driveway—he was always aware of things like that, even when it likely had nothing to do with him. SUV or pickup, he had decided, from the deep sound of the engine. He was mildly surprised when, a minute later, someone knocked on his door.

He was less surprised to find his brother on his doorstep. They occasionally dropped by each other's homes. That had been the sum total of their relationship outside of work, until a little over a year ago when Duncan met Jane, who insisted on inviting Niall to dinner and suchlike. He'd been Duncan's best man at the wedding, too, an odd experience.

Am I his best friend? he had wondered. *If I were getting married, who would* I *ask to stand beside me?*

The answer had disturbed him. Duncan, of course. But sometime in the past year he'd settled into the realization that he loved his big brother, who probably loved him, too. The fact that they weren't very good at showing how they felt didn't mean the emotion wasn't there.

"Hey," he said now. "What's up?"

"Nothing." Duncan followed him in then looked around with the exact same, faintly appalled expression he had every time he came there. It said, *How the hell can you live in a shoebox?*

The main room of the cottage had a kitchenette, table with two chairs, sofa, one bookcase and a stand with a TV and DVD player. Not much floor space left over. It was as if the place had been designed for child-size furniture, although that wasn't the case. Enid had told Niall that her husband had decided they needed a rental, and had built the cottage with that in mind. He hadn't wanted to give up too much yard, though; apparently he'd had a big vegetable garden. Niall didn't mind the close quarters, but obviously Duncan did. His visit would be short. It wouldn't take long before he'd start looking uneasy, possibly claustrophobic, and would depart as abruptly as he'd arrived.

Niall poured coffee and carried the mugs to the table.

"Thank God," his brother said, seizing one.

Niall stared at him.

"It's Jane. Now that she's pregnant, she can't

stand the smell of coffee. She's sick to her stomach," he said gloomily.

"Morning sickness."

"And midday, afternoon and evening sickness." He grimaced. "Apparently that isn't uncommon, and it'll pass in maybe another month."

Niall grinned. "Curtailed your sex life, has it?"

Duncan mumbled something that might have been, "Killed it."

He decided not to torment his big brother. They talked about work; Niall had been cleared to go back at the beginning of the week and had taken up the reins again with relief. Duncan wanted to know if he was bothered any by the shooting, and he shrugged. Duncan raised his brows.

"No more than you'd expect," Niall said finally.

"I've never shot anyone."

"I expected a few nightmares," he admitted. "Like last time."

His brother nodded; they'd talked some, after Niall had killed the crazy who had been stalking Jane and had had a knife to her throat.

"Seeing that little girl and thinking she'd been killed…" He cleared his throat.

"Not your fault."

"Sure it was," Niall said sharply. "It was my job to control the situation."

"And you did. There's not a person who looked

at what happened who didn't think you did everything possible."

He only shrugged again.

After a minute Duncan got up and poured himself a second cup of coffee. "How's it working with the new landlady?" he asked, letting the subject of the shooting go.

Would he understand why Niall had spent the past week hiding inside the house, sneaking in and out when he had to go somewhere?

Maybe not. Niall wasn't even sure if *he* understood.

"I'm thinking of looking for another place," he said. "I've been keeping an eye on the classifieds."

"Why?"

Why? *Because I'm attracted to a woman who has two kids and would be insulted by the idea of recreational sex. Because it's killing me, seeing the expression on the boy's face every time he looks this way. Because I feel a whole mess of things I don't understand.*

Yeah, that about summed it up.

"They're noisy," he said. "One of the kids keeps knocking on my door. Because I haven't played the bagpipe in weeks."

Usually his brother would have been getting restless by now. This evening, he wasn't. He sat there, relaxed, his eyes steady and penetrating. Déjà vu. When Niall was a kid and Duncan sensed he had a problem, he would look at him that way, too. He didn't ask a lot of questions, only waited. A tactic that usually worked.

Not this time, Niall thought grimly. He wasn't ready to admit to anyone, even his brother, that he'd been behaving like a shit because he was scared. Of something.

After a long time, Duncan nodded. "She said hi when I crossed the yard." He paused. "Pretty little thing."

"Cute kids, too. The little girl…" He stopped himself.

"The little girl?"

"She's having trouble with ear infections." That wasn't what he'd been about to say, but it would do. "Engine Company 12 could tie her to the hood when they go out on a call."

Duncan flashed one of his rare and therefore startling grins. "See what I have to look forward to?"

Jolted, Niall said, "You of all people."

Duncan's smile died. "Of all people?"

Oh, hell. He hadn't meant it that way. His most distant memories of Duncan were good ones. Niall had trailed his big brother as only a determined and devoted four- and five- and six-year-old could, and Duncan had been patient and kind. Increasingly, Niall had trouble remembering either of his parents with any clarity, but Duncan, who had always been there, stayed crystal clear.

"Never pictured you as the kissing-babies type," he said. "That's all."

His brother shrugged. His face was never very expressive, but for a moment Niall would have sworn he saw sadness there, and that stung because he was responsible for it.

"You heard from Conall?"

He always asked. Niall shook his head. "Not for..." He had to think. "Three or four months."

"They'd let us know if he went down."

In the line of duty, Duncan meant. The youngest MacLachlan brother worked for the U.S. Drug Enforcement Agency. It sounded as if he was undercover as often as not. He seemed to get off on risk and had a gift for losing himself in another identity. Not for the first time, Niall reflected on the fact that, while all three of them had become cops of one kind or another, the MacLachlan boys had had three entirely different motives. Power, for Duncan—control. For Conall, a need to live on the edge. And for Niall...that one was a little harder to define. Neither of the above, was all he could say for sure. Lately it had occurred to him that he didn't know himself nearly as well as he'd believed.

"Yeah, we'd be informed. You know Conall isn't good at staying in touch."

Duncan gave a short, humorless laugh, which Niall understood. Con had resented their big brother with a passion Niall hadn't altogether understood. He hadn't spoken to Duncan since he'd graduated from college. Once upon a time, Niall had figured Duncan didn't much care. Now he knew better.

After a moment, Duncan rapped his knuckles on the table, stood and took his mug to the sink where he rinsed it out. "I'm off," he said.

Niall surprised himself by saying, "You and Jane okay? I mean…together?"

"Sure we are." Duncan's hard face relaxed into a smile. "She had a difficult childhood, you know."

Niall nodded. She hadn't said a lot, but some.

"We should be an accident waiting to happen, but it's not like that. She makes me happy. I make her happy. Sometimes we fight, but it's okay." He hesitated, his gray eyes holding Niall's, as if he wanted to be sure he was listening. "Don't shut yourself off," he said finally.

Niall snorted. "Have you been possessed by Dr. Phil? Oprah?"

His brother smiled again, clapped him on the shoulder, then left.

Niall hesitated at the open door before step-

were lucky to get in quick to see the ear, nose and throat guy. He wants to take her tonsils and adenoids out. Surgery is scheduled for a week from Friday."

He felt a stab of alarm. "Is it risky?"

"You didn't have your tonsils out?"

Niall shook his head. "I think my younger brother did, but I guess I was too little to think much about it."

"It's outpatient surgery. It's not like...like they're cutting her open, exactly. But they do knock her out and...it's scary for me, okay?"

He nodded. After a moment, he sat on the bottom step, his back to the newel post. "Does she know?"

He thought Rowan's arms had tightened around herself, as if to contain the fear she'd admitted to. "Not really. She's four. I'm not making a big deal out of it."

"Desmond?"

She shook her head.

"What will you do with him while..."

"We'll manage something," she said shortly.

"I'm sorry." He didn't even know why he'd come over here to talk to her, why he was saying any of this. Dr. Jekyll and Mr. Hyde, he thought, at war within him.

"For?"

"Being such a jackass." He hesitated. "Hurting Desmond's feelings."

"I'm glad you're human enough to have noticed you were."

"I'm human." Maybe. He wasn't always sure. He didn't feel what most people did.

Didn't used *to feel what other people did.*

The realization came out of left field, stunning him. He couldn't deny it, much as he'd have liked to. Lately, he'd been a mess. The shift had begun a while back, when Duncan got involved with Jane and his and Niall's relationship changed. But the day Niall had found Enid dead then had been involved in the shooting had been a sort of watershed. Or maybe that wasn't it at all; maybe it was the day Rowan and her children moved into the house and gave him an up-close-and-personal view of something unfamiliar and disconcerting.

Tempting.

As loving as their small family was, it had an obvious vacuum. Daddy was missing. He'd tried a couple of times, however awkwardly, to fill the vacancy. An experience that scared the crap out of him.

So why are you over here talking to her? he had to ask himself again, and was unnerved by the answer.

I'm still tempted. I liked the way Desmond looked at me. The feel of his hand in mine.

He'd liked more than that. He'd liked easing the strain on Rowan's face. He'd liked the warm, trusting weight of the children in his arms. He liked seeing the softness of Rowan's eyes close up, studying the fine texture of her skin, imagining her small hands on his body and his big ones on hers. He liked her smell, the sight of her hair slipping out of the ponytail, the delicate shell of her ears and the very female swell of her breasts. The love and patience in her voice when she talked to her kids.

She made him feel things he didn't trust. They all did. *I can't go there,* he thought desperately. But he also knew he couldn't keep hurting them the way he had.

"Desmond hasn't given up on me," he heard himself say.

"Give him time," Rowan muttered.

"No. I..." He almost choked on it. "I'll try."

He felt her scrutiny; for once, couldn't meet it. "Why?"

Damn it, why did she have to keep asking that? He didn't *know* why.

"Because it seems to matter to him." At first he thought that was the best he could do. But then more words came to him, ones that felt strange in his mouth, like a food he'd never tasted. "Because...I needed someone when I was a kid."

He couldn't even hear her breathing. She spoke at last, very softly. "Did you have someone?"

"Duncan. My brother."

"That was him who just left, wasn't it? I've seen him on the news."

"Yeah."

This silence all but made him squirm. He looked down to see that his fingers were beating an uneasy rhythm on his jean-clad thigh. He stilled them, waiting for her judgment.

"All right. But if you hurt Desmond, I'm going to hurt you." Her voice was lioness fierce. "Is that clear?"

He looked at her finally. She was glaring at him. What could he do but nod?

She did the same, hers sharper and not very friendly. Then she stood, went up the steps and into the house. She eased first the screen door then the door closed quietly, probably to avoid waking the kids. But he heard the lock snick, and next thing he knew the porch light went out, leaving him in darkness.

He might have smiled, except he felt too weird, as if he was having an out-of-body experience.

Why did I open my big mouth? But he knew. He would have broken the next time the kid came up to his back door and knocked, then stood there waiting instead of going away. Each time he'd done that, Niall, sitting rigid on the other side of that door, had been able to feel the intensity of his hope and then his disappointment.

This was payback, he decided. Duncan could have abandoned him and Conall and didn't. He sensed some similar need in the kid, even though he didn't altogether understand it. He couldn't be a father, but maybe he could be a friend.

He stood and made his way back across the dark yard, glad that Rowan, in her snit, had forgotten to take the dog in with her. Sam bumped companionably against his leg with each step he took. Amused at himself, Niall wondered what would happen when Super Sam's tunnel finally made it under the foundation and into the crawl space. Would he keep digging, or would he turn his attention to gnawing his way up through the floor instead?

The picture he had of the dog's head popping up in the middle of the room brought a low laugh from his throat. He told himself that was why he felt…lighter. Why when he went to bed he thought he might actually sleep tonight.

THE ROAR OF THE MOTORCYCLE heralded Niall's arrival home from work Friday afternoon. Wearing a short-sleeved dress shirt, tie and slacks, he strolled over to say hello. Already tugging the tie loose, he might have been any other guy grateful to be freed from a hard day at work, except most of those other guys didn't wear a gun in a holster at their waists along with a badge clipped to the belt. Desmond's face lit at the sight of Niall, which made Rowan anxious. He had already asked a whole lot of questions about that gun and badge. Did he have some idea of Niall as superhero? Darn it, she thought—as if Niall didn't make her anxious on plenty of levels already.

She said hello, hoping he hadn't noticed the dark circles she got under her eyes whenever she had one of her migraines. His gaze seemed to sharpen on her face, but they were both distracted by the sound of a car pulling into the driveway behind Niall's Harley. Recognizing the sound of the engine, Rowan groaned under her breath. Neither of the kids heard her, but Niall did and gave her an inquiring look.

"Grandma and Granddad," she said resignedly. Boy, did they know how to pick their time. Here she was, in grubby shorts and T-shirt, sweaty, trying to dig out a flower bed despite the distant thud behind her right temple. A few feet away, Anna was contentedly making mud pies thanks to a wet circle provided by the water hose. Des, boylike, had spent the day rolling on the grass with Sam, climbing the old apple tree and pedalling hard in an attempt to learn to ride a two-wheel bike while she raced along holding him up. He was even dirtier than his mom.

The past little while, he had been attempting to train Sam to sit. The dog had somehow conned him out of a whole bunch of treats despite the fact that his butt had never descended to the ground. Desmond, sitting on the grass, had begun explaining his plan to Niall, but now he swiveled to face Rowan. "*They're* not taking me swimming, are they?"

"No. For goodness sakes, I don't even know if either of them can swim." Rowan frowned. "I suppose they can. But Des… I don't know if I can take you tonight, either."

"What?" He shot to his feet. "But you *said!*"

"You know I had a headache earlier."

"But you said you feel better."

She wouldn't have come outside if she hadn't, but the headache had been creeping back. "Yes, but we have that potluck tomorrow so the kids and parents in Anna's new preschool can meet. I have so much to do tonight." She glanced at Anna to realize she was getting soaked. "Oh, honey. Let me turn the water off."

Her daughter's lower lip stuck out. "No! I want more mud." She grabbed the nozzle, and the trickle ran over her bare, muddy legs.

Des crossed his arms and glowered. "Mo-om!"

None of them had heard the gate opening and closing. Now, Donna stared from one of her grandchildren to the other. "What on earth is going on here?"

"We're having fun, that's what," Rowan snapped, feeling as sulky as her kids.

She heard a choked sound and leveled a look at Niall, who had conditioned his expression to bland. His eyes, though... She'd have sworn his eyes smiled.

Desmond ignored his grandparents. "It's not fair! I don't want to go to some dumb potluck tomorrow. It's not my friends. You said you'd help me swim so I could be in the same class as Zeke. Anna always gets everything *she* wants," he exclaimed.

"I do *not!*" his sister shot back.

Donna, stout and permed, wearing blue polyester slacks and a crisp blue-and-white striped blouse, reached for Desmond's hand. "These children need to get clean," she announced.

With a sense of impending doom, Rowan saw that Glenn hovered with an expression of distaste aimed at her.

Sure enough, bad went to worse. Desmond wrenched away from his grandmother. "I don't hafta go get clean! Mom didn't say I hafta. Mom, I want to go *swimming.*"

Anna must have suddenly noticed how cold the water coming out of the hose was, because she threw it away from herself and the stream caught her grandfather's legs. He hopped back, a bellow escaping him. And Rowan realized that her migraine was no longer creeping back—in fact, despite the medication she'd taken earlier, she felt as if someone had taken a mallet to her head. The tableau in front of her was oddly sharp and yet unreal. Her stomach took an unhappy roll and her temple throbbed.

"I wasn't expecting you," she said to Glenn and Donna, desperately trying for politeness when she really wanted to say, *Why are you here when I didn't invite you?*

After a sharp glance at her, Niall spoke up quietly. "I told Des I'd take him swimming one of these nights. Why don't we make it tonight? In fact—" he smiled at the boy "—if you'll give me a minute to change clothes—and you'll go get cleaned up like your grandmother suggested—we'll have dinner, too. Just you and me."

Desmond's face lit with hope. "Can we get a burger? I really want one. And French fries?"

"Sure." He raised his eyebrows, his gaze meeting Rowan's. "If that's okay with your mom."

"Please." She bit her lip, making herself add, "Are you sure?"

"Why don't you let Grandma and me take you instead?" Glenn said. "You can come home with us and we'll grill cheeseburgers on the patio. In fact, you can both spend the night if you want.

Your mother doesn't look like she can take care of you right now."

Desmond all but flung himself at Niall. "I'm going with Niall. I can, can't I, Mom? Please?"

Anna scrambled the couple of yards to attach her muddy self to Rowan. "I wanna stay with Mommy. I don't wanna spend the night at Gramma and Gramp's."

Glenn snorted. "Anna, you're too old to be clinging like that. And who, may I ask, is this?" He apportioned his glare between Rowan and Niall. "Do you have any idea who you're trusting your son to?"

"Detective Niall MacLachlan." Niall held out a hand. "And you are?"

"*I'm* these children's grandfather. I'm not sure I appreciate your interference, Detective."

Rowan had seen Niall's gray eyes remote; now she saw how chilly they could become.

"I wouldn't call befriending a nice kid interfering. And I'm not what you'd call a stranger. Enid knew and trusted me."

Oh, Lord, I'm going to be sick, Rowan thought, but from sheer willpower looked her father-in-law in the eye. "*I* know and trust Niall, too." In a different tone, she added, "Des, go get cleaned up and grab your swimming stuff. Don't forget the towel. Glenn, you're closest to the faucet. Would you mind turning the water off? Thank you. Anna, honey, I think you and I need to take a nice shower together." With all the steel in her, she once again looked at her parents-in-law. "Glenn and Donna, I don't mean to be unwelcoming, but this really isn't a good time. Perhaps you'd come to dinner one night next week? I'll be sure to call when I figure out the best night."

Both of their faces froze. No one else moved, either. That weird clarity of vision continued for Rowan and she wanted, quite desperately, to go inside, take another pill and lie down with Anna cuddled up next to her.

Could this get any worse? Sure, why not? she thought semihysterically, *Mom or Dad could show up, too.*

"Well!" Donna said, her voice small. Glenn put his arm around his wife.

With a sinking sensation, Rowan realized she really had hurt their feelings. She had to try to make this better. "You know I get migraines," she explained. "This hasn't been a great day...."

"Wouldn't it be natural to turn to us for help?" the other woman said stiffly.

Yes, it would be, she thought guiltily. And maybe she should have. It wouldn't have killed the kids to have spent the day with Grandma and Grandpa.

"You've helped so much." That sounded weak. "I don't like to keep asking."

"They're all we have left of our Andrew."

Her grip on the shovel seemed to be all that was keeping her upright. "I know."

Niall strode over, lifted Anna into his arms and turned Rowan toward the house. "Excuse us," he said brusquely to Glenn and Donna. "It's obvious Rowan doesn't feel well." His voice was a shade huskier than usual; angry, she realized in surprise.

As far as she knew, her parents-in-law were still standing there when Niall swept her and the kids inside. "Upstairs?" he asked, and she nodded. Carefully, afraid her head might disconnect from her body. "Are you sure you're okay with Anna?" he asked.

"You'll nap with Mommy, won't you, sweetie?" she asked.

"Uh-huh. I like to nap with Mommy."

"Okay." He all but deposited her and Anna in the bathroom, made sure she didn't need anything, then followed Desmond to his bedroom. Within minutes, man and boy were gone, leaving the house in blessed silence.

She had the feeble thought that he couldn't possibly have wanted to take a six-year-old boy swimming during a crowded public session at the city pool after he'd worked an eight-hour or longer shift doing…whatever detectives did, when they weren't having shoot-outs in bank parking lots. But he'd volunteered. *I'll try,* he'd said, and he had been the past couple of days. She only hoped tonight's effort wouldn't wear out whatever altruistic urge that had him, as he put it, befriending a nice kid. Because if tomorrow he ignored Desmond again, well, she might have to steal his gun and shoot him, even though he'd been a lifesaver when she needed one.

A moment later she stood with her eyes closed under the beat of hot water in the shower, the small slippery body of her daughter held close, and wondered if Niall MacLachlan, with those large, strong hands, had ever given a woman a massage.

CHAPTER FIVE

NIALL HADN'T SEEN hide nor hair of either of the kids or Rowan today since he got home. Feeling restless, he prowled the small confines of his cottage. Was she embarrassed by yesterday's scene? Mad because he'd intervened?

He hadn't been able to tell when he brought Desmond home at nearly eight o'clock. She'd been waiting at the back door, her face pale and pinched, her few freckles standing out in sharp relief. Niall's mother had gotten migraines; he hadn't thought of them in years, hardly ever thought about *her.* But now he remembered the expression on her face and the way she'd disappear into a darkened bedroom for up to two days at a time after saying, "All I ask for is quiet."

Even when he'd been really little, Niall had known she meant it. They'd all tiptoed around until she was better. Duncan couldn't have been more than seven or eight—barely older than Des—when he'd first had to take charge of his younger siblings because Mommy couldn't and Daddy... Well, chances were Daddy was in the slammer. Niall didn't remember so well what ages he'd been when his father was home or not home for those stretches of time he hadn't understood then.

He was glad he'd been able to give Desmond a good time. The kid had been subdued at first, but by the time he gingerly inched into the swimming pool he'd also been chattering in his completely uninhibited way.

"I can put my face in, but I don't really like it when people splash. 'Cuz then I can't close my eyes fast enough. You won't splash me, will you?"

"Promise." The pool wasn't especially crowded, maybe not surprising when the day was so nice outside. People might have gone to the river or a lake today, instead of an indoor pool. There were families there, though, mostly kids shepherded by parents. Wearing board shorts, Niall hopped in, dunked himself in the cool water and surfaced, pushing his hair back from his face. "Your turn."

They actually made some progress. It was true that Desmond could float, although he tended to sink if he didn't kick at the same time. Not enough body fat to provide buoyancy. Niall dredged up the memory of long-ago swim lessons. Who'd taken him? he wondered. Mom? Dad? Duncan, who wouldn't have been able to drive yet but could have ridden his bike over with Niall?

From those memories, he demonstrated the arm stroke and patiently helped Desmond practice, first standing and bending over, then actually swimming. They even got to a first lesson in turning your head to breathe, although hadn't quite mastered that yet when Niall decided it was time to play instead.

There was a slide for the small fry, which Desmond loved.

"Mom showed me how to plug my nose," he confided. "See?" He showed how he took a big puff of air, swelling out his cheeks, squeezed his eyes shut tight and gripped his nose tightly.

They played tag. They floated on their backs and stared up at the ceiling. They took turns sinking to the bottom of the pool to hunt for a penny Niall had had the foresight to bring. Together they showered in the communal shower in the locker room along with other men and boys, and got dressed together.

"This is the first time I've been in here," Des said in awe, sneaking glances around. "'Cuz with Mom I have to go in the *girls'* dressing room. Mom says when I'm bigger I can come in here by myself, but she says I'm not that big yet."

"Probably not," Niall agreed, amused. He'd noticed the way the boy appraised him in the buff, puffing out his own chest and dipping his head under the showerhead exactly the way Niall did.

Over dinner he asked if Desmond remembered his dad. "Yeah." He was silent for an unnatural length of time for him. "Kind of. I was five when he died, you know. And I'm six now."

"Do you miss him?"

He nodded. "Dad used to pick me up and let me ride on his shoulders. And he'd sit with me while I was taking my bath so Mom didn't have to. And read to me sometimes. He was real good at reading stories." He poked at his fries without picking one up. "I have a picture of him next to my bed. I'm glad, 'cuz…well, sometimes it's getting hard to remember what he looked like. You know?"

"Yeah." Niall had to clear his throat. "I know."

"Did your mom and dad die?"

"No. But I haven't seen either of them since I was fifteen years old. My big brother, Duncan, raised my younger brother and me."

"How come? Where did your mom and dad go?"

"My father was arrested and went to jail." He didn't let himself react to the awe and horror on the boy's face. "My mother… I guess she didn't want to take care of three kids by herself." Could he even blame her?

Yes, he thought. *Yes, I can.*

Desmond was quiet again. "I'm Anna's big brother," he finally volunteered.

"I know. She's as lucky to have you as I was to have Duncan."

"Except, I don't think I could take care of her without Mom."

Wishing he hadn't awakened the worry he saw in those brown eyes so like Rowan's, Niall smiled. "You won't have to. Your mom isn't the kind to ever leave you. I think they'd have to drag her away kicking and screaming."

"I've never heard her scream. And she doesn't kick. Except—" his forehead furrowed "—she's real quick with her foot when Sam tries to get in the house when he's not supposed to. Like when he's muddy."

Here it was the next evening and he was alone, but Niall smiled again when he recalled how admiring Des had sounded. "You're real quick with your foot, too. Maybe it's 'cuz you're both grown-ups," he had added.

Niall shook off the recollection. *I should be glad Rowan and the kids are nowhere to be seen. This way I have the evening to myself.*

His irritability didn't subside. He wanted to know if her headache had gotten better, whether Desmond had had fun at the potluck even if he didn't know any other kids going in. Probably,

Niall realized, that's where they were now. *All* having a good time.

Did Rowan date?

Man, he didn't like the kids' grandparents. Maybe they were luckier in Rowan's parents, except…why had she taken her children to live with the Staleys if she had a good relationship with her own mother and father?

He swore and went to get his bagpipe. A few minutes later, he was absorbed in tuning the chanter. The peace that playing this most ancient of musical instruments brought him vanquished the restlessness.

DESMOND OPENED HIS CAR DOOR. "Why is Sam howling? Is he hurt?"

Her own car door open, Rowan listened. "I don't think that is Sam. Or…" She hesitated. "Not only Sam."

It was music, she realized, but out of her experience. Notes slid from one to the other in a haunting refrain that lifted the hair on her arms. She thought of state funerals, of bowed heads and tears. The word *lament* wasn't one she'd ever used in her life, but it was the only word she could think of to describe this music. Her throat clogged momentarily. This was the saddest sound she'd ever heard.

"What on earth…?" she whispered.

Then she realized that Sam *was* chiming in with an occasional, sympathetic howl. So were several other dogs in the neighborhood.

"Mommy?" Anna sounded scared.

"It's a bagpipe," Rowan realized.

"What's that?" Desmond had come around the car to stand close to her, the way he did when he was uneasy.

"A musical instrument." She gave herself a shake. "Here, honey." She helped Anna out of the car seat, grabbed the empty casserole dish and locked the car.

She opened the gate, but Super Sam didn't come running to greet them. She finally spotted him on Niall's small porch, sitting in front of the closed door staring at it, looking as pathetic as Desmond had when Niall ignored his knocks. The dog lifted his nose and loosed another long wail.

Dear God, *Niall* must be playing that music. The sound was too powerful, too visceral, to be a recording. Why hadn't Gran ever said?

Because she was nearly deaf, of course.

"It's scary music." Anna buried her face against her mom's neck.

Rowan pressed a kiss to her head. "No, sad. Bagpipes can be cheerful, too." Couldn't they? Yes, of course they could; Irish jigs were played on a bagpipe, she thought. This, though, could hardly be said even to have a melody; it was as if the man playing the music was expressing some inner hurt. Mourning.

She hustled the kids inside and firmly shut the door, which did not, unfortunately, shut out the music. If he was still playing once they were ready for bed, she'd have to go talk to him.

As she supervised teeth brushing and the donning of pajamas, it occurred to Rowan to wonder why she leaped to assume that was Niall playing. Maybe he had a friend over, or it was his brother. She might not have noticed a car parked out at the curb. But for some reason she knew. This would be his instrument. She'd seen the same emotions in his eyes often enough. Loneliness. Pride. Grief.

Don't be ridiculous. You're imagining things.

No.

She was tucking Desmond into bed when the lament came to an end, the last notes hanging in the air. Rowan held her breath, waiting for the music to start again, but it didn't. She should have felt relieved, but instead was unsettled. As if something was missing.

More silliness.

Anna, worn out by meeting so many new people, fell asleep readily. Rowan read to Desmond as she did most nights. He was reading himself now, but not well enough to enjoy it yet. She kept her voice soft, lulling him to sleep.

Was it possible to play a lullaby with a bagpipe? she wondered idly.

She reached out and gently smoothed his hair, recognizing the utter relaxation of sleep.

They'd had a good time, all of them, even Desmond who'd found other kids his age at the potluck, including a boy and a girl from his kindergarten class. Most of the families came with mother and father, which gave Rowan a pang, but there were others with a single parent. Mostly mothers, of course, but she'd met one man with two preschoolers. Someone told her he was raising his kids alone after his wife had left them.

Plenty of us do it, she'd told herself sternly. She didn't want a man. A father for her kids, yes, but not if it meant having sex with him.

Other women enjoyed it.

Other women's husbands didn't get off on giving them pain.

No surprise, she had a flicker of imagining Niall cupping her face, bending his head…

She shivered.

If Drew had been like that, there must be other men who were, too. If there was one thing Rowan had learned, it was that you couldn't tell from the outside what was really going on behind closed doors.

Wow, she thought, standing in the hall outside her kids' bedrooms, *I'm in a mood.* And after such a good afternoon and evening.

It had to be the music that had set her off. It had been like...like a long, drawn out sob, making her shudder with the memory of every grief she'd ever known. Her marriage. Her husband's death. Her realization that she couldn't depend on her parents the way she thought she could. Her loneliness.

Rowan hated feeling sorry for herself.

"So don't," she said aloud.

There were things she could, and probably should, do, but she wouldn't. She could see if there was something good on TV, or read. Maybe even something that would make her laugh.

Or she could sit outside and enjoy the night, now that it was quiet. The rose that clambered up the porch railing was in bloom, scenting the air. Rowan wished she'd thought to ask Gran what the name of it was. Now she'd probably never know.

Without consciously making a decision, she went downstairs and out through the kitchen. She didn't turn on the porch light. Light did fall through the kitchen window, but not directly onto her. It was like a nightlight, she decided whimsically, settling onto the glider Gran had loved. One foot folded under her, the other on the porch, she set herself to rocking. Sam appeared out of the darkness, mellower than usual. Worn-out, probably, from playing accompaniment.

Why wasn't Rowan at all surprised when Niall appeared, too? He seemed to materialize, a wraith taking on solidity once he chose to let her notice him. He was barefoot, she saw, without looking directly at him. Bare-legged, too, in cargo shorts and a T-shirt. He sat on the top step, not far from her, and didn't say anything for a long time.

She glided back and forth and finally let her gaze settle on him, his shoulder leaning comfortably on the newel post of the railing, face in profile to her. He was mostly in shadow, but she'd have been able to see his face even if her eyes were closed. A strong face, not exactly handsome but unforgettable. Mostly, she thought, it was his eyes. They weren't like other people's. They were usually so flat, so distant. Only occasionally did she see an emotion in them that twisted her heart, and she didn't even know why.

"Headache better?" he asked finally without looking at her.

"Uh-huh."

"Migraine?"

"Yes. I don't get them often, but they're miserable."

"My mother had migraines." He made a sound;

a sigh? "They'd knock her out for a couple of days."

"I can't afford to let them knock me out. I take pills."

"Supermom."

She wished. "Most moms do what they have to do."

He averted his face, and she felt a sharp stab of regret, remembering what Desmond had passed on about his family.

"Was that you playing the bagpipe?" Rowan said after a while.

"I wondered if you'd heard. I haven't played in a few weeks."

"Because of us."

His shoulders moved, although she couldn't exactly call it a shrug. "Enid made an ideal land-lady for me."

"You wanted one who was deaf, not someone who appreciated music."

For the first time, Niall glanced at her. She saw a flash of teeth as he smiled. "Not everyone be-lieves bagpipes create music."

"What I heard was…sad."

"It was a lament. I played not long ago when a cop was killed in Tacoma. At his funeral."

She imagined the stillness among the mourn-ers as they listened. The way their skin had prickled as that peculiar instrument raised grief to an art form.

"I told the kids that bagpipes can make happy music, too."

"Dance music. Yes."

"How did you learn to play?

"My father. The MacLachlans are Scottish." His tone was dry. "My grandfather emigrated. Dad still had a bit of an accent. He taught all of us boys the bagpipes. I'm not sure whether Conall has an ear or not, and Duncan quit playing when he got angry at Dad. I suppose he was rejecting everything Dad stood for." He was silent for a long time. "Me, I was angry, too, but…I've always been able to express myself with the bagpipe."

"You were angry because your father went to prison?"

"Des told you?" He didn't sound surprised. "I suppose that was it. Although it had as much to do with the decisions he made that got him sent there."

She didn't ask. Couldn't ask. But she wanted to.

"He dealt drugs." Niall was gazing across the yard as if he saw more than the lights on in his cottage. "Trafficked in them, I guess is a better way to describe it. He occasionally held a regular job, but we all knew he hated it. He lived for the rush of adrenaline, for the big payoff."

"And you and your brother became police officers."

He laughed, low in his throat. "All three of us did. Most ironically of all, Conall is with the DEA."

"Because of what your father did?" This was the strangest conversation. Neither of them were quite looking at each other. The quiet and the darkness and the scent of roses made it dream-like, as if tomorrow they could both pretend they hadn't held the conversation at all.

"No, I doubt it's that simple. Although I suppose I can't speak for my brothers."

"Then…why?" she asked softly.

"I think for Duncan there was that rage." He tipped his head back, as if to gaze up at the stars. "He's likely in line to become police chief. Duncan is…all about being in charge. Funny, I was thinking about this the other day. Conall has always been reckless. He likes the adrenaline rush, too. I don't hear from him for months at a time because he's undercover with Mexican smugglers or some crime organization. I couldn't live like that."

"No," she murmured. She couldn't imagine that Niall had in him the ability to sublimate his personality to that extent. He would always be himself. Aloof, wary, sad.

"Me, I suspect I followed the path of least resistance. There wasn't anything in particular I wanted to do with my life, so I followed in Duncan's footsteps." There was a pause, then his voice changed. "Turned out law enforcement suited me, or I probably wouldn't have stuck to it. And why the hell I've been going on and on about ancient history, I don't know."

"Doesn't playing the bagpipe take you back? Make you remember your father?"

"Mostly not." From the clipped sound of that, it was clear confidences were at an end. In fact, he eased himself to his feet. "I'll leave you in peace."

She took a deep breath. "You don't have to."

There was an unnerving moment of silence, during which the glider slowed. Rowan knew her cheeks were flushed and was grateful he wouldn't be able to tell. What on earth had gotten into her? She didn't understand, only knew that she craved his companionship.

"All right." He sat down again.

Mortified, she couldn't think of a thing to say. Was he itching to escape?

"You were glad to be able to move here," he said in a quiet, slow, deep voice.

Rowan gave a choked laugh. "You noticed I'm not crazy about my parents-in-law."

"Hard not to." He sounded apologetic. Then thoughtful. "The kids didn't look all that excited to see them, either."

"No. Well, Anna's okay with them. They spoil her, you know."

"But not Desmond?"

"With Desmond, it's different. They want something from him."

His head turned; she knew he was looking at her. "What?"

"For him to be Andrew, reincarnated. His father," she explained. "It's almost creepy, how desperately they want to believe he's just like his dad. It's so intense, I can tell it freaks him even though he doesn't know what they're asking from him."

"How did your husband die?"

"A car accident. His fault. He was speeding. He…liked to drive fast." He'd scared her sometimes, when she was in the car with him. To his credit, he'd never exceeded the speed limit when either of the kids were in the car. "He went off the road. Thank God he didn't hit anyone else."

"Didn't you own a home?"

"I thought we did. Turned out we owed more than it was worth. And there were other debts." So many, ones she hadn't known about. She'd believed them to be solvent, even prosperous. Drew had had a good job with the county. Wasn't he the stereotype of reliability?

Niall didn't say anything for a bit. With a strange sense of desperation, Rowan wondered if this was why she'd wanted him to stay. So she could tell him things she could never say to anyone else.

"How long did you live with your parents-in-law?"

"Fourteen months. I would have asked Gran, but…"

His voice held a smile. "Enid? And two small kids?"

This time Rowan's laugh loosened something in her. "Yeah. That's what I thought, too. Only in the end, she rescued us after all."

She looked away from Niall, wondering at her own melodrama. Rescued? Things weren't that bad at the Staleys. Only uncomfortable.

"Your parents?"

"In the middle of getting a divorce, and acting as if they're about nineteen. '*He* said. *She* said. Why don't *you* talk to your father,'" she mimicked. "It feels surreal."

His low chuckle was almost as good as a touch. A hug.

The thought crept sideways into her mind— what would it feel like to be held by Niall? His shoulders were so broad. She could tell he was strong. Could he be tender and affectionate without…without wanting more? Without wanting something unpleasant?

"You have great kids. You're doing all right, Rowan."

That made her eyes sting. "Thank you. And… and thank you for…you know. Trying, the way you said you would. You were our hero yesterday. The scene would have been way worse if you hadn't stepped in."

"Would it? I had the impression I made them mad."

"Only because you kept them from having their way." She sighed. "I guess I've been a coward. Maybe I should try to make them understand what they're doing. Why I *have* to pull away."

"You haven't said anything?"

"I've tried, in a beating around the bush kind of way. It upsets Donna, which gets Glenn's back up." She sighed. "I wish they lived farther away. Or I lived farther away."

"Your parents nearby?"

"Dad is. He's still in their house here in town. Mom claims now she always hated it. She's gone to stay with my aunt Mina in Portland. I'm sure she'll be back when…well, she gets over Dad."

Despite everything, this silence felt relaxed.

Niall leaned down and scratched Sam's neck. The dog's tail thumped and he leaned into the caress.

"So. Anna's surgery is Friday."

Her stomach knotted. "Yes."

"What time of day?"

"Early. We have to be there at seven-thirty."

He made a sound, impossible to interpret. "Your dad going with you?"

"I didn't ask him." Her mind boggled at the thought. She loved him, but he'd been a sort of weekend father even when he wasn't. Mom did the practical, have-to-be-done things: the diapers, the parent-teacher conferences, the bandage on the skinned knee, the talks on serious subjects. Dad was good for fun. She simply couldn't imagine him volunteering to accompany her to the emergency room the way Niall had. There was a reason, after all, that she hadn't asked if she and the kids could live with him. And that he hadn't offered. It was partly the succession of women he was dating, but not entirely.

Suddenly terribly conscious of the man sitting not too much more than an arm's reach away, Rowan felt a lump form in her throat. *I want you there Friday,* she admitted, although she would never, ever say it aloud.

"Do you miss your husband?"

Wow. That came out of left field. Her movement on the glider became jerky as she tried to figure out how to answer.

"Yes." Honest. "And no." Honest, too.

He looked at her, his face shadowed. "Not a perfect marriage?"

"Is there such a thing?" She hated sounding so bitter.

"I don't know." Niall hesitated. "My brother sounds happy, but they've only been married a year."

It hadn't taken her a year to realize how unhappy her marriage was making her.

"You think you know someone." That burst out of her.

"That bad?" he asked gently.

"No." She made herself take a few deep breaths. "No. It was…complicated. Drew was a good father. He really loved his children."

And her. She believed he'd loved her, too. In fairness, they hadn't had a bad marriage except in the bedroom, and maybe he couldn't help that.

Inexplicably, Rowan felt compelled to go on. "I wouldn't have stayed with him otherwise. My parents, well, Dad didn't do his part. I wouldn't put up with that from a man."

"Or even from your tenant." Amusement deepened his voice.

Maybe she should be embarrassed, but Rowan

laughed instead. "I sounded awfully demanding, didn't I?"

"Yeah, but I don't blame you. I was blowing hot and cold. That's confusing for a kid."

For a woman, too. She had the sudden, aching hope that he wouldn't go cold on her again. This—having a listening ear, an adult to talk to who didn't criticize, didn't have an agenda— felt amazing. She couldn't even imagine what it would be like to have this all the time.

Her arms closed around herself. Of course she didn't want that. She was envisioning some sort of Norman Rockwell relationship, mom and dad and the kids, but Norm hadn't painted mom and dad in their bedroom.

She stole a look at Niall sidelong, not knowing whether to be glad or sorry that she couldn't see him any better. Would a man who could be so gentle and patient *hurt* her?

He hadn't seemed interested in her that way at all, although a few times she'd seen flickers of expression that had made her wonder. Maybe he needed a friend, too. Or felt a sense of obligation for some reason. Because he'd cared for Gran? Or because Des reminded him of himself in some way?

"What if I come with you Friday?"

"What?" She stared at him.

"I'd like to come Friday."

"You're serious."

"I'm serious."

Rowan gulped. "Don't you have to work?"

"I can take the morning off."

Her chest burned. Probably she should make some polite disclaimer, but he wouldn't have offered if he hadn't meant it, would he? "I would love it if you could come."

"Good." He rose to his feet then. "I'll wish you good night. We should leave by seven on Friday?"

"Ugh. Yes."

He laughed. "Sleep tight."

"And don't let the bed bugs bite."

Niall was disappearing into the darkness. Dematerializing again. But his voice floated back. "Thanks to Super Sam, you probably have a few."

How wonderful it was to be smiling when she slipped back into the house. Feeling relief and joy and, yes, trepidation, because why *was* he being so nice? But she was so grateful that he was.

He was the kind of man she could…

No! Don't even think it. Not happening.

Okay, then. But she still felt happy. And yes, Niall MacLachlan was the reason why.

CHAPTER SIX

"I HEAR YOU'RE TAKING the morning off," Duncan observed. They were at the dinner table Thursday night, and Jane, as well as Duncan, watched Niall with interested faces.

Well, damn. He'd been glad of the dinner invitation because he'd felt the need to have a day away from Rowan and her kids. It wasn't easy when they lived so close. With the long, light summer evenings, they were often outside. Even if Desmond didn't come knocking, Niall would hear them: a laugh from Rowan, or a remonstrance for one of the kids. Sam would bark, Anna giggle. There would be the whack of plastic bat against a whiffle ball. And Niall would find himself drawn outside. It wouldn't hurt him, he'd think, to give the kid some batting tips. Or hoist Anna into the branches of the apple tree, then stand below to guard her. Give Rowan a momentary break. After all, it was summer. He didn't want to huddle inside, did he?

"Good lasagna," he said to his sister-in-law

before looking at his brother. "I am taking a few hours off tomorrow. Is that a problem?"

"How can it be? The city must still owe you a month or more of vacation."

He made a noncommital sound.

They waited. Disgruntled, he realized Jane, formerly more impatient, had soaked up some of her husband's techniques.

"One of the landlady's kids is having surgery in the morning. Tonsils and adenoids. The little girl. I volunteered to go along and help distract her son," he mumbled.

Jane's eyes were bright with astonishment. "That's...really nice of you."

He scowled at her. "You didn't think I could be nice?"

"Well, yes, but... Not that way. Or at least—" She looked to Duncan for help.

"This Rowan isn't your usual kind of lady," Duncan said.

"It's not like that. We're not involved."

"You seem pretty involved."

"I mean, it's not, uh, sexual." He flicked a glance at Jane, with her rich blue eyes and warm brown hair. "Or romantic."

Romantic. Good God. Had he ever used that word in his life?

"You're not interested in her, then." Duncan sounded intrigued. A year ago, he'd have been unlikely to ask at all about any relationship Niall had with a woman. He certainly wouldn't have pursued it beyond a casual inquiry. He'd changed, though. Was it like a smoker who'd quit, and was now ardent to reform everyone else? The thought filled Niall with alarm.

The question filled him with alarm, too. Because of course he was interested in Rowan. What man wouldn't be, seeing that luscious, petite body day in and day out, half the time clad in no more than shorts and tank top that bared a disturbing amount of smooth flesh gaining a warm, golden tan?

He also knew he didn't dare take that attraction anywhere. Duncan was right—she was different, not Niall's kind of woman. He'd taken to repeating that to himself half a dozen times a day. It was one of the many reasons he was dodging her and her children tonight. He'd hoped for distraction, not an inquisition.

"She's got kids," he said shortly.

Jane's mouth opened, then closed. Thank God. He didn't need anyone to point out that Rowan's children weren't necessarily the stopping point that kids usually were for him, that he *was* involved with them, whether he wanted to admit it or not.

The fact that he cared about them made it all the more essential that he not make a move on their mother. That would only increase expectations. Ones he couldn't fulfill. He was trying to help them out a little, not make things worse for them down the line when he moved out.

"Are you still looking for another place?" his brother asked, as if reading his mind.

After a moment, he shook his head. "As long as I play the bagpipe before the kids' bedtime, Rowan seems okay with it. I like the cottage. I've even gotten used to the dog." A grin tugged at his mouth. "Did I tell you he likes to dig?"

They laughed at his tales of the homely dog's attempts to tunnel to God knows where. "He's made it into the crawl space. I'm pretty sure he's spending the nights digging holes underneath the cottage, but who's to know?"

They laughed some more, and the subject got changed. Niall found himself watching Jane, though, gently rubbing her belly when she stood up to clear the table and bring dessert. Duncan was watching her, too, an expression on his face that shook Niall. The stone man had feelings. It shouldn't still surprise him, but every so often he caught something new on his big brother's face. Tenderness or another kind of softness that made emotions Niall didn't understand threaten to break free inside him, too.

He couldn't let that happen. Not feeling much of anything was safe. The decision had been an unconscious one for him; he was in his twenties before he realized he'd made it and when. By then, he didn't know how to unmake it even if he'd wanted to, and he didn't. Look at him lately—he couldn't help feeling things, and he didn't like it. Why suffer from recurrent heartburn if you didn't have to?

But he could be nice, could relate well to people, without getting emotionally involved. He relaxed now, thinking it over. Yes, in a way he guessed he *was* involved with Rowan, Anna and Desmond, but it wasn't and didn't have to be deeply emotional. So it was okay, as long as he kept it that way.

He lingered at his brother's until near dusk. He could see lights on in the main house when he got home. He went inside himself, decided reluctantly that it was too late to play the bagpipe, and grabbed a beer from the refrigerator. He should hit the sack soon, even though it was early by his standards. If he wanted coffee, a shower and maybe breakfast before they left for the hospital in the morning, he'd have to be up not much after six. The thought made him grimace. He'd always been a night owl. His one regret at giving up patrol had been also giving up the night shift.

Rowan was probably getting the kids in bed about now. No, Anna would already be down for the night, but Rowan had been letting Des stay up late. Realizing where his thoughts had drifted, Niall swore aloud. This was one night when he wouldn't watch to see whether Rowan came out on her porch, as she often did at this time of night. Instead, he retreated to his bedroom, where he piled pillows against the headboard and stretched out to read.

He had his window open, the screen keeping out night flying insects. He smiled to hear snuffling and then scratching as Sam squeezed himself under the cottage.

A high, terrified scream rent the night. It sounded so damn close, he all but fell over the edge in his lunge to get out of bed.

Swearing, Niall snatched up the gun on the nightstand and ran for the front door. Damn it, damn it, damn it. It had to be one of the kids who'd screamed. Thank God he hadn't stripped off his jeans yet.

Halfway across the lawn it occurred to him that he might be overreacting. He was going to feel bloody stupid, barrelling into the house only to find Anna had had a nightmare. But the sense of urgency didn't leave him, and he didn't slow down.

The back door was unlocked. Why the hell didn't she lock it? Somebody could have walked right in! The lights were still on downstairs. He saw no one.

"Rowan?" he bellowed.

"Niall?" He heard a sob of relief in her voice. "I'm upstairs."

So was he by that time. Anna was crying in her bedroom, but Rowan appeared in Des's doorway, shock and fear on her face. Her eyes dilated at the sight of the gun he held at his side, but all she did was swallow.

"What is it?" he said roughly.

"Desmond saw somebody looking in his window."

"What?" His first instinct was to reject it; maybe the kid had had a nightmare. But then he pictured the outside of the house and the flat roof of the carport that was right beneath Desmond's bedroom window.

Without a word, Niall turned and ran back the way he'd come. Before he made it outside, he heard Sam barking furiously at the gate. When Niall unlatched it, they both raced out. With a chill, he saw a stepladder that usually hung on one of the support posts was set up beyond his motorcycle, at the edge of the carport. He boosted himself enough to see that no one was up on the roof. Of course the bastard would have taken off when Desmond screamed.

Dropping back to the ground, Niall went after the dog around the front of the house. Sam had disappeared. Even knowing he'd been too late getting out here, Niall held his gun two-handed and investigated every damn shrub in Rowan's yard and the next one, too. He'd have given a lot to have a high-powered flashlight but made do with light from the streetlamps.

Had somebody intended to break in? Burglars usually had more sense. Daytime was safer, or the middle of the night when residents were all sound asleep. Maybe Desmond's window had been dark, but Rowan had still been up and other lights in the house were on. Hell, the back door was unlocked.

Wait. If Des's bedroom light had been out, how had he seen a face at the window?

Niall walked out to the street and whistled. He listened hard and finally heard the hard click of claws on pavement and then the pant of breath. Sam appeared, running down the middle of the road. Niall wondered if he'd caught the son of a bitch. He'd have probably licked him if he had.

Then Niall remembered the deep, vicious sound of that bark and wondered. Sam might be ugly as sin and dumb as a box of rocks, but he still had the protective instincts of his species. And he was unquestionably Desmond's dog, for all his easy affection for the rest of the family and even for Niall.

Rowan was still upstairs when he got back. She sat on the top step, one arm around each kid, huddled against her. Sam bounded up ahead of Niall and flung himself at them. Desmond toppled backward, his arms around the dog.

Rowan's eyes fixed on Niall's face. "Did you find anyone?"

He shook his head. "Why don't you tuck Anna in?"

The little girl clutched her mother convulsively. "I don't wanna! I wanna sleep with you."

"Yes. Okay." Rowan stood with her daughter in her arms and went into the one bedroom Niall hadn't yet breached. "I'll tuck you into my bed, honey, but then I need to talk to Niall before I go to bed." Her voice became a soft murmur as they disappeared.

Niall crouched before Desmond, who now sat up with one arm around Sam, leaning against his boy.

"Can you tell me what happened?"

The boy's head bobbed. When he spoke, his voice trembled. "Mommy hadn't pulled my curtains yet. I was…I was putting my pajamas on when I saw him."

"Your light was still on."

"Mom turns it off after she tucks me in."

"But your mother didn't see this face?"

He shook his head. "No, just me. She hadn't come yet. I think she was brushing her teeth. She said she was going to bed real soon, too, because of us having to get up so early."

A Peeping Tom. Niall felt both relief and a resurgence of rage. The six-year-old boy had been alone in his room, naked, and some creep had been peeking in the window.

Did this particular creep like boys? Or had he hoped for a little girl? Or even the mother? Niall couldn't see how the scum could have known which bedroom he'd be looking into.

No. Wait. Within a week of moving in, Rowan had replaced the heavy dark curtains with ones she'd made herself. The kids had picked out their own fabrics. Someone standing outside could guess that the pink ones with unicorns signaled girl and the green ones with dinosaurs were a boy. Niall had noticed the new curtains as soon as they were hung. He'd also noticed that Rowan had replaced the ugly tan blinds in her—formerly Enid's—bedroom window with sunny yellow blinds and sheer white curtains.

A Peeping Tom who liked boys, then.

Desmond described the face he'd seen as pale and "kind of regular," which Niall interpreted to mean no mask and probably no covering of panty hose to blur the features. Definitely Caucasian. Likely no beard or mustache. Otherwise, all the boy could say was that someone was looking in, and then he'd screamed and he thought the face disappeared.

Hell, it could even have been a woman.

Desmond didn't want to sleep in his own room, either. No surprise there. Niall gave Desmond a hard hug and said, "See you in the morning, buddy," then waited while Rowan escorted the kid into her bedroom in turn.

"I hope you have at least a queen-size bed," he said when she returned.

Rowan made a face. "No such luck." She hesitated. "Can we go downstairs?"

Sam bumped open her half-closed door and disappeared into her room. She looked after him with some resignation. "I suppose tonight…"

They went as far as the kitchen. Neither sat down.

"You don't think he was imagining it?"

"No." Cold and hard, Niall said, "Your stepladder was set up so that somebody could climb up on the carport. And Sam heard somebody. The minute I opened the gate, he went tearing out and around the house. He might even have caught him, I don't know. I searched your yard and the one on the corner. The Fishers' on the other side doesn't have much of anyplace to hide."

She nodded, still looking scared.

"Sam must have run a couple of blocks at least. It took him a while to come back when I called."

"Was somebody trying to break in?"

"I doubt it," he said grimly. "I suspect it was your classic Peeping Tom." Seeing her distress, he added, "I know it's upsetting, but they're usually harmless. I'll check tomorrow to find out whether there have been reports of anything similar in the neighborhood."

"We shouldn't call the police now?"

"I am the police," he reminded her.

She shivered, closing her eyes. "Thank you. I'm so glad you were here."

He scraped a hand over his unshaven jaw. "Hearing him scream took a couple of years off my life."

"Mine, too." Rowan shivered again, and Niall finally couldn't stand it another minute.

He crossed the couple of feet separating them and wrapped her in his arms.

Not until that moment had he remembered that he wasn't wearing a shirt or paid attention to the fact that she had on a sheer, sleeveless white nightgown with her shorts and sandals on beneath. She'd been in the middle of getting ready for bed, then, when Des screamed.

Now that he'd consciously acknowledged what she was wearing, Niall could see the swell of her breasts and the darker circles of her nipples through the fine fabric even though those breasts were now pressed to his bare chest. Which meant he'd been noticing, all right, even when he was narrowly focused on the kids and the disturbing event.

Her arms closed around him, too, and she pressed her face against his shoulder. Her hands splayed on his back, the tension in her fingertips feeling as if she was trying to grip his flesh to hold on tight. Her body trembled and she was panting, each breath stirring his chest hair.

Niall moved his own hands in a soothing rhythm on her back even though he didn't feel all that calm and comforting. He was angry and aroused both. A part of him wanted violence; he didn't like having his hunt thwarted. The creep had picked the wrong house. Obviously he hadn't known a cop lived so close.

At the same time, Niall wanted sex. He'd wanted her from the first glance, when he still thought Enid's granddaughter was probably married. Having her in his arms was shaking his usually unshakable control. How could she *not* notice how he was reacting to her? But he couldn't bring himself to let her go.

She smelled good. Something like the rose that grew over the railing of her back porch. He'd noticed it before. Not strong, like perfume. It was more subtle than that. Her shampoo, maybe. He closed his eyes and inhaled the scent.

He had to back off. Quick.

"Mom? Aren't you coming to bed?"

The worried call from the top of the stairs came as a relief to Niall. He gently squeezed her upper arms and stepped back. "We'd both better get to bed." His voice came out low and rough. "Uh…is there a lock on Desmond's window?"

Her cheeks were pink and her eyes didn't quite meet his, which made him guess she had noticed he'd been feeling more than a desire to offer her support. But she nodded.

"Yes, of course. Thank you, Niall."

He wished her good-night and left, waiting on the doorstep until she turned the dead bolt before he started down the steps and across the lawn. Niall quietly let himself out the gate, walked the perimeter of the house and yard and then hung the stepladder back up.

Tomorrow it would go in the locked garage. If the creep came back, he'd have to be carrying his own ladder.

Sleep, Niall suspected, wasn't going to come easily.

"THERE HAVE BEEN A COUPLE of reports that might match up with our guy," Niall told Rowan the next evening. He had stopped by briefly when he first arrived home from work, to find out how Anna was recovering from the morning surgery, but he hadn't said anything then about the Peeping Tom and Rowan hadn't asked.

Somehow she'd known that he would come back later. He didn't every night, although she'd made a habit of taking some quiet time out on the porch almost every evening after she'd tucked the kids in. Her excuse was that the house was hot and she liked the cool night air. She didn't like acknowledging how much she hoped he would come over to talk to her.

Please don't let him have guessed.

Tonight she had barely sat down on the glider when he appeared, moving as silently as always, settling in his usual spot on the steps before he said a word.

"They back in their own beds?"

She gave a huff that was almost a laugh. "Are you kidding? Not a chance."

"Yeah, I guess that was asking for too much."

"Really, I don't mind."

She thought his glance was searching, although she couldn't be sure in the darkness. But she saw his nod.

That's when he told her about the other police reports.

"One kid saw a face in his window, like Des did. The other call was from a man who noticed footprints in the flowerbed right under his kid's bedroom window. He'd been weeding the day before, putting in new plantings, so the earth was soft. Not good enough prints to take an impression, even assuming anybody would have bothered when no crime was committed except trespass, but the cop who wrote up the report guessed the shoe size as a man's eleven or twelve."

"Near here?"

"One was six blocks away, the other maybe eight blocks. Which suggests he lives in the neighborhood."

"I'm tempted to tear down the carport."

"You'd be sorry come winter."

She felt a spurt of temper. "Then what do you suggest?"

"Blinds on Des's window," Niall said promptly. "Make sure no one can see in."

"That's it?" She didn't know why she was suddenly so agitated, so mad, but she was. The idea of her children threatened in any way was unbearable. She'd been so grateful to find sanctuary here, in Gran's house, and now it didn't feel nearly as safe. She resented that.

"Rowan, I meant it when I said most Peeping Toms don't go beyond that."

"But some do."

His pause suggested he didn't want to answer, but he did. "Sure, a few. Even then, they're not likely to break in to a kid's bedroom."

"What do they do, coach his sports team instead?"

"I'm afraid so."

She gusted out air, hating this new feeling of vulnerability. "Great."

"You know I'll do my best to catch him."

"How?" Rowan challenged.

"I'll talk to every cop who patrols this area." Niall sounded grim. "I might do a little prowling after dark myself."

"You really think it's someone who lives nearby."

"Oh, yeah."

"Then why hasn't this been going on all along?" She stopped. "Or…has it?"

"It might. I didn't look back far. It's also possible the guy moved here recently, or something triggered a new behavior for him. There's no way to know until we catch him."

"Do you think he was, um, hoping for a little girl?"

"No." Niall pointed out that the curtains on her kids' bedroom windows were a pretty clear signal. "Besides, both the other reports involved boys in Desmond's age range."

She shuddered.

"He seemed okay this morning," Niall ventured after a minute.

Des had chattered some about last night's excitement as they drove to the hospital, but Niall was right; the subject hadn't come up again all day until bedtime rolled around.

"Did I thank you for coming with us this morning?"

"Yeah. And it was no biggie," he replied, a smile in his voice.

"Of course it was. You're so great with Desmond." *And me.* Yes, he'd been everything she needed, too. A solid, mostly quiet presence, an occasional touch. He was *there,* when it counted.

She was having a hard time looking at him tonight. This morning she'd been scared enough about Anna she hadn't thought about those few minutes in the kitchen last night, but now she couldn't help it. The way he'd held her had felt wonderful. And then she'd become aware that he had an erection. Part of her had wanted to bolt, but another part of her… Well, she'd shocked herself, because her body had wanted to burrow against him. She had become suddenly, acutely aware of his bare skin, of the power of the muscles under her hands and the soft fleece of chest hair layered over more muscles. She could hear his heartbeat, smell the faint odor of sweat and something more indefinable: *man.* And she'd felt cramping and heat low in her belly and between her legs. It had been so very long since Rowan had felt sexual desire, it had taken a stunned moment for her to recognize it. She'd just been thinking, *What kind of masochist am I?* when Des called for her.

What she still couldn't understand was that, whatever common sense told her, she hadn't wanted Niall to let her go.

She had wanted him to kiss her.

This was surely no more than a primitive biological response, something she was wired to feel, she told herself rather desperately. He'd helped with Anna, and been so kind to both the kids, and when Des screamed Niall had come roaring to protect them. Some cavewoman part of her brain had decided she ought to grab him and hold on with everything she had. Which meant sex.

I don't want sex. I don't.

So why did something inside her quiver now every time she saw him?

Why did she keep wondering what it would be like if he did kiss her? Whether he could be tender in bed? Whether she could trust him?

And how foolish was that?

The thing was, he'd been astonishingly trustworthy even though she knew, *knew,* that he'd never meant to get so sucked into their lives and that every time he joined them he was bemused at himself. She could see it on his face. *What in the hell am I doing?* And yet he kept meeting her needs and her children's as if not doing so wasn't an option.

Rowan wished she understood him better. She wished she didn't have to fear that, one of these days, he'd simply fade from their lives the same way he disappeared these evenings after sitting and talking with her. She imagined it so vividly: him walking away and never coming back, leaving behind no explanation. He hadn't given her the slightest indication she or the kids could count on anything permanent from him. And *that* was scary, because—heaven help her—she had come to depend on him. Going back to being alone would be hard.

"I'd better wish you good-night," he said. "I imagine Anna will be waking you up regularly."

"She's pretty miserable," Rowan agreed. "But it'll be worth it if she quits being sick all the time."

"She might even be able to take up swimming."

"I hope so."

"I saw Donna and Glenn when they came by this evening," he said after a silence.

"They wanted to find out how Anna was." They hadn't said anything objectionable, but they'd scarcely looked at Rowan or spoken to her even though she'd called the minute Anna was out of surgery to let them know it had gone well. This evening she'd seen how Glenn stiffened when Des told him that Niall had gone with them to the hospital. It would have been politic of her to invite them to come with her instead, but the choice had been no choice at all. She and Desmond both had needed Niall.

He nodded, understanding what she didn't say as well as what she did, Rowan suspected. "I've never given you my phone number."

She hadn't thought about it, but no, he hadn't.

"I keep my cell with me all the time. I want you to put my number on speed dial."

"You're scaring me."

He shook his head. "I don't mean to. But if I'd had music on last night, I might not have heard Desmond scream. I want to be sure you can reach me. Okay?"

She nodded. "Okay. I'll go get my cell phone."

He waited where he was until she came back. Then he stood and came to her, taking her phone out of her hand. She watched as he entered his name and number, determined she didn't have any other numbers on speed dial and made his own number one.

He laid the phone in her hand, then carefully folded her fingers over it.

"Thank you." She couldn't seem to help how tremulous that sounded. His touch and standing so close to him brought a resurgence of all those confusing feelings from last night.

"Rowan." His voice was scarcely over a whisper.

Her mouth formed the word "Yes?" but it may have been soundless.

He was staring down at her, even though he actually stood a step below Rowan. His eyes were shadowed, but she couldn't look away from them anyway.

He lifted one hand to cup her face. His fingertips were rough textured but astonishingly gentle. With his thumb, he caressed her lips, which parted. Her tongue touched the pad of his thumb—not intentionally, she hadn't made any such decision, but somehow it happened anyway, and it was as if the dampness was an electrical conductor. Her body quivered; he groaned.

He bent his head, and she got her wish. Niall kissed her.

CHAPTER SEVEN

ALARM MELDED WITH THE HUNGER that had made him reach for her. What was he *doing?* Whoa.

Too late, because his lips were on hers. And, oh damn, her mouth was soft. It quivered, too, only a tiny bit, but the feeling was both erotic and wrenched something uncomfortable in Niall's chest. Was she *afraid?*

Unsure, he kept the kiss gentle even though he wanted to dive in. He brushed his mouth back and forth, savoring that little tremble. Then he traced her lips with his tongue. When she stayed still as a mouse caught in the open, head tipped back and eyes closed, he took a chance and nipped at her bottom lip. A soft sound slipped out of her. An "Ohh." Wonder? Pleasure?

His body hardened painfully. He slid his hand around to capture the back of her head. Her hair was as silky as it looked. Sunshine. Summer. Everything pretty and hopeful that he knew.

With his other hand, he captured one of hers and lifted it to his shoulder. Then her other one. Her fingers tightened on his taut muscles, squeezing and releasing, like a cat kneading. Did she have any idea she was doing that?

He nibbled at the corner of her mouth, then pressed kisses against the plump satin of her cheek. He licked her cheek, too, one lap to taste her salt and perfume. Another sound escaped her. A moan.

He liked that she didn't wear earrings, had never pierced the lobes. He grazed one with his teeth, then suckled it.

She kneaded him some more. He edged forward so their bodies were in contact, knees to breast, and he did like the rich, deep cushion of her breasts against his chest.

"Kiss me back," he whispered as he trailed his lips back to hers.

Her breath hitched. "I—I'm not very good at…"

"Yes, you are." He rubbed their mouths together with a little more force, enough that he could taste the damp flesh just inside. Sweet. Of course she tasted sweet. The cliché made him smile. He'd kissed plenty of women who tasted of beer or some godawful flavor of toothpaste—he'd slept with one organic nut who swore by a toothpaste that all but made him gag. But Rowan's flavor was cinnamon, he thought. He loved cinnamon.

"Open up," he murmured.

He lifted his head enough to see her face, raised as if in rapture. Waiting. But when his mouth came back to hers, she parted her lips. Niall didn't know what instinct it was that kept him gentle, but it occurred to him that she kissed like a virgin, surprised by sensations she didn't recognize. A woman with two kids, as frozen in astonishment as an inexperienced fifteen-year-old.

And she made him feel like a horny fifteen-year-old himself. Knowing he wasn't getting any, not tonight, and damn near desperate in his disappointment.

But enjoying what he *was* getting, even though that voice in the back of his head insisted, *Big mistake.*

How could this be a mistake when it felt so good?

He ran the tip of his tongue along her teeth, so smooth he knew she'd already brushed. Like pearls. He hoped he didn't have bad breath. His tongue wanted to thrust once it found its way past her teeth, but he didn't let it. He flirted, and her tongue finally, shyly, came out to play.

What he felt most was a funny kind of pleasure because she *was* responding. Their tongues slipped and slid, teased and coiled. She was panting. Still kneading, but harder. He was pressing against her, stopping himself from rocking his hips by sheer willpower, but she was doing some pressing of her own now, too. Melting, maybe.

He had to stop, before the point of no return. There was no way in hell she was ready to take this any further, and he and his voice of common sense had to have a serious talk before he got himself in over his head, too.

Yes, finally! You're thinking, the voice approved.

Not with much coherence, because this felt unbelievable. Halfway chaste as it had been, it was the best kiss of his life. Hands-down, no competition, he wanted to keep doing it forever. But didn't.

Instead, he licked his way out of her mouth, sucked gently on her lower lip, nuzzled her nose and then kissed the tip of it. And lifted his head.

She stayed suspended for a few heartbeats before her eyes opened and she stared into his. "Oh, my God," she breathed.

He smiled, hoping he didn't look as triumphant and stunned as he felt. "Good night, Rowan."

"I—I need to go in." She hadn't managed to back up yet, but then neither had he.

"Yes. Anna will want you."

"Anna."

Niall's smile widened. If he was going to suffer from intense frustration, he at least liked knowing that he'd addled her to the point she didn't sound sure she remembered her daughter's name.

He disentangled his fingers from her hair, rubbing silken strands between his fingertips as he went. Then he took one of her hands from his shoulder, pressed an openmouthed kiss to the back of it, and lowered it to her side.

She gasped and, as if stung, snatched her other hand away.

"Go on in," he murmured. "Lock up."

She didn't know that he never went into his house at night after sitting and talking with her until she had gone in. These warm summer evening rendezvous weren't dates, exactly, where he felt compelled to be a gentleman, but...they were something. Something out of the ordinary. There were nights he didn't let himself come over to her porch to visit, but he still stood watch by his window until she satisfied her need for peace or gave up waiting for him, he wasn't sure which, and went back inside.

She swallowed and finally retreated a step. He almost groaned in distress at losing contact with her body. Right at that same moment, Rowan's expression sparked with shock.

"What am I *doing?*" she gasped.

"Making out," he said a little drily, although it was the tamest make-out session he'd had since he was a boy. He hadn't even tried to grope her.

Next time.

No. Think this through first. She's got two kids, remember?

Yeah, yeah. From the look on her face as she edged back, a repeat wasn't in the cards for the near future, anyway. It burned a little, that she was obviously so horrified. *She* was the one who lurked out here every night trying to tempt him, wasn't she? So where did she get off, looking as if he was the devil incarnate?

"Good night," he repeated, his voice harsher, harder.

She'd backed up against the kitchen door. Niall turned and walked away, into the darkness. He hoped she didn't notice the gun he'd tucked into the waistband at the small of his back. He wasn't going back to his cottage, not yet. He'd heard excited voices out on the street not long back, kids playing whatever gangs of neighborhood kids did play these days. Probably not cops and robbers anymore, more likely some demon and enforcer thing from Nintendo or an Xbox game, but same old same old. The younger boys were probably already tucked in snug, but the pervert might not be that particular about age. He might like eight- or nine-year-old boys, too. Niall was going to widen his patrol tonight. He wasn't sleepy, and he guessed his prey wouldn't be peeking in windows of houses too close to Desmond's, not after the uproar the other night.

He paused beside the gate, though, and saw the kitchen door shut. He didn't doubt she'd locked it. It would be a while before Rowan might get lax on security again. He guessed the hair on the back of her neck still rose every time she remembered her little boy's scream.

Sam wanted to go with Niall, but he deftly slipped out the gate without the dog, however tempting it was to take him. He still suspected Sam was too stupid to be any use.

Tonight, Niall imagined himself as a soldier behind enemy lines. In Vietnam, maybe, rather than the sparse, dry landscape of Iraq or Afghanistan. A jungle, where he could slip from one bit of cover to another, avoiding light cast from houses and headlights and streetlamps. He watched for other moving shadows, and tried not to think about that once-in-a-lifetime kiss.

"DAMN!" NIALL SMACKED his fist against the wall.

He'd missed the creep by two blocks. Two G-D blocks. If only he'd gone left instead of right, or right instead of left…. It didn't matter, only that somewhere, sometime last night he'd made the wrong decision.

Maybe if he *had* taken the dog….

And maybe not, too.

It had been two days, and so far he was batting a big fat zero.

"What's your interest, Detective?" the patrol sergeant asked him. He was an old-timer, pushing retirement. Niall happened to know that Duncan was hoping to ease Lewicki that direction when he had the opportunity.

"This guy is working *my* neighborhood." After a moment Niall grudgingly added, "He targeted my landlady's kid."

"Exposed himself?"

"No. Watched the kid get undressed."

Last night the Peeping Tom had unzipped and worked his dick right in front of a window, where to all reports two young brothers had stared in consternation until one of them sucked in enough air to let out a screech worthy of being an air alarm. According to the boys' mother, they were supposed to be getting ready for bed, but they'd resumed play with army action figures instead. The Peeping Tom had likely gotten impatient at their failure to strip and decided to excite himself a different way.

A couple of patrol officers wandering by had stopped to listen to the conversation.

"Maybe if you're lucky he'll pick your window," one of them said, laughing.

Niall turned a stare on the fool, which shut him up. "What if it was *your* kid?"

"Don't have any."

"Use your imagination," Lewicki barked.

Mildly surprised, Niall eyed him.

"I have grandchildren," he muttered.

"So, what are you planning to do?" Yet another uniform had joined the conversation. He was laughing, too. "Set up a stakeout?"

"I'll think of something."

"You guys bored over in the detective division?"

Niall ground his teeth. Hell, he probably looked like Duncan right now. Duncan's dentist swore his golf game would be supported down the line by the caps he'd have to put on all of Duncan's molars.

"These guys escalate," Niall said tensely.

"Most of them don't," the original jerk retorted.

"Enough do." Niall stared hard from one face to another. "You know what? This is our town. There are a whole bunch of kids who don't feel safe in their bedrooms anymore. It may be a long time before they feel safe again. If you think that's okay, maybe you should be looking for another job."

He stalked away, hearing only silence behind him except for one murmured, "Amen." Lewicki.

No surprise, Niall's own lieutenant cornered

him a couple of hours later. "I hear you have too much time on your hands."

Niall explained again. He was using minimal department time on this. He was taking it personally. He didn't say, *And if that's not okay, you can shove it,* although that's what he was thinking.

The lieutenant was surprised enough to give him the go-ahead, as long as he didn't neglect his other cases. Niall was chagrined to realize how startlingly he'd violated his cool-as-the-click-of-ice-cubes persona. He'd showed emotion, something he didn't do.

Because he didn't feel it.

Except he was feeling too many things these days. This sense of outrage was only one of them.

Rowan had not come out on her porch last night. In fact, she and the kids stayed in all evening. He'd thought about knocking to ask how Anna was, but decided against it. He and his voice of common sense had indeed conversed, with an undecided outcome but a definite increase of caution. Unless he envisioned himself as a devoted husband and father, a mow the lawn every Saturday morning, sell the Harley in favor of a child-friendly van kind of guy, he needed to steer well clear of Rowan Staley and her kids. And yes, that was proving to be astonishingly more difficult than he would ever have dreamed, but he was good at sliding away at any hint of emotional involvement, wasn't he?

So why was he advertising to the entire department that he was seriously pissed because one particular little boy had had the shit scared out of him?

He rubbed the heel of his hand over his breastbone to quell the ache beneath and leaned back in his desk chair.

Because I like the kid. That's all.

Good enough, he decided. If some pervert had peeped in Enid's bedroom window, Niall would have taken that seriously, too. *Don't complicate this,* he thought. Mostly it pissed him off because it was his neighborhood. Call him territorial. Whatever.

Frowning, he flicked away the memory of a small hand grasping his trustingly. He had calls to return. A job to do.

ROWAN LAID HER HAND ON her daughter's forehead. She looked feverish, but she didn't feel hot. Mostly she was fretful. An unhappy whimper escaped her.

A glance at the clock told Rowan she could safely give Anna another dose of her pain medication. Her doorbell rang just as she was measuring out the strawberry-flavored medicine.

She'd almost forgotten that her father had said he was stopping by.

"Dad!" she said with a smile when she answered the door, and then her eye fell on the stylish blonde woman with him. One who was certainly no older than late thirties. The girlfriend *du jour*.

Not that her father didn't look good. He could easily have passed for a man ten years younger. His hair had only recently silvered attractively at the temples, a fact that infuriated Rowan's mother, who had taken to coloring her hair years ago.

"Sweetheart." Her father smiled broadly and stepped forward, kissing her cheek. He tugged the other woman forward. "I'd like you to meet Michelle Ross. Michelle, my daughter."

Rowan couldn't believe he'd done this.

Behind her, Anna started to cry.

Rowan couldn't think what to do but stand aside and say, "Come in. Please. Anna's hurting and I need to give her the next dose of painkiller."

"Painkiller?" her father said, following her. He or the girlfriend—Michelle—closed the front door.

"I told you she was having her tonsils and adenoids out."

"Right." He sounded embarrassed. "I suppose

I didn't realize…. You had yours out, didn't you?
I don't remember it being much of a fuss."

She didn't remember him being there at all.
He'd probably slithered out of miserable kid
duties in his usual way.

When did I get so bitter? Rowan wondered,
appalled. *Maybe when I realized how unhappy
Mom was.*

But had it all been Dad's fault? Rowan didn't
know. She was disconcerted to realize how little
she understood her own parents' relationship,
considering she'd been there for much of it.

"Pumpkin," her father said with delight, bending to give Anna a surprisingly gentle hug. "Not
feeling so good, huh?"

"Grampa," she whispered and sniffled.

"Here you go, honey." Rowan helped her swallow her medication, then laid her back against
her pillows. "Er…coffee?" she asked her dad and
the woman. "Lemonade?"

"Too hot for coffee, unless you have iced?"
Dad could see the answer. "Lemonade would be
fine. Michelle?"

"Lovely," she said with an embarrassed smile
for Rowan. So she, at least, had noticed that her
hostess was less than thrilled by her presence.

Dad, of course, was oblivious. They stayed to
visit with Anna while Rowan went to the kitchen.
Was Dad trying to impress this girlfriend with

what a fabulous grandparent he was? Worse yet—was he serious about her? Did she want children of her own? Rowan didn't know whether to laugh or cry at the idea of her father starting a new family now.

Oh, Mom.

She served tall glasses of lemonade and they all sat making polite conversation while Anna drooped and finally fell asleep. Her father had been there for twenty minutes before he noticed Desmond wasn't around. "Where's my best bud?" he asked, and Rowan tried not to embarrass him by displaying her incredulity.

"At a friend's house. He should be back soon." Zeke's mom was going to walk him home so Rowan didn't have to disturb Anna.

Michelle asked to use a restroom and looked astonished to be told the only one in the house was upstairs. The moment she was gone, Rowan turned to her father. "What's this all about, Dad? Why did you bring her here?"

"Every time I mention her, you start talking about something else," he said grumpily.

"You've put me in an awkward position."

"Because I introduced a new friend of mine to you?"

"Friend?" She couldn't help sounding scathing. She stole a quick glance at Anna; yes, she was definitely asleep.

"I think she might be important, Rowan." He leaned forward, elbows on his knees. His expression was warm, cajoling. "Is it wrong for me to want my daughter to meet her?"

"You're still married. To Mom."

"For another few weeks. Neither of us is making a pretence that there's a chance of getting back together."

Rowan was suddenly, irrationally furious. She leaped to her feet. "Do you have any idea how uncomfortable this makes me?"

She hadn't heard the sound of the toilet flushing, but the footsteps on the stairs registered. Thank heavens.

"You have no idea—" her father bit off.

"No, I don't. I don't want to. I want you to be my father. Grandpa to my kids. Not...not..."

The tension in the room had to be obvious. Michelle returned, her expression wary. A sharp rapping on the back door made Rowan want to scream.

Please not Glenn and Donna. I can't take that. My life is a mess.

She didn't even know what was wrong with her. She'd overreacted. Her poor father. Mom and he *were* getting a divorce. Men and women did date other people before their divorces were final. Mom's hurt and anger were infectious. But if Dad had showed up with a nice woman his own age, Rowan didn't think she'd be as both-ered. It was...the *egoism* that had him flaunting pretty young women. He didn't want to admit his age.

"Excuse me," she said, and went to the back door. Her knees weakened at the sight of Niall framed by the glass. Thank God.

When she opened the door, his narrowed gaze went past her. "I saw a car out in front. Not your in-laws?"

No, worse.

Silly. Of course this wasn't worse.

She shook her head. "My father and...a friend."

Those gray eyes studied her with the intensity that was all his. "Anna?" he said after a minute.

"She finally fell asleep. And Des is over at Zeke's."

"Good. Hey." He squeezed her shoulder. "Relax."

She wanted to lean on him. Just tip forward until her cheek was against his chest and his arms were around her and he was supporting her weight entirely.

Not something he'd volunteered for.

"Would you like to meet him?" she asked wryly. "Or would you prefer to flee while you can?"

"Introduce me." His face gave no clues as to what he thought.

She nodded and led the way to the living

room. Her father was polite when she introduced them, but he didn't look pleased. Michelle's initially startled expression and glance at the gun at Niall's waist was replaced by a faint flush of color in her cheeks. Her reaction made Rowan take another look at him. He was in cop mode, she realized, nothing like the relaxed guy who played T-ball with her kid. The guy who wore cargo shorts and went barefoot. This Niall MacLachlan wore dark slacks, white shirt and tie. The gun and badge added an air of intimidation. His face was completely closed even as he shook hands and smiled.

How did he *do* that?

"So you're the renter." Her father didn't sound very friendly. Had he noticed the way his girlfriend looked at Niall?

"That's right."

"I trust you don't usually wear a gun around my grandchildren," her father said.

"Dad!" she exclaimed.

Niall's eyebrows rose as he met her father's eyes. "I'm a police officer, Mr. Cooper. Carrying a weapon is part of my job. Which is keeping the citizens of this community safe. Are you asking whether I leave my weapon lying around where one of the kids can get to it? No."

"I'm sure you understand my concern," her father said stiffly.

Niall didn't say anything.

The back door banged open. "I'm home!" Desmond yelled.

Anna startled and began to cry. Rowan scooped her up. "It's okay, honey. Shh. I'm sorry."

Showing some sense or maybe compassion, Michelle tugged at Rowan's father's arm. "Keith, maybe this isn't the best time with poor Anna not feeling good."

Des burst into the living room followed by Zeke's mother, Jillian.

"Grandad!" Des cried, but then he spotted Niall, his face lit and he flung himself at the impassive cop instead of his grandfather. "Niall!"

Niall gave him a quick hug. "Meet your grandfather's friend," he said.

Amidst the greetings, Rowan saw the way her father bristled at Desmond's enthusiasm for Niall. She'd have more sympathy with him if he'd actually dedicated himself to spending any time with his grandson.

Introductions began all over again. Likely sensitive to the atmosphere, Jillian stayed only for a minute. She corralled Zeke, who Rowan hadn't even noticed until now, and departed, while successfully, for a second time, keeping Sam from making it in. Wouldn't that have been the last straw? A dog rampaging through the living room, leaping with customary enthusiasm on the visitors. Rowan braced herself for Niall to make his excuses, too, now that he knew they didn't threaten her or the kids' safety. Instead, he simply stood there, rocklike and as expressionless. His stance spoke for him. *I'm not going anywhere.*

The undercurrents were many and confusing. Rowan found she didn't care why he was refusing to leave. She didn't want him to go. She was still staggered by the rush of pleasure she'd felt at the first sight of him since he'd kissed her.

Finally, Dad and Michelle left. "Keith didn't tell me your daughter had just had surgery," the blonde woman murmured. It made Rowan realize she might be a perfectly nice woman. Probably was.

I wasn't fair.

She made an effort to be friendlier now, and gave her father an affectionate kiss on the cheek. "Sorry, Dad. Anna hasn't been sleeping well, which means I'm not getting much sleep, either."

"It's okay," he said gruffly, hugging her. For a moment he was her daddy, and she felt young and vulnerable and loved despite everything. "I haven't seen enough of you lately."

Des walked them out to the car, chattering, which seemed to please her dad, too.

"Anna's still hurting," said Niall.

Rowan nodded. "It hasn't been the best couple of days."

"I heard her crying last night."

During the middle of the night, he meant. She winced.

"I'm sorry."

"Don't be. Not your fault." He sounded gruff, too. Dad always did when he felt emotional and was trying to be manly about it. Was that what Niall was doing, too? The idea made Rowan blink.

"Tell you what," he said. "Why don't I order a pizza? Des and I can go pick it up. I don't know what Anna's eating…"

"Jell-O. Ice cream." Rowan made a face. "Pudding. Weirdly enough, just what the doctor ordered."

He laughed. "Okay. Do you need us to stop at the store, too? Are you running low on ice cream?"

"Would you?" she said in relief. "Yes. Please."

She was going to find her purse to give him money; he told her not to be ridiculous, she could pay him back if she insisted. "The pizza's on me," he added.

He made her give him a list so she wouldn't have to grocery shop tomorrow. And then he took Des away and left Rowan free to persuade

Anna to eat a cup of butterscotch pudding and drink some milk.

Rowan was almost embarrassed at how grateful she was, how excited for Niall and Des to come home. It scared her, this feeling. He was almost too good to be true, somehow always there when she needed him most. Someday he wouldn't be. She couldn't rely on him too much. She couldn't.

The most alarming part was that she knew if he did keep coming around, he would want more than a kiss. She was afraid she'd give it. And then what? She'd endured her marriage for the kids' sake. Was she really thinking of putting herself through something like that again?

I can't. I can't.

But she was invaded by heat every time she thought of the kiss, and it made her wonder. Niall wasn't anything like Drew. Being with him might be different.

She couldn't prevent the fear that swelled in her at the idea, though. Maybe she should listen to the fear, not be reckless.

Assuming, of course, she ever had to make that decision. She hadn't even been sure Niall was attracted to her until he kissed her. And maybe that had been a moment of idle curiosity for him. He *had* been the one to end it, firmly sending her inside to bed. All she had to do was think of the essentially solitary man she knew, the one who played haunting laments and seemed so reluctant to get drawn into their lives, to see that he wasn't looking for a real relationship.

Then why did he keep coming to her rescue?

And why, like the proverbial moth to a white-hot lightbulb, did she want him to kiss her again, and maybe even ask for more?

CHAPTER EIGHT

NIALL SAT ON HIS OWN small porch in the dark and reflected on the previous evening. Voice of common sense, where the hell were you?

What was he doing, pretending he was—what?—a dear friend of the family? A beloved uncle?

Daddy?

He winced.

He and Des had gone grocery shopping, which had included innumerable debates about what kinds of ice cream to get, whether Mom usually bought two-percent milk or whole, whether Mom would approve of the several heavily advertised breakfast cereals Desmond picked out. Whether they had to buy the broccoli she'd put on the list.

Then they'd picked up the pizza, the boy marching happily at Niall's side and wanting to carry the box even though it was too big for him.

Anna had decided to sit at the table with them while they ate pizza and drank soda. Afterward they all had ice cream. Then, when Anna got whiny, Niall volunteered to take Des swimming again. The words popped out of his mouth and he'd expected to feel appalled, but no, damn it, he'd had fun the last time they went. And the gratitude and warmth in Rowan's eyes were more than adequate recompense.

Or so he'd told himself at the time.

He and Desmond had fun again. The lessons had started, and the kid was getting the hang of breathing while doing the crawl stroke. The only bad moment had come as Niall stood in chest-deep water holding out his arms to Des, who wanted to jump in but was scared to, and he saw a fellow cop. Charlie Spears was a detective, too, but a known family man. Niall saw at a glance that he was there with two kids, a boy and a girl. He was carrying the girl, whose legs were latched around her dad's waist, while he held the boy's hand.

Charlie stared blankly at Niall before recognition and then astonishment crept onto his face. "MacLachlan?"

Desmond turned to stare at the man who'd come to a stop poolside. The two boys studied each other with open curiosity.

"Spears?"

"I've never seen you here." His gaze went to Desmond. "I didn't know you had any kids."

Niall gritted his teeth—damn, there he went again—at the surprise in the other man's tone.

"This is Desmond," he said. "He's my land-lady's boy."

"The one who…?"

Was everyone in the department talking about his quixotic quest?

"Yes," Niall said hurriedly.

Spears introduced his two. Turned out his girl would be starting kindergarten that fall, his son second grade. Des was friendly. Charlie and his kids finally moved on, but the rest of the time Desmond and Niall were in the water he was aware of occasional incredulous glances.

What the hell? he decided recklessly and refused to let the audience keep him from having a good time.

He'd kept on with the uncharacteristic behavior, too, hanging around while Rowan tucked Des into bed and then sitting out on the porch with her. She asked a few questions that got him remembering his childhood, back when his family still seemed normal to him.

"Yeah," he said, smiling, "I was okay with having a little brother until he started to walk, and then he became a major aggravation. We got to be friends once he learned to ask before he played with my stuff."

Her glider had gone still as she listened to him talk. "Why is it I can't picture you as a little boy at all?"

"I was carrot-topped, freckled and skinny, if that helps." He was still smiling, remembering his young self.

"Is your younger brother redheaded, too?"

"No, Conall looks more like Duncan. Mom was dark-haired. Dad was the redheaded one." He didn't much like thinking about that, the idea that he'd taken after his father in any way. Except he knew he did. Now and again he'd look at himself in the mirror and have the disquieting experience of seeing his father. He wasn't all that much younger than Dad had been, the last time he saw him.

Strange thought.

"The musical ability came from him, too, didn't it?" Rowan said softly, as if she'd read his mind.

"I suppose so." He frowned, uneasiness stealing over him. He half expected that sometime when he was playing the bagpipe at the Highland Games or maybe in a parade, he'd look up and see his father. Should he talk to him, or turn his back the way he knew Duncan would? Niall had never decided.

He stilled his fingers when he realized they were playing a nervous beat on the step beside him. He didn't know whether he'd talk to his father if the occasion arose. He did know that he didn't like talking *about* him.

"That your dad's girlfriend?" he asked.

Rowan pushed the glider into motion. "I suppose." She paused. "The latest, anyway."

There was something in her voice. He tried to make out her expression. "Did he, uh, have other women while he was married?"

"He's still married," she snapped. Then let out a huff of air. "Their divorce is almost final. According to Mom he's been dating practically from the day she moved out."

"But not before?"

She was silent for a long time. "I don't know," she finally admitted. "I don't think so. Mom calls all the time. I think she'd have said."

"Is that the kind of thing you'd tell your daughter?" Man, he hoped not.

"She's been telling me lots of things I wish she wouldn't. It puts me in the middle. You know?"

"Yeah." He wasn't sure that was actually true, being as he didn't have parents who called him. Shouldn't she be grateful that her mom and dad both loved her and wanted to talk to her about anything at all?

Maybe not. He had a vague and completely unsubstantiated belief that kids should lean on parents and not the other way around, at least until old age changed the dynamic. His mouth curled into a smile unpleasant enough he wouldn't have wanted Rowan to see it. Once in a while he surprised himself with some stupidly naive belief, and this was one of those times.

"I'd better go to bed," he said, suddenly needing to get away from her.

But to his dismay, when he rose to his feet she did, too, and temptation had him stifling any internal warnings. "Rowan," he said. Only that. Voice husky. Hand outstretched.

She stared at him from shadowed eyes. When she finally moved forward it was slowly, her steps halting, as if she battled some fears or cautions of her own.

He quit breathing as he waited to find out whether she'd come to him or not. Finally, hesitantly, she laid her hand in his and let him tug her forward until their bodies bumped. The sensation was indescribable. He tried not to let himself examine how he felt. Why would he be almost lightheaded with something that might have been relief?

Maybe only because he needed to breathe. He *could* breathe now that he was threading his fingers through the silken strands of her hair.

He had to start almost from scratch with this kiss, so shy was she again. She pursed lips that were firmly pressed together, as if she were going to kiss Anna or Desmond. Niall had to coax again, and the whole thing should have been about as erotic as the first, terror-making kiss of two twelve-year-olds who'd agreed to "go together" without ever having had a real conversation.

Not so. It was unbelievably sexy. More so than the openmouthed, panting, grinding hips together kind of kiss.

As his lips played with hers, Niall was too engrossed to analyze what he felt. He was aroused, but fine with not taking this very far. With enjoying it for what it was. Sexy, yeah, but also sweet and...magical.

It wasn't until she'd gone inside and he was walking through the darkness back to his cottage that he thought in shock, *Magical?* What had he done, stumbled through some portal into another dimension? Lost his frigging *mind?*

Now it was the next evening, and he was still wondering.

Rowan Staley and her children were the kind of complication he'd spent a lifetime avoiding.

With perfect clarity, Niall thought, *I need to get laid.* By someone who bore no resemblance to Rowan.

It took him a minute to dredge up a memory of the last time he'd had sex. There had been a long dry spell even before Enid died and Rowan moved into the house. The last time was...that dark-haired attorney. He struggled to remember her face, her name. A weird name, he did

recall that much. Something to do with jewelry…
Cameo. That was it. Yeah, yeah. Cameo Burke.
He could call up a picture of her body better than
he could of her face, which embarrassed him a
little. She was tall and supple, leggy and bold.
She should have been everything he wanted in
bed, but he had to play the game first: flirtation,
romantic dinners, conversation. After a couple of
times, it wasn't worth it. He didn't call her back,
deleted the couple of messages she'd left on his
phone. Knew he'd been a bastard and didn't care.

Somewhere in there—maybe exactly then—
he'd caught his first sight of Rowan visiting her
grandmother. She must have been around before;
at the time he'd figured he had been lucky to
miss her earlier. He had stepped out his front
door and seen her through the open gate getting
out of her car. Stretching. His gaze was caught
by her very generous breasts. Small waist. Luscious ass as she leaned into the car to get something out.

"Something" turned out to be a little girl who
clung to her like a limpet. Des must have been in
school, Niall realized now. But Anna had been
enough to chill him. Wow. He'd felt extreme lust
for a woman with a *child?*

After that, he'd tried really hard not to look
when he saw her around. Went out of his way not
to meet her. But now, his heart beating heavily

in panic, he wondered if she'd been responsible for the fact that he hadn't called Cameo again or worked up the interest to start anything with another woman. The fact that he'd been celibate for…damn. Eight months? Nine? The longest stretch since he'd turned sixteen or so.

So how could he possibly be so content with kisses that were tame by anyone's standards?

I really need to get laid.

What scared the crap out of him was discovering he couldn't think of another woman who stirred a single cell of his body. He made himself picture a couple of movie actresses who were usually good for a fantasy or two.

He felt…nothing.

Until he had a flash of Rowan's face when he'd lifted his head from last night's kiss. Her lips, soft, damp, parted. The long line of her throat, the slow, reluctant way she'd opened her eyes, and the slumberous look in them before shock supplanted it.

His memory of the throaty little sounds she'd made a couple of times.

Fully aroused, Niall groaned.

He was in such trouble.

ROWAN DREADED DINNER at the Staleys, but had to go. She should have them at her house; she'd promised, holding off because Anna's surgery was a good excuse to postpone. But she hadn't been able to turn down an invitation. When she explained that Anna's throat was still sore, Donna promised to have the little girl's favorite cream of tomato soup and ice cream for her. Desmond, as usual, got quiet during the drive over. Rowan couldn't blame him; *she* felt reluctant and sulky, too.

I wanna have pizza with Niall instead.

Her mouth curved into a smile at the childish whine her inner teenager had managed.

Yep, she and Des were in harmony there. Niall was more fun than Grandma and Grandad.

Only once again a couple of days had gone by without her setting eyes on Niall. It was silly to feel hurt, of course; they were neighbors, landlady and tenant, maybe friends, not anything more. Except that he *had* kissed her—twice—so maybe they were "more" although she wasn't sure how to define it. He hadn't asked her out. They weren't committed to each other in any way. He might even be seeing another woman right now, which would explain why his cottage remained dark some evenings.

At the very least, he was busy, or maybe he hadn't been in the mood for the whole family scene. Especially *her* family. He'd certainly gotten an up-close-and-personal look at her whole, messy world. Unpleasant in-laws, philandering father, sobbing, clingy little girl, needy boy.

Needy woman?

She still couldn't believe she'd kissed him— let him kiss her that way. Or that it had been so lovely. Tender. Patient. The really astonishing part was that she wasn't so sure she'd have stopped him if he'd gone on. Slipped a hand beneath the hem of her T-shirt, even stripped it off over her head. Heck, carried her down the porch steps, laid her on the lawn and made love to her. She'd wanted him to, so much, even though she also didn't.

At some point his amazing control would shatter, right? And then he'd get rough or impatient. He'd quit bothering with seduction and just *take*.

And even if he didn't…well, it was uncomfortable for her once the actual sex part started. The penetration. Maybe it was a quirk of her body, but surely if she was capable of enjoying it, she would have at least once during her marriage.

So why did she want to find out if it *could* be different?

She knew the answer. Niall made her feel things. Lots of things. So many things, it made her mad when he disappeared from their lives like this, even if she had no right whatsoever to react that way.

She sighed so gustily Desmond said, "Mom?"

"Yes?"

"We don't have to spend the night tonight, right?"

"Nope. We're having dinner, that's all."

"Okay." He lapsed into silence again until she parked in the Staleys' driveway.

Dinner smelled good, and she had to admit it was nice to eat someone else's cooking. Donna had fixed some of Desmond's favorite foods: fried chicken, mashed potatoes, peas instead of one of the yuckier vegetables his mother made him eat, blackberry crisp still warm from the oven with vanilla ice cream melting atop. The Staleys were eager to catch up on the kids' lives, and Rowan relaxed, remembering how many pleasant meals they'd all eaten together. Yes, they could be difficult, but they cared, and that counted for a lot. Donna especially really did try to please the kids; she might have opinions on healthy eating, but she did pay attention to what they enjoyed, too.

Rowan looked around, thinking about other good times here, too. Both the Staleys were rigid, but Donna at least had seemed to understand that kids needed to do things like fingerpaint and help cut out Christmas cookies. They'd bought them an easel and Glenn had somewhere found a square of vinyl to lay under it. From here, Rowan could see it was still set up in the kitchen. Anna's sandbox had come from them, too. And, while Glenn had grumbled plenty about Super Sam, neither of them had ever suggested getting rid of the dog. Considering how many holes Sam had dug in Glenn's lawn and flowerbeds, that tolerance was a biggie.

Listening to Des tell his grandparents about his swim lessons and the friends he'd made and how he was starting to get excited for school to start, Rowan began to feel chagrined about how much she'd limited their time with the kids since the move.

Anna piped up, "I get to go to school, too."

Donna turned a disapproving face on Rowan and said, "You're absolutely determined to go through with this?"

She wasn't quite chagrined enough to back down on this particular issue. "You mean preschool?" Rowan kept her tone cheerful for the kids' sake. "Of course I am. A year from now, Anna will be starting kindergarten. Preschool is a great way to make that transition. And she's excited about it, aren't you, honey?"

"Uh-huh." But she didn't look all that excited, mainly because she still didn't feel very well but also because she was a little hazy about what preschool actually was.

"Listen to her, for goodness sake, Rowan." Donna turned a flashlight beam of coaxing on her granddaughter. "You'd rather come stay with Grandma and Grandad every day instead, wouldn't you, pumpkin? Remember what fun we had last year?"

Anna's lower lip pushed out. "I wanna go to school like Desmond."

"But when he was four, Desmond didn't go to preschool, did he?" Donna sounded sugary sweet. "Preschool is babysitting for little girls and boys whose mommies and daddies have to work and can't be with them. Ones who don't *have* grandmas and grandads to take care of them."

Rowan became aware that she was clenching her teeth. *I will not react, I will not react.*

Ignoring her, Donna continued, "Since your mommy is so determined to have a job instead of staying with you, your grandad and I think you should come here daytimes. And maybe Desmond could even come here when school lets out, until Mommy can pick you both up."

Rowan set down her fork. "I get off at the same time school lets out. Des won't have to go to after-school care except once in a while, and he won't mind because his friend Brett will be there."

He'd been watching his grandmother warily. After a glance flicked at his mother, he exclaimed, "Yeah! It's fun. I bet preschool is fun, too."

Donna's carefully plucked and drawn-in eyebrows arched. "All day? I wouldn't think so."

Tears promptly welled in Anna's eyes. "Mommy said I could go. She said I'm a big girl, not a little girl!"

"She's going to cry?" Glenn exclaimed in disgust, balling his napkin in one fist and tossing it onto the table. "She behaved better than this when she lived with us."

Anna did burst into tears. Rowan pulled her onto her lap and pressed a kiss onto her head. "Oh, sweetheart, it's okay. Of course you're a big girl!" She glared at her parents-in-law. "Grandad didn't mean to sound mad. He's surprised because you hardly ever cry, do you?"

"She's been crying lots lately," Desmond told them all.

"Possibly because she needs structure and firmness," Glenn declared.

Anna cried harder.

"Or because she had surgery five days ago." Rowan pushed back her chair. "Donna, I feel terrible leaving you with the cleanup, but I think I'd better get the kids home."

Flustered, her mother-in-law rose, too. "You're leaving already? But we so wanted to spend some time with our grandchildren. We've hardly seen them at all."

Rowan almost groaned from guilt. Their feelings had been hurt since she moved out, she knew that, but surely they could see that this wasn't a good time?

"I'm sorry, but I suspect Anna needs another dose of her pain medication. I didn't think to bring it."

"Are you sure it's not that man you're living with?" Glenn growled.

"What?"

"Do you think we're blind?" His face was red with anger. "We saw what was going on."

Desmond slipped from his chair and scuttled to her side, needing the reassurance of contact. Anna buried her wet face against Rowan's neck.

"If you're talking about Niall, he rents the cottage from me, just as he did from Gran. He's a kind man who's been nice to the kids. We most certainly don't *live* with him. I can't imagine where you got the idea we do," she said, very, very calmly.

"Obviously you turn the kids over to him any time he feels like taking one of them even though you won't let their grandparents see them at all," said Glenn, expression ugly.

"You're exaggerating. We're here, aren't we?"

"To eat and run." He snorted and pushed back

his own chair. "I don't know why I'm even talking to you. With Drew gone, you don't want anything to do with his family, do you? And after everything we did for you."

This had to be a nightmare.

"That isn't true." Desmond, she realized, was pressed hard against her now, scared by this bizarre scene that had erupted from nowhere. Anna's breath was hitching in awful little gulps. "I'm grateful for everything you did, but it was time we stood on our own feet. Surely you can understand that."

"You mean, you couldn't spend time with a man while you were living here. You put your husband out of your mind pretty damn quick."

In her shock, she thought, *I won't descend to his level. I won't.* "I will not talk about this in front of the children." She looked at her mother-in-law, who seemed to be in nearly as much shock as Rowan was. "Donna, thank you for making such a nice dinner for us. Good night."

She marched out, hustling the kids with her. With days so warm, they hadn't had to collect coats or anything but her purse, left on the living room sofa. She buckled them into their car seats without once turning her head to see if Glenn had followed them out to glare.

As Rowan drove away, Anna was still crying with those strange, hitching breaths, as if she was having trouble getting enough oxygen, while Desmond appeared to have shrunk.

Rowan had driven several blocks before she could summon something like a normal tone. "Well, Grandad was sure in a bad mood tonight, wasn't he?"

"Why was he mad about Niall?" Desmond asked in complete perplexity.

Good question. She had to think about it for a minute, trying to untangle her own anger and shock and bewilderment.

"Your grandparents miss your dad. He was their son, you know. Their little boy. Maybe it's especially hard for them because they didn't have any other kids."

After a minute Des dipped his head.

"When they saw how much you liked Niall—" *how much* I *liked Niall, too* "—they were afraid you'd forget your own dad. It's hard for them to see us moving on with our lives without your dad."

Desmond didn't say anything for a long time. Rowan couldn't tell if Anna, in her misery, was even listening. They were almost home when Desmond spoke. "Would Daddy not like it that sometimes I kind of think of Niall like he's *almost* my dad?"

All she could think was, *I'm responsible for this.* The necessity of concentrating as she turned into the driveway, set the brake and turned off the car gave her a moment to think. How could she address this without encouraging him?

"I know your dad would be glad Niall can do stuff with you," she said carefully. From somewhere, she summoned a laugh. "Your dad knew I'm not any good at T-ball or soccer."

"You're not a very good swimmer, either, are you?" said Desmond, sounding more like himself.

Still laughing, Rowan shook her head. "Nope. I wish I'd learned when I was your age, but I didn't." She hesitated. "Des… Niall *has* been nice, and he does cool things with you, but he isn't your dad. I don't think he really wants a family, not full-time. So it might be better if you think of him as a friend. He could move away any time, you know, or…or get married and start a family of his own."

While she watched, Desmond brooded.

"Why can't he marry us?" he finally exclaimed.

"Honey…" Rowan collected herself. "I know your dad wouldn't mind if I remarried, not if it was someone who loved me and really wanted to be your father. He can't be here, and I believe with all my heart that he wants us to be happy. But that doesn't mean Niall is that person. He's been nice to us, but he doesn't feel that way about me. I'm not sure he's ready to be a dad at all. You know he doesn't always have time for you."

Desmond hung his head, but his expression was stubborn. She hadn't convinced him. Maybe he guessed that a part of her wished Niall would marry them, too. Probably that's what made her explanation more than a little incoherent.

Fortunately, Desmond moved on to more questions as they got out of the car and went into the house, mostly about what Dad would mind and didn't mind and did Mom think he could *see* them? 'Cuz Des bet Dad wanted to beat up that guy who looked in the bedroom window, huh, Mom?

The worst part of the whole, hideous evening, as far as Rowan was concerned, was the creeping sense of shame she couldn't quite shake off. Had it really been so obvious to Donna and Glenn that she was attracted to Niall? Did they actually believe she was bringing a man who wasn't her husband into her bedroom, right across the hall from her kids? And was that exactly what Niall expected she would do?

As they crossed the yard, she didn't even let herself look toward the cottage, beyond noticing from her peripheral vision that the lights were on.

She didn't go out to sit on the porch after she tucked Anna and Desmond into bed. After darkness fell, she made sure neither the back porch light nor the kitchen light were on, in case either would have encouraged Niall to come knock on the door.

She went to bed early, pretending to read, when really she struggled with a barrage of questions quite different from Desmond's, starting with the biggie.

Why had Drew stayed so close to his parents when they were so awful? She knew he'd often felt angry with them, especially his father. She wished, not for the first time, that he'd talked to her more. Explained some of those mixed feelings he obviously had.

But some of her questions weren't so different from Desmond's. How would Drew feel about her kissing another man? About her feeling so much more than she had in her husband's arms? And why should she feel guilty, when Drew had hurt her so much?

She closed her eyes and remembered the way he'd gather her into his arms afterward and hold her close, his voice low and sad, if also husky from physical satisfaction. "I'm sorry, love. So sorry. Thank you for giving me what I need. If only..."

But he'd never finish. He'd never say, If only we could *both* enjoy this. Because his way meant they couldn't.

Was it mostly her fault, the way she'd always

believed? Or—and this was the most innocent explanation—had Drew not known how to
arouse her, how to make her want his touch, his
body? What she didn't want to believe was that
her husband had needed to hurt her. That he'd
taken pleasure in her every gasp of pain even
though he was ashamed when he was done.

She turned off her lamp and lay staring into
the darkness, into the past.

Of course, she knew. But she couldn't hate
Drew anyway. She could be angry, yes, but she'd
loved him, too, and felt pity because he couldn't
seem to help himself.

And she thought, finally, *I don't care what
Drew would think about Niall.*

If Niall wanted her, could she be brave enough
to find out whether sex could be as glorious as
it was depicted in books and movies instead of
painful and degrading as it had been in her experience?

What made her even more afraid was the
knowledge that making love wouldn't be an ex-
periment for her. Fun and liberating if it went
well. She couldn't do it at all if she weren't in
love with him. And she couldn't shake off the
feeling that the last thing Niall would want was
a woman's love or expectations.

CHAPTER NINE

SATURDAY MORNING, NIALL SAT at his small table, ate a bowl of tasteless multigrain cereal and listened to the voices drifting in from outside. Desmond yelling something, Rowan answering, Super Sam barking.

Would Rowan be pissed because he hadn't been around the past few days? Man, was this niggling sense of shame what guys in a relationship had to put up with all the time? If so, he didn't want any of it.

Except, he did want to go out there and... He frowned. Find out whether Anna was better enough to give him one of her big, sweet smiles. Kick the soccer ball around with Des. See Rowan. That was all. See her.

His heart felt like that soccer ball when it had just been booted hard. The pain of being dented, the rebound effect, the soaring high.

He didn't want her to look at him distantly, the way she did after he'd hurt her little boy's feelings. He wanted her shy smile, too, so like her daughter's in the way it lit her whole face.

He kept sitting there, telling himself he was lingering over his coffee, really feeling like a gutless wonder.

The last inch of coffee in the mug went cold. With the *Times* spread on the table in front of him, he read about the Seahawks training camp and exhibition games and didn't give a flying you-know-what. His belly felt as if the cereal was being digested into concrete and he stared toward the windows, the slice of sky he could see, the leafy branches of the big apple tree. The woman and children he couldn't see.

His phone rang, and he grabbed it in gratitude. The name he saw on the screen surprised him: Conall. His little brother hadn't called in months.

"Hey," he said in greeting. "I thought maybe you'd been buried in a shallow grave somewhere in Baja."

His brother laughed. "Not me. I'm too quick, too smart. Too mean."

"Too lucky. So far."

"Luck comes into it once in a while," Conall admitted.

Niall could hear his smile, so charming women went *splat!* like flies beneath a swatter. Conall had always been good with girls. You'd think they could see through it, but they never seemed to. Conall didn't mean anything the smile promised. Beneath the surface ability to get what he wanted, he was intense, wired and lacking, seemingly, any ability to feel real emotion. He'd picked the right life for himself, but Niall expected it to be a short one. Speaking of...

"Used up one of your nine lives lately?" he asked.

"Maybe." Pause. "I got made. Had to dive off a fishing boat into the Sea of Cortez and swim for what seemed like miles with searchlights spinning overhead and bullets pinging every time I came up for air. Here's the surreal part: I had a whale surface near me. About crapped my very wet pants when it blew." He sounded cheerful.

Niall shook his head, laughing and swearing both. He edited Conall's stories for Duncan's ears. Duncan didn't need to know that Conall had what amounted to a death wish. Or maybe he only believed he was immortal, as if he had never matured from a stupid sixteen-year-old kid who played chicken with his buddies out on the highway in the middle of the night.

Niall had scraped a few of those kids off the pavement when he was on patrol.

"So how are you?" Conall asked. "Make any good arrests?"

"I shot a bank robber." As he told the story, he wondered how many men Conall had killed. Did you eventually get completely inured? He found he didn't like the idea of the eager toddler he remembered having grown into a man cold-blooded enough not to feel anything when he killed someone.

"That's your second kill this year, isn't it?" Matter-of-fact, merely curious.

"Yeah. That makes me a statistical anomaly among cops. Most of us go a lifetime without having to use the gun on the job."

"It's not your style," Con mused.

"No." A shriek outside momentarily caught his attention, but he decided it was a happy one. "You should call Duncan," he said abruptly.

There was a moment of silence. "Why? Does he have terminal cancer?"

"His wife is pregnant."

This silence felt different. "You're going to be an uncle," Conall finally said.

"*We're* going to be uncles."

"You can't tell me Duncan gives a rip if he ever hears from me again."

Niall rocked his chair back on two legs. "He always wants to know if I've heard from you."

"Why do you care?" his brother asked with seeming genuine puzzlement. "You hated the son of a bitch's guts every bit as much as I did."

"No. I pretended I did because I didn't want to admit to anyone how pathetically grateful I was that he was there."

Conall spit out an ugly obscenity. "Don't give

me that shit. Duncan got what he wanted out of it. It was the ultimate high for him. Snap the whip and we had to stumble over our feet falling in line."

"No," Niall said again. "Do you know how much he gave up? How desperately he wanted to be gone? He was more normal than either of us until then. He'd have gone off to college and partied and screwed girls and, yeah, gotten a four-point-O because Duncan didn't let himself make big mistakes, but he'd have had a life. Mom killed something in him when she did what she did."

"That's bull." But Conall didn't sound as sure as he wanted to.

"We're getting to be friends." It felt weird hearing himself say it out loud, but good, too. "Real brothers. I've been…remembering. He was good to me when I was little and a pain in the butt. Even later. Do you know how many hours he spent with me helping me develop the shot that got me on the varsity team? How many hours he put in on that heap of junk car making it look good and run, too?"

"The one he destroyed with a baseball bat?"

That was a low point, sure. Not so long ago Niall would have said he'd never forgive Duncan for what he did. Maybe he'd truly become an adult at the moment when he realized his brother had done what he did out of love, not rage.

Niall hadn't had his license that long, and he'd started rebelling against his brother's authority. The first six or eight months after Mom ditched them all, Niall had been too dazed to do anything but what Duncan asked. If eighteen-year-old Duncan had shrugged and left for college, Conall, then twelve, would probably have gone to a foster home. Niall, who'd already been in and out of juvenile hall half a dozen times, would have been sent to a group home instead. Even then, he'd known how utterly he would have been screwed. He'd already been lashing out trying to get his mother or father to notice. With any possibility of somebody really giving a damn gone, he'd have been lost. He knew himself well enough to recognize that.

But he'd gotten cocky, actually believed Duncan would never desert them and that it was safe to rebel. Or else felt that inexplicable need to test Duncan. *Are you really here to stay?* Into drugs and alcohol and girls and showing how fearless he was by speeding and—yeah, even playing chicken a few times, and winning, too— Niall might as well have walked onto the Burlington Northern train tracks, waved his arms and said, "Here I am," as the train bore down on him.

Duncan had yanked him back the only way

he could. Conall, too. Conall had been emulating Niall and one-upping him. He'd have been on the train tracks before long, too.

Duncan grounded Niall, but didn't ask for his car keys. He pretended not to hear Niall steal out of the house, but he was waiting when Niall got home around three in the morning, piss-faced and triumphant, because what did Duncan think he was going to do about it? Now Niall remembered the other emotions sliding under the surface like Moray eels, a ripple, a frightening dark slide of movement only half-seen. A part of him had been scared that Duncan wouldn't do anything. That he didn't care enough to take hard action any more than Mom or Dad had. That night had been Niall's challenge. Make me clean up my act. Please.

When he got home and sauntered in, glad to see the lights on in the house but secretly scared, too, Duncan had hauled Con out of bed, grabbed the baseball bat kept in the coat closet, marched both younger brothers out onto the lawn and ordered them to watch. Then he'd laid into Niall's car. The car Duncan himself had helped lovingly restore. He'd smashed the windshield, the hood, the trunk, the roof. He'd utterly and completely destroyed the car while Niall and Conall stood out in the cold watching in shock.

It had been the most terrifying spectacle of

Niall's life. Duncan had turned around, said, "You lost the privilege of having a car. From now on, when I tell you to do something, you do it. When I tell you not to do something, you don't. Got it?"

Niall had been trembling, Conall crying. Lights had come on in neighbors' houses; somebody had called the cops, because they could hear an approaching siren. Duncan had had some major explaining to do.

It was years before Niall realized there had been no explosion of rage. That, in fact, he'd been set up. Duncan had given him every opportunity to screw up because he'd decided the only way he'd keep the upper hand over his brothers was by scaring the shit out of them.

It worked. It also destroyed any remnants of brotherly camaraderie. They obeyed, and hated him. He'd been willing to pay that price.

Even then, Niall had loved him, too.

But Conall, he thought, didn't. Or had forgotten that he once did.

"He did what he had to do," Niall said now. "We wouldn't have listened to him any other way. Mom let us run wild because she didn't care enough to do anything about it."

"I know that." Conall's voice was tight, unforgiving. "I know I should be sending him goddamn Father's Day cards, but I choose not to, okay?"

"He's changed," Niall tried to explain. "Since he met Jane."

"If anything will ever get me back to your little corner of the world, it will be curiosity over how any woman could marry him. Do they have an electric blanket to warm his ice-cold blood at night?"

He should let it go, but couldn't. "We wouldn't have had a chance without him."

"I know that!" his brother yelled. He breathed heavily. Controlled his voice if not his fury. Or was it pain? "But I don't have to see him or talk to him ever again. Don't try to guilt me into something I won't do."

Niall's chair dropped back to the floor. He closed his eyes and pinched the bridge of his nose. "You're right," he said quietly. "I'm sorry. Lately I've been thinking a lot about the past. Seeing it differently. But I don't have to lay it on you."

More silence. He began to wonder if Conall had hung up on him. But then he spoke. "Something's changed."

"What do you mean?"

"You. I've never heard you sound like this."

"I haven't changed."

"You have. God. Don't tell me it's a woman."

Niall's gaze involuntarily went to the front window again. He heard a laugh outside. Rowan.

He made a noise that was supposed to be scathing but didn't quite come off. "Good thing you're not a detective."

"That's it." Conall laughed in disbelief. "Not you. It's got to be a temporary sickness. You'll get over it, man. Who needs that kind of shit? Not us."

Niall got him off the subject. They talked for a few more minutes before ending the call. He dropped the phone on the table with a thunk and speared his fingers into his hair.

You'll get over it, man. It's got to be a temporary sickness.

It had to be, he thought desperately. A wife and family... He wouldn't know what to do with them. How to make it work. How to stick, how to believe she would, that he could trust her not to walk like Mom did.

How to believe that he himself was more like Duncan than he was like their parents; that he would be capable of sacrifice for people he loved.

Duncan was all about responsibility. He'd made *duty* a grim word. But Niall had come to understand that his big brother cared. He would never let Jane down. No matter what. When his kids needed him, he'd be there.

Niall's throat felt thick. It was hard to swallow.

He had the stunned realization that he'd never believed he had it in him to measure up to the man he admired more than any other in the world: Duncan. He'd spent the past fifteen years or so trying, but he was no closer to believing.

Or am I?

The thought was the equivalent of an earthquake, way down deep in his bedrock. Once he'd understood that Duncan loved Jane, Niall would have died to save her for his brother. He would have sacrificed his life if necessary to save the bank teller in the parking lot that day, and he didn't even know the woman. He knew he'd do the same without question or hesitation for Rowan or her kids.

If he was willing to do that, could he also change how he lived for them? Give up his solitude, overcome the gut-deep fear of tying himself down to anyone or anything, even a piece of ground and a house?

He felt as sick as if he had a hangover. He couldn't believe he was even thinking things like this. He'd kissed Rowan. Twice. Hung out with her and the kids a few times. Lost his head over a minor threat to Desmond. Stepped between her and her in-laws. Her and her dad.

I want to stand between her and the world, when she needs me.

And he was out of his flipping mind.

Rowan had lingered in her kitchen as long as she could without it looking weird. She didn't know why she felt so shy with Niall's brother and his wife, but she did.

Yesterday Niall had asked a little awkwardly if he could barbeque in the backyard. "You and the kids can join us," he'd said. "Jane's having a baby. She might like to talk to you."

Uh-huh. Because she couldn't find any other woman who'd had a baby before. Like mother, sisters, friends, coworkers, random women in line with her at the grocery store…

But truthfully, Rowan was curious about his brother and the wife. She'd seen Duncan come and go, exchanged nods and greetings from a distance, but never talked to him. Otherwise Niall never had anyone over. If he got together with friends—or women—it was elsewhere. But here was her chance to be nosy. Maybe understand him better.

And she was hiding in her kitchen under the pretence of finishing her potato salad and getting drinks for the kids.

The back door opened and Jane MacLachlan stuck her head in. "Hi. Can I help?"

At first sight, she'd intimidated Rowan. She seemed so confident. She was beautiful, elegant, graceful and easily six inches taller than Rowan besides. Rowan felt short and squat beside her.

"Almost done," she said cheerfully, scraping chopped celery into the bowl from the cutting board. "Sorry. I should have been organized."

Jane came the rest of the way into the kitchen, looking to see what she was doing. "Yum. I love potato salad. I brought baked beans. I hope you like them."

"One of my favorite foods, except I've never made them from scratch."

"Surely there's something I can do."

Once they were bustling around the kitchen together, Rowan began to relax. "Your kids are darling. Desmond cracks me up. Is he ever shy?" asked Jane.

Rowan laughed. "Very, very rarely. He's the kid you see grinning at total strangers the second he learns how to smile. Anna is a little more suspicious."

"I like Anna. I'm more like her."

"Me, too," Rowan admitted. She hesitated and glanced at the other woman. "Um…Niall tells me you're pregnant."

Her hand fluttered briefly to her belly. "I am. Duncan and I gave ourselves almost a year after we got married, then decided to start a family." She made a face. "I never expected to get pregnant the first month we tried."

Rowan grinned at her. "Haven't you heard? All it takes is once."

"I guess I didn't believe it."

"You and every teenager in America."

They both laughed.

"Do you know yet whether you're having a girl or a boy?"

She shook her head. "I haven't decided whether I want to know." She rolled her eyes. "Duncan does, of course."

"Why 'of course'?"

"He's a control freak. He comes to every appointment with me and always has this list of questions. My doctor probably dreads seeing us coming. I can hardly wait to see Duncan when I'm in labor. He won't be able to do a thing but hold my hand, and that will kill him." She sounded as if she was savoring the notion. Jane's gaze met Rowan's. "I love him. I do. It's just that, uh, he needs taking down a peg or two now and again."

"He and Niall look a lot alike."

"They do." Jane propped a hip comfortably against the edge of the counter. The pregnancy showed when her shirt draped right. "Are you asking if they are alike?"

Rowan nodded.

"Then my answer is…I don't know. I don't think so. Niall doesn't seem driven to control everyone around him the same way. But the truth is, I don't feel as if I really know him. I remember one of the first times I met him thinking that he's surrounded himself with an inpenetrable force field. He was relaxed, pleasant, sexy..." She grinned. "He does look like Duncan, after all. Anyway. I looked into his eyes and absolutely could not tell what he was thinking. Not a hint. I told myself he had his cop face on...."

Rowan nodded at that; she knew exactly what Jane meant.

"But if so, he lives behind that face all the time. Or at least, I thought he did."

"What do you mean?"

"I looked at him a few minutes ago. He had Anna sitting on his shoulders. She was clutching onto his hair and giggling."

Rowan had seen out the kitchen window.

"Meantime, he was roughhousing with Desmond and he was laughing and I had never seen anything like that expression on his face before." She snitched a carrot stick Rowan had just prepared. "I saw joy."

And it awed her, Rowan could tell. She felt that now-familiar constriction in her chest. She had seen both expressions on Niall's face. Only she hadn't known how rare that open delight was.

"I think," she said, "he really likes the kids. But he's not sure he should. Sometimes he goes into hiding. We don't see him for days at a time. It's as if he can only take so much."

"It's new to him," Jane said gently.

"Well, I have to admit I was looking forward to meeting you and Duncan. To give him some context. You know?"

Jane laughed. "I know."

They ferried the rest of the food outside, where Duncan was flipping burgers on the grill while Niall manhandled the shrieking kids and occasionally grabbed the dog when he made a feint for the platter of hamburger patties.

They all sat at the picnic table, Anna on Rowan's knee and Des beside Niall, and chattered as they dished up and ate. Rowan watched the two brothers, astonished at a certain way they turned their heads or the echo of a mannerism. If there were major personality differences, they weren't evident in this setting. Duncan threw back his head and laughed often; Niall told incredibly juvenile jokes that had Desmond in hysterics. Now, how would he know those? she marveled. Once in a while, Rowan intercepted a glance between his brother and Jane that made her cheeks flush. Once she saw him touch Jane with tenderness that made her chest ache with envy. Drew had loved her in his way, but he'd never looked at her like that.

She'd probably never looked at him the way Jane did at her husband, either.

Rowan was very careful not to look directly at

Niall at all, except when he was talking and everyone was watching him. Those nights he and she had sat out on the porch, she hadn't been able to see his expressions. Sometimes his voice was so gentle, or it lowered to a deep, velvety texture. When that happened, what would she have been able to see on his face?

She shivered a little, and concentrated on dishing up more baked beans for herself and Anna both.

"When are you expecting?" she asked Jane.

"December." She grimaced. "I'm hoping the baby doesn't come late. I always thought being a Christmas baby would be the pits."

Desmond wanted to know why, and his eyes widened at the idea of only getting a heap of presents once a year instead of twice. "*My* birthday is October 22," he told them. "Anna's is March 27. I'm gonna be seven."

"I'm four," Anna said.

Niall smiled at her. "You'll be five on your next birthday." He glanced at his brother. "Wasn't that the year I had chicken pox?"

"What's chicken pox?" Des asked.

The adults all shook their heads at the marvel of children protected by a vaccine from one of the scourges and rites of passage they'd all survived. Niall was able to resume his story, about a birthday party from hell. It had been held at a pizza place and he started to cry in the middle of it, which was when his mother discovered his first spots. The other mothers weren't thrilled.

Grinning crookedly, Duncan said, "Half the kids got it, too—although they'd probably all been exposed already. *I* got it from you, and was seriously unhappy. Con never did get chicken pox."

"It's supposed to be awful if you catch it as an adult," Rowan said. "He should probably get the vaccine."

Niall laughed. "The big bad DEA agent covered with itchy red spots. There's a picture." His face sobered. "He called yesterday."

Des was sliding under the table to feed part of his hamburger to Sam. Something in the odd nature of the silence pulled Rowan's gaze from her son to the two men and even Jane. She and Niall both were watching his brother, who had gone still and expressionless.

"Did he?" he said finally. He tossed a black olive in his mouth. Chewed, swallowed and asked, "Any news?"

"He had to take a swim from a fishing boat in the Sea of Cortez and said a whale surfaced right beside him. You know that noise they make when they blow out? He said it was surreal, the two of them momentarily out there in the dark together."

Rowan saw the glance the two men exchanged.

Had to take a swim from a fishing boat? She wasn't sure she wanted to know why anyone would *have* to do anything like that.

"But he's okay?" That was Duncan.

"He says so. He'll be transferred to another region."

The older brother nodded.

"He's not the kid I remember anymore."

Duncan reached for his wife's hand. Rowan wasn't sure he'd even been aware he was doing so.

"Conall hasn't been that kid since he was nine or ten years old. Something went wrong in there."

Niall nodded.

Jane's expression was troubled; Rowan watched them all surreptitiously. She knew enough from what Niall had told her to be sure their childhood had been nowhere near as rosy as her own.

Maybe, she thought, she should be more forgiving of her parents. She'd been lucky in so many ways, able to start a family of her own in full confidence that she had it in her to be a good mother because she'd had a worthy role model.

Did Niall know how wonderful he was with her two children? What an amazing father he'd be? She switched her gaze to his brother's face, currently as grave and withdrawn as Niall at his most inpenetrable. Did Duncan doubt his ability to be a father? Hadn't he already proved himself with his brothers?

She found herself looking at where his hand and Jane's were linked, and saw that his knuckles showed white. So he and Niall *were* alike in needing to hide intense emotions. It was unsettling to think that these two men, both emotionally damaged, worried about their youngest brother because "something went wrong" when he was little.

Oh, Lord. What?

"Maybe he'll get up our way," Duncan said at last. "You haven't seen him in…"

"Four or five years." Niall frowned. "I flew down to San Diego."

Nobody said anything else. Even the kids were staring at the adults now.

"Apple crisp, anyone?" said Rowan.

They all burst into speech. Rowan took orders; no ice cream for Jane, ice cream *separated* from the cobbler for Desmond 'cuz he didn't like the crusty part getting soggy, all of the above for the two men.

She felt a tiny bit relieved to escape into the house.

CHAPTER TEN

NIALL DEBATED ALL WEEK whether he should ask
her. He performed in public, yes, but he had
never, not once, taken anyone with him to watch.
On occasion he saw someone in the crowd who
knew him; he lived with the unease that someday his father would be there, perhaps even wearing the clan MacLachlan tartan as he did. But he
didn't tell women he slept with that he played the
bagpipe, much less share that side of himself.

It wasn't Rowan he would be inviting, he
tried to tell himself. Not exactly. It was the kids.
Desmond especially would enjoy the Highland
Games, with the bagpiping and drumming, fiddling, dancing and traditional Scottish athletic
events. They'd all heard Niall play; a couple of
times now, he'd stood out on his porch to play the
bagpipe with the kids sitting at his feet listening
and watching with something like the awe he'd
felt when he was small watching his father.

He was embarrassed to wonder if Rowan
would think it was silly, a grown man, an Ameri-
can, a cop, for God's sake, dressing up in a kilt

and wearing the traditional black knife—*Sgian Dhub*—in his sock. He wasn't even sure he could explain why, for such a private man, he sometimes needed an audience for his music.

But finally, midweek, when he sat in his usual spot on her porch step with her in the glider, he said, "The Highland Games are this weekend."

"I've never been."

"I'm playing in the solo competition."

"Really? Can we come watch you? Or would you rather we didn't?"

"I was working my way up to inviting you. I thought the kids would enjoy it. The dancing is impressive, there's a sheep dog trial going on, fiddlers, bands playing. Some strong-man competitions." He hesitated. "I'm going Saturday. If you're not busy."

"We would love to come," Rowan said promptly.

She asked what time, they discussed the likelihood of the day being hot, and then fell into silence. Time to say good-night.

He most often kissed her now. Not always; he wouldn't let himself sometimes, or Rowan seemed especially skittish and he didn't like the idea of frightening her. He hadn't asked her yet *why* a widow with two children was clearly alarmed by a man's touch. A part of him didn't want to know, because he expected it would make him angry.

Tonight he stood and waited, leaving the choice to her. After a moment she stepped forward, her voice soft. "Thank you for asking."

He cupped her cheek. "I hope you like it. The music," he said huskily.

"I like hearing you play, even though you choose such sad music."

"Not always," he said. "The piece for Saturday, though… It's a folk song, I guess you could say. Not a lament, but not cheerful."

A small laugh escaped her. "I can't picture you playing a bouncy reel. Sorry."

"I do sometimes." With his thumb he explored her lips. He loved her lips—the shape, the way they quivered at his touch. Most of all the taste. "I will someday soon."

He kissed her then, letting loose some of the hunger he'd been keeping penned as if it was a wild animal snapping to be released. She wasn't so shy tonight, and that made it harder to stay gentle.

His tongue didn't play with hers, it thrust purposefully into her mouth, and he let one of his hands capture her breast, so full it spilled over his fingers. Her nipple peaked through her bra and thin knit T-shirt, pressing into his palm. He wanted his mouth to be there. He heard himself groan as he kissed her harder, deeper, fingers in her hair gripping her head, pulling it back. He kissed her throat tonight, licked the hollow at the base of it, and she took gasping breaths that lifted her breasts in a quick, uneven rhythm.

His body ached, but he made himself back off. Gradually let her go, because he knew she still wasn't ready. His frustration was building, though. This was ridiculous. He'd never had to court a woman like this. He didn't date women who didn't want the same thing he did.

She was different. Everything about this was different. Niall knew it, resented it and liked it all at the same time.

Rowan backed away from him, not looking behind her. She banged hard enough into the door to cause an audible thump and mumbled something to herself. He imagined her blushing. Anticipation heated his blood. He was going to be uncomfortable for a while, until his arousal subsided.

He shouldn't have sat talking to her for so long. He'd intended to go hunting tonight for the pervert, as he did every couple of nights, but he thought it was too late now. Kids were all snug in their beds with lights out.

Sam walked him back to the cottage and looked longingly inside but plopped his butt down on the porch with a sigh when Niall didn't invite him.

"Good dog," Niall murmured, and resigned himself to going to bed with a stubborn hard-on.

EVEN THE KIDS WERE awestruck at the sight of Niall in Highland regalia. Rowan was struck speechless.

The fact that he was wearing what was, essentially, a skirt didn't reduce his innate dignity at all. The effect was masculine, sexy and very formal.

The Clan MacLachlan tartan was a red, blue and black plaid threaded with a thin line of green. There were variations on it, he explained to all of them; the tartan had changed with the centuries, and different colors had been worn for dress-up occasions versus hunting, say. Above the kilt he wore a short-waisted black argyll jacket that she'd be willing to bet had been custom tailored to fit his broad shoulders. The knee socks were blue, and there was a dagger thrust into one. From his waist hung a sporran, a small bag. With his dark red hair and eyes the color of a loch under a winter sky, he might have stepped from another century, another place.

"Okay," Rowan said, "I feel seriously underdressed."

Niall laughed. The kids were in their usual shorts and sturdy sandals, Rowan in midcalf-length chinos, comfy sandals of her own and a filmy, short-sleeved white shirt open over a tank. "You'll be more comfortable than I will," he told her. "The kilt and jacket are both wool. Although I will be able to take advantage of any cool breezes coming from down below." He shot her a wicked grin.

Rowan knew her eyes had widened. Heavens—was it true that men didn't wear anything beneath a kilt? While he drove, she kept sneaking glances at the way the plaid lay over his thighs, catching glimpses of knees that were larger and bonier than hers.

Thinking about the possibility he was naked beneath the kilt became something of an obsession during the forty-five minute trip, interrupted, fortunately, by the necessity of answering the kids' questions. But every so often she'd steal another glance, know her cheeks were coloring, and feel…funny. Like she wanted to squirm in her seat. She had to press her legs together to contain that odd, cramping sense of *need*.

Please don't let Niall have noticed.

Probably he did wear underwear. Performances must sometimes take place on windy days. She imagined practical white briefs like Desmond's beneath the kilt.

"Why the smile?" Niall's voice was low and husky.

Gulp. He must have noticed her peeking. And blushing.

Why not be honest? "I had this sudden picture of a whole bunch of bagpipers—" *lie, lie, only you* "—caught in a good breeze."

His laugh was husky, too, as though he needed to clear his throat. "Some of us wear something under there." Pause. His gaze momentarily left the road and met hers, his eyes glinting with amusement but also holding a certain amount of heat. "Some of us don't."

She turned her head away from him and bit back a moan. It was a moment before she could say with convincing lightness, "And you?"

"Don't."

Dear God.

They were nearing the fairgrounds where the games were being held this year. Rowan spotted a bumper sticker on a car ahead of them and laughed.

"Support your local piper."

Niall smiled. "My favorite is 'Blow it out your bagpipes'."

They all laughed, especially Desmond who was at that age to love simple humor.

They could hear music from the minute they got out of the SUV. Fiddlers playing a dance tune, a far off cry of a bagpipe. Voices, shouts, laughter. Rowan found herself rising on tiptoe to try to see everything. In one direction, the sheepdog trials were going on and she wanted to watch, but she could also see a performance of dancers ahead.

Half the men and boys in the crowd wore kilts, and some women and girls, too.

"There are competitions for kids, too," Niall explained. "Drumming and fiddling for the younger ones. Blowing the pipes takes so much lung power, most kids can't do it until around ten years old."

"You make it look easy."

"I work up a good sweat."

They wandered for the first hour, watching dancers and some of the athletics, including a competition Niall called caber, in which big men wearing kilts ran carrying what looked like a telephone pole and then threw it astonishing distances. Shot-putting must have originated in these early games, she realized, watching men heaving a heavy iron ball. The effect of seeing them in bright T-shirts and kilts was startling, as was the flashes of massive thighs as they twirled to throw and the kilt lifted.

Anna was entranced with the dancing, Desmond the bagpipes and fiddlers. They all had fun watching the sheepdog trials. Des cackled at the idea of Sam on the field with a herd of sheep. Niall gave one of his deep, slow laughs.

"Yeah, I bet our Sam could break records for scattering sheep."

She was careful not to look at him. Had he heard himself say "*our* Sam"? Why did that make her heart squeeze? Maybe because, as he said it, he was also lifting Des high with one arm and his other hand rested lightly on Rowan's back.

He took his hand away and was quiet for a bit after that, though, which made her think he had noticed what he'd said and been dismayed. She'd rather think he was withdrawing as he psyched himself up to play.

They sat in the very front when he performed on the main stage. Rowan had the impression this individual bagpipe competition was one of the big draws of the games. She didn't have the ear to judge in any way, but was riveted by Niall when he played, the "bag" of his pipe tucked under his left arm, the blowpipe in his mouth, his fingers flying on the chanter. She'd learned enough to know it was the drones—the sticklike appendages that protruded from the bag—that made bagpipe music so distinctive. In most wind instruments, there was a fraction of a pause, at least, while the musician drew breath. With the bagpipe, the drones produced continuous sound.

The piece he played was haunting and melancholic. If it was a folk song, it was telling about a tragedy, of which Scottish history had plenty to choose from.

He got rousing applause and whistles, but when he joined Rowan and the kids he shook his head. "I'm off today."

"Really?" She tried to decide if he looked upset.

"Haven't been practicing enough lately." He shrugged. "Listen to this next guy. He's really good."

Not upset; his tone held admiration and friendship. After the competition she bought ice cream for the kids while he talked with other musicians. Watching him surreptitiously, she remembered Jane's observations. It was true, Rowan thought. Even though Niall stood amongst the group of men and laughed with them, he somehow still held himself apart.

Something changed on his face when he turned to look for her and the kids, though. His expression lightened when he saw Rowan, relaxed into a smile as he strode toward them, seemingly aware of the people around them only in the sense that he occasionally had to adjust his pace or divert from a direct path.

Anna had been sagging in her arms. He reached automatically to take her, and Rowan let him.

"Hold still. I've got to wipe her face."

"Chocolate ice cream, huh?" He grinned down at her little girl. "Good?"

"Uh-huh." She laid her cheek against his shoulder.

"Getting tired?" he asked Rowan.

She nodded. "I think we'd better call it quits, unless there's something you think we should stay for."

Niall shook his head. "Come on, buddy," he said to Desmond. "We can walk back to the car by the sheepdog trials and see if any of them have managed to best Sam yet."

Desmond grinned. "Maybe there are sheep all over the parking lot. We could take one home for Sam to practice on."

"That'd go over well with your grandparents," he said drily.

Rowan suppressed a shudder.

"I've got to tell you," Niall continued, "I don't think Super Sam has it in him to be a sheepdog."

"How come? Sam's *smart.*"

Niall's laughing, sidelong glance caught Rowan's. She felt a hitch in her pulse at the silent communication.

"It's not all about being smart," Niall said with a gravity at odds with that smile. "Some of it is instinct. Certain breeds *want* to herd from the time they're puppies. If Sam had that kind of instinct, he'd be herding you and Anna. My guess is Sam's breed—" the infinestimal pause likely had to do with the obstacle of imagining Sam as *having* any identifiable breed "—hunted something like rabbits or weasels. You know how much he likes to dig."

"Yeah!" Des brightened. "Sam's a hunter."

"And tunneler," Niall murmured for Rowan's ears only.

She giggled.

He unlocked the SUV and put Anna in her car seat as gently and deftly as if he'd been doing it her entire life. They bumped across the field that had been turned into a parking lot and hadn't been on smooth roads for five minutes before he flicked a glance at the rearview mirror.

"Out like a light."

"Anna?" Rowan started to turn.

"Both of them."

Sure enough, Desmond had slumped at an uncomfortable-looking angle and was sound asleep, as well.

"They had fun," she said.

"Do you think so?"

"I know so. I did, too."

"Good." He was quiet for a minute. "I was afraid you'd think it was silly."

Rowan blinked. "Silly? What do you mean?"

"Dressing up in kilts and folk costumes. Heaving heavy objects great distances for no reason.

Playing musical instruments most people would consider irrelevant."

"What I saw was people celebrating their roots. A culture. Having fun. Playing amazing music." She looked at him shyly. "When you play, I get goose bumps. I can all but see you standing on a battlefield, piping as men fall and die all around you." Rowan shivered. "I can see why bagpipes are so often played at funerals."

He made a noncommittal noise, but his shoulders had loosened, his fingers on the steering wheel relaxed. He really had been worried that she'd see him as ridiculous. As if Niall MacLachlan could be any such thing.

"You really don't wear any underwear under the kilt?" Horrified, Rowan realized she'd blurted it right out.

A satisfied smile curled his mouth. "I really don't."

"Oh."

"Had it on your mind, have you?"

"Maybe." She tried to sound dignified.

He laughed, low and smug. "Good."

She wasn't going to touch that one with a ten-foot pole. Or should she say, with a caber? Rowan thought with humor.

"Do you win the competitions sometimes?"

He glanced at her. "Yeah. Actually, I do. Winning isn't so much the point for me, though.

I'm…well, I was going to say not competitive, but that isn't true. Of course I am. Mostly I like to perform. Listen to other pipers, talk about the craft. I'm sorry neither of my brothers kept playing."

"I wish I'd had brothers or sisters," she heard herself say. "Mom…I think she had some miscarriages. She warned me when I got pregnant with Desmond. She was afraid it might be familial."

He nodded and said nothing for several miles. "You never talk about your husband."

"I don't?"

Niall shook his head. "What did he do for a living?"

"He worked in the assessor's office. It was something he fell into right out of college and never left. His father was disappointed." She grimaced. For all that Drew had risen to sainthood now in his parents' eyes, when he was alive they had often disapproved of his decisions. "He'd have liked Drew to come to work in the bank with him. Drew had majored in business, I think to please his father. He talked about going to law school, but…" She shrugged.

"But?"

"Glenn blames me. Because I got pregnant. I might feel bad, except I don't think Drew actually wanted to go to law school."

Niall had lapsed into silence, and she was

glad. When she looked at him, she saw that the lines on his forehead had deepened, as if he was brooding about something. Her down-to-earth side suggested he might have a headache, but he had an air of preoccupation, as if he'd forgotten she was there.

Would he go into hibernation now for three days? Because he'd let himself open up too much today? Was it a way of running away from unwelcome emotions? Maybe he craved solitude? Ending up living in such proximity to her, two young children and an admittedly annoying dog must have been an unwelcome surprise, she thought, venting a sigh she hoped didn't reach his ears.

When they reached home, both kids woke up, although Anna was disoriented and grumpy. Niall let Rowan take her daughter while he transferred the two child seats to her car. Sam barked frantically on the other side of the gate until they opened it and he could jump all over them.

"Thank you," she told Niall. "We had a good time. Didn't we, kids?"

Anna nodded.

"Yeah!" said Desmond.

"I'm glad," Niall said. He carried his bagpipe. "I can hardly wait to get changed."

"You look…" Rowan stopped.

He smiled. A slow, sexy smile that made his eyelids heavy and created heat low in her belly.

"Good." She cleared her throat. "We like you in a kilt."

The kids clamored to agree. Of course, Desmond in particular worshipped Niall. Des would think *anything* Niall did was awesome.

Sad to say, so did she.

Except, she amended in a hurry, when he hurt all their feelings.

THE MAN HAD BECOME increasingly cautious during his evening outings. He'd had a couple of close calls, and he didn't like being interrupted when one of the boys saw him. He was particularly unhappy about the one occasion, when he had climbed onto the roof of the carport. In scrambling down, he'd wrenched an ankle and had to make up an excuse for his wife's benefit. And that damn dog had caught up with him within two blocks! How had he gotten out? They never let the idiot dog out unless he was on a leash.

He snorted at the notion that anyone had imagined the dog was of any use. Of course Super Sam—a ludicrous name for a particularly dumb animal—hadn't known what to do when he did catch the man. His bark had been surprisingly deep and ferocious when he first raced out of the yard, which had alarmed the man initially before he realized there was no reason to worry. Not about that dog.

What did worry him was the increase in patrol cars prowling the neighborhood evenings. It would seem parents had believed their kids and called in reports.

He shrugged. Concentrating a few extra patrols in the neighborhood was political. A face in the window? No crime committed? The cops wouldn't take any of it seriously. He rarely strolled down the sidewalk where he'd be seen by a patrol officer anyway.

He'd given thought to taking his car and driving across town, but that carried pitfalls. He'd have to make up an excuse for where he was going to his wife, who thought nothing of his before-bedtime walks. In a strange neighborhood, he'd have to start from scratch identifying targets, too. And there was the risk that someone would notice the car, perhaps even jot down a license plate.

No, better to stick to his usual patterns. How fortunate that so many young families lived nearby.

He smiled as he crossed a dark lawn, studded with thick, tall rhododendrons. There was one right outside this boy's window. Really it ought to have been pruned, he thought with disapproval. The yard wasn't kept up well at all. The boy's clothes tended to be shabby, too. Clearly the house was a rental. The boy stood out among others his age, however, with a freckled face, an infectious grin and a thin, strong body. He'd be an athlete when he was older, the man felt sure.

Edging between the stiff, scratchy branches of the rhododendron and the peeling clapboard of the house until he stood to one side of the bedroom window, the man felt that irresistible tingle of anticipation. He had been looking forward to peeking in this boy's window, to seeing him without those too-worn jeans and ragged T-shirts.

His blood seemed to thicken in his veins as he watched the boy take pajamas from a drawer.

NIALL STARED IN FRUSTRATION at his map, where he'd marked sightings in red. Too scattered as yet to provide much guidance. Rowan's house was easily a mile and a half from where the latest incident had occurred, almost directly north. It would have been handy if two of the others had been equidistant east and west, allowing him to draw a circle. Peeping Toms, men who exposed themselves, even rapists, often operated within a certain perimeter of their own homes. It was rather like a wild animal who'd staked out a territory. They had a comfort level near home, an accumulated knowledge of their prey.

But in this case, two other complaints came from homes within a couple of blocks of each other, northwest of any theoretical center; the third house was perhaps six blocks directly south. In fact, there was something of a cluster up that way. Desmond was the anomaly, Niall reflected. Almost too far from the others to fit a usual pattern.

He grunted. He was drawing conclusions without enough evidence. He knew damn well the guy was peeking in half a dozen windows a night. The creep would get to some after lights were out, the curtains or blinds would be fully drawn, or the kid would change to pajamas in the bathroom. Most of the time, he would be disappointed. He'd have to work for his occasional success. And ninety-nine percent of the time he wouldn't be spotted at all.

That enraged and frustrated Niall. He was beginning to feel foolish, spending several hours most nights patrolling the neighborhood as dusk turned to night. He knew he was wasting his time; it would take a stroke of unlikely luck for him to stumble on this guy. He also knew he'd become the butt of jokes on the job.

His determination had yet to flag, though. Desmond hadn't wanted to sleep in his own room for damn near two weeks after the incident. He liked his new blinds, but Rowan had told Niall that every night she had to make a big production out of checking the lock on the window, turning the wand to be sure the blinds were as tightly closed as they'd go, drawing the curtains besides and checking their hang. And then the boy who'd never been afraid of the dark begged her to leave his door open and the hall light on until he was asleep. He'd had nightmares, too, that had torn her from sleep and scared Anna.

Desmond was something special. A great kid. Despite losing his father, despite nasty grandparents, he had this optimistic thing going. He expected to like people. Until this happened, life hadn't taught him to be suspicious yet. Now some pervert trying to get his jollies had stolen a little of Desmond's trust in his world.

Anger renewed, gaze still fixed on the map, Niall thought, *I'm going to get you, you bastard.*

After which, he thought grimly, the judge would slap the guy's hand, soothe it with lotion and send him home to start preying on little boys again.

But he'd have a record. The next time, cops would know where to start.

His eyes narrowed. It was likely, wasn't it, that Desmond was on the outside of this guy's territory. Somehow Des had caught his eye. But odds were he lived closer to the other four targets. Niall's finger slid over the map.

Perhaps… Gut instinct kicked in and his finger settled. About *there*.

CHAPTER ELEVEN

ROWAN SAW NIALL exactly twice that week. Sunday he had vanished entirely. Monday he came home from work and disappeared into his cottage, not to reappear until, presumably, Tuesday morning when he left for work. She didn't actually see him go. That afternoon she and the kids were out in the yard when he got home and he stopped to wrestle for a few minutes with Des, talk to Anna, who was holding a tea party for her dolls, and exchange pleasant and entirely meaningless conversation with Rowan. His face relaxed a little when he focused on the kids, but went impassive when he was talking to her.

Wednesday she had no contact with him; Thursday she took Desmond and Anna to Des's friend Zeke's house for a barbecue and they lingered nearly until bedtime.

Friday night, she didn't even know why she went out and sat on her glider after the kids were down. She didn't *want* Niall to cross the yard. She was too angry.

But at the same time, she wasn't surprised

when he did materialize out of the darkness and take his usual seat on the porch steps. The anger balled in her chest and she stared straight ahead and kept the glider moving smoothly.

The silence stretched. She refused to look at him and had no idea whether he was looking at her.

"I'm sorry," he said eventually.

"For what?" she said, managing to sound mystified and indifferent.

"For not being around much this week."

Much? Try *ever*.

"You're my tenant, Niall," she said flatly "Your only obligation to me, besides paying the rent on time, is to be reasonably quiet and not trash the place. It's fine." It wasn't fine.

"Tell Des I've been busy."

She'd gotten good at reading nuances in his voice, as many times as they'd sat talking in the dark. Now, he felt awkward. Maybe he was even ashamed of himself.

He should be.

"I think he's figured that out."

He was quiet for a while. "God," he said at last, explosively.

For the first time, it occurred to her that something might be going on in *his* life. Maybe a really dreadful case. But she did read the local newspaper, and surely she'd have seen something about any recent murders.

"Busy at work?" she asked politely.

He stood, in that quick, eerily lithe way he had. "No."

In response to the movement, Sam scrabbled out from beneath the porch, where he'd dug one of his burrows.

Rowan's chest ached. *Don't ask, don't ask, don't...* "Then what are you swearing about?"

"I don't have any excuse," he said. "I get... I don't know."

"Hermitlike?"

His laugh held not an iota of humor. "Something like that."

"It's okay, Niall. You don't owe us anything."

"Except the rent money."

Her fingers were knotted together, hurting. "Right."

"Maybe we can all do something together tomorrow."

"We have plans." Oh, Lord, now she'd have to think of an outing.

He was quiet, still standing at the foot of the stairs. "Okay," he said at last. "Good night, Rowan."

Still, he waited. She wouldn't even look toward him. Nothing in the world would have made her go into his arms, if that's what he thought.

Jerk.

"Rowan," he said softly.

Abruptly, she planted a foot to stop the glider and stood. "Good night." She turned and went into the house, letting the screen door snap closed with unnecessary force.

To hell with you, she thought, mad at herself because she felt like crying.

ROWAN WOKE UP MISERABLE and feeling the beginning of one of her headaches the next day, but she announced to the kids that they were going to the beach, and go they did.

She actually took them to Padilla Bay, an estuary where fresh water flowing into the bay had created an especially rich habitat for wildlife. The bay was so shallow that when the tide was out, miles of mudflats were exposed. They visited the interpretive center, where even Anna had fun with hands-on stuff like buttons she could push to hear the calls of local birds. Des was wide-eyed learning about "who eats whom in the estuary." They ate their picnic lunch, deposited the remnants in the car, then walked part of the Shore Trail and, with the tide well out, Rowan let the kids play in the mud left behind. One of Anna's shoes got sucked right off her foot and she cried when Rowan couldn't find it despite digging in slimy, thick mud.

"Maybe one of the clams wanted to make a home in it," she suggested.

Anna whimpered. Des stared in fascination at the spot where his sister's shoe had disappeared, *slurp*.

"Cool," he declared.

"You wouldn't actually want your shoe back," Rowan pointed out. "We'd never get it clean again. Look at the one that's left."

They all looked at it, then at Des's and Rowan's feet, not to mention her hand and arm, black up past her elbow. Yuck.

"You need new shoes before school starts anyway. Maybe we can go tomorrow."

"I don't wanna shop," her son objected, but Anna brightened. She'd become a little princess lately and liked clothes. She put together bizarre combinations, but Rowan didn't mind.

"Okay," she said, sniffed once and decided she wanted down. She took off her other shoe and was prepared to fling it, too, into the mud when Rowan grabbed it.

She didn't think her lecture on ecological preservation impressed Anna much, although Des at least looked thoughtful at the idea of one of the birds or fish eating something that might kill them. They'd been lucky already to see a great blue heron flapping its awkward way into the air.

Anna walked barefoot most of the way back

to the car, letting her mom carry her only once they reached the parking lot. Both the kids had developed tough feet this summer, running wild around the backyard. Rowan loved that they could do that. They'd been so much more constrained at their grandparents' house. There, they weren't supposed to rip holes in the knees of their jeans or get grass stains on new clothes or scrape themselves climbing a tree. They were expected to *behave*.

She had an attack of guilt, contributing to the headache that had made a comeback. She *still* hadn't invited her in-laws over for dinner. Maybe she'd call tonight and suggest they come tomorrow, for Sunday dinner.

After parking in the carport at home, she let Desmond run out to the street to collect the mail and carry it in. Rowan pretended that she didn't care Niall's motorcycle was gone. Once in the house, Rowan made the kids take baths and then let them put in a movie. Quiet time would be good for all of them.

She took some more painkiller and made herself a cup of tea before she flipped through the scant pile of mail.

One envelope looked official. It was from a law firm, she realized, hesitating before she opened it. Not the firm that had handled Drew's will. This one wasn't in Stimson at all; they were in Mount Vernon, the next county over. What on earth? She slit it open then read in astonishment that cramped into terror.

The attorney, one Elliott Bateson of Bateson, Young and Voight, was writing to inform her that Glenn and Donna Staley intended to sue for custody of their grandchildren, Anna and Desmond Staley, on the grounds that Rowan was unfit to raise said children.

She heard the roar of Niall's Harley turning into the driveway, the cough as he turned off the engine. Eventually there was a knock on the back door. Rowan had no idea if she said, "Come in," or not. What she did know was that he walked into the kitchen, saw her face and removed the letter from her shaking hand so that he could read it.

HE'D NEVER FELT ANYTHING like the fury that overtook him as he read the chilly legalese. He dropped the letter and squatted to bring himself to Rowan's level. Her face was white with shock, her eyes huge and dilated. Her hands, when he took them in his, were icy.

He squeezed them. "Rowan. Listen to me." He sensed the huge effort it took her to focus on his face. "They don't have a leg to stand on. You're a great mother. You don't do drugs, you don't drink booze, you don't leave the kids alone. You own your own home, you have a job. They're being spiteful. That's all. You know that, don't you?"

Her teeth chattered.

He muttered a curse. "What are you drinking?" He lifted it and took a sample taste, then dumped a couple of teaspoonfuls of sugar in from the bowl on the table and pressed the mug into her hand. "You need sugar."

She drank so clumsily, tea dripped from her chin when he took the mug away.

"Talk to me."

"I'm scared."

"This is nothing but a threat," he told her. His hands had come to be holding both of hers, warming them. "What I don't understand is why they're making it."

"I don't, either," she whispered. "I—I knew their feelings were hurt that I took the kids and moved out. But surely they didn't expect us to stay forever!"

"It seems they did." Disturbed by her shock, he rose from his crouch and pulled one of the chairs close so that he could sit more comfortably and keep holding her hands. Time to fill in the background. "I take it your husband was an only child?"

"Yes." She frowned. "Well, there was a cousin of Drew's that lived with them for a few years. Donna's sister's boy, I think. His mother had some kind of problem, but she came and took him away when he was, I don't know, seven or eight. Drew said his parents were upset."

Niall nodded. "Okay, that might be part of what's behind this."

She was still remembering. "Drew said he never saw his cousin again, so it was worse than just having him go back to live with his own mother. Maybe she hadn't wanted Donna and Glenn to have him in the first place? I don't know."

It might be ancient history, the details irrelevant at this point, but Niall found the story bothered him. "What about your husband's relationship with them?" he asked.

Rowan let out a long breath that seemed to take some of her rigidity with it. Her face had more color now.

"I never understood it," she admitted. "There was this weird push-pull. You know? It was like he hated them and loved them both. I swear through our entire marriage we never had a week that we didn't get together with them at least twice, but Drew also never seemed happy when we were with them. I suspect he wanted approval he never got. You know them. I don't think they're *capable* of approving wholeheartedly of anyone or anything."

"So he kept working to please them."

She looked at him. "I suppose that was it. I'm ashamed now that I didn't give more thought to it. They mattered to him, so I didn't let myself resent his dependence on them. But I wish... Oh, I wish I'd never let them talk me into moving in with them." She swallowed convulsively. "If I hadn't been so desperate..."

"They could have helped you financially without insisting you be under their control," Niall said harshly.

"That's what they did, isn't it?"

He hated the expression on her face. He could tell she was judging herself instead of her disagreeable in-laws. *I should have seen,* she was thinking. *I should have found another way. How could I have been so stupid?*

"But this..." she said finally, helplessly.

"Pretty much guarantees you'll sever the relationship they did have with their grandchildren. Why would they do that?"

"Because it's not a threat. They intend to carry it out and they think they'll win." Her breathing became ragged again. "I don't understand."

His eyes narrowed. "Have they criticized anything in particular recently?"

She half laughed. "That's all they do. Specifically, they're horrified about my plan to put Anna in preschool. And any suggestion Desmond might go to after-school care days I'm running late."

"In other words, you're keeping the kids away from them." When she nodded, he asked, "Anything else?"

Her eyes widened, her pupils fluctuating in size. Color came and went in her cheeks.

"Rowan?"

"You." Her voice was small, scratchy. "They didn't like it when you took Desmond swimming that one evening when they wanted to take him home with them. And…and Glenn said…"

His fury rose again in a hot tide. "He implied we have something going."

"Yes." Rowan closed her eyes for a moment, as if gathering herself. "He said you were 'that man I have living with me'."

"You told him I'm not."

"Of course I did."

He had to say this even though everything in him revolted. "Would it be better for you if I move out?"

Her gaze flew to his face. "No! No. You're… you're good for the kids. You pay the rent. You came running when Des screamed. You held my hand when Anna had surgery. You've been…" She hesitated over this. "A friend. I won't let them isolate me. I'm entitled to friends."

"But they've guessed it's more than that, haven't they?" he said softly.

"What?" Rowan formed the word almost soundlessly.

He shouldn't have let the prick of irritation he felt at being labeled a *friend* make him say something he hadn't meant to. But it was still there, and it stung.

"Am I really nothing but a friend?"

She stared at him, her eyes stunned and wary both. But pretty, too, that warm, melting brown.

"Am I?"

"Mommy?" Des called from the living room.

Niall jerked. He'd heard the television and known the kids were there, but in his worry for Rowan had blocked their presence from his mind.

She muffled her moan, but Niall heard it. "You're in no shape to be Mommy."

Her chin came up. "I'm *always* Mommy."

Yeah, but she looked like hell. A frown gathered on his forehead. It wasn't only the shock of this letter, he suddenly realized. "Do you have one of your headaches?"

She sagged. "Yes."

"Mo-om?" came a louder yell.

"Just a minute," she called back.

"Is there anyplace they can go for the evening?" Niall asked. "Or, better yet, to spend the night?"

He expected her to argue. The fact that she didn't told him how distraught she was. Worse come to worst, he'd stay himself, give her some time out. But he thought she needed more than that; she wouldn't completely relax if her kids were in demanding distance. And he and she needed to talk.

"I— Zeke's invited Des before. He has a little sister, too. We were just over there, but I'll bet if I asked…"

"Do it," he said. "I'll distract them."

He went to the living room and learned that their movie had ended and they wanted to know if they could put another one in. He talked to them for a few minutes, and then Rowan appeared.

"Hey. Jillian called to ask both of you to spend the night. Zeke and Elena are really excited."

It took some persuading. Anna thought she might get scared. Rowan promised she'd come get her if she did. She explained that she had one of her headaches and needed to lie down.

In the end, she pulled herself together enough to help them pack but let Niall walk them over to the neighbor's house.

He went back to Rowan's to find she was right where he'd found her last time. She'd sunk down at the kitchen table again as if her legs couldn't hold her. Her face was wan, her eyes glassy.

"Do you have prescription stuff for your headaches?" he asked. "Have you taken it?"

"Of course I have." There was only the smallest spark of indignation.

"All right," he said. "Here's the plan. You're coming home with me. I'll cook dinner while you relax."

"The kids…"

"I gave Jillian my number."

Rowan looked at him, and he had the uncomfortable feeling she was seeing deeper than he wanted. "Are you sure?" she said, and he knew that wasn't all she was asking.

Am I sure?

Hell, no! His chest felt crowded, as if his heart or his lungs had become too big for his rib cage. But he'd gotten himself into this. What could he say?

"I'm sure."

After a moment she gave a tiny nod.

He escorted her across the yard. Ridiculous, when he was renting the cottage from her, for it to feel so momentous that she stepped inside. Had she ever been in here?

"Yes, once between tenants," she told him when he asked. "The only furniture was the table and chairs."

"I don't have a lot, but I don't need much for this place." He steered her to the leather sofa. "Sit. Lie down, if you'd feel better."

She demurred at that. He had one of those socks stuffed with rice or beans or something that could be heated in the microwave and used to soothe sore muscles. He warmed it and draped it around her neck. She sat back with a sigh, her eyes drifting closed.

Niall stood above her, looking in a way he rarely had the opportunity. For one, she was almost always in motion. Talking to one of her kids, holding one, laughing, cooking, gesturing. At night, when they did their best talking, it was always in near-darkness. Mostly he liked that; both of them, probably, felt freer when they didn't have to read expressions and could concentrate on the subtleties of tone. There had been times, though, when he'd deeply regretted not being able to see her.

At the moment, no one would have called her pretty. Not with her face so pinched. Maybe she hadn't slept well last night, maybe it was the migraine, maybe distress only, but something had given her shadows as dark as bruises beneath her eyes. Her lashes, fanned on the bruise-purple skin, were long but not dark; he hadn't seen her yet bother with makeup. She looked so damned vulnerable right now, with her eyes closed and the tracery of blue veins on her lids, her face utterly still.

Then she sighed, and her breasts rose and fell, and even though he noticed, he wasn't stirred to lust. He *was* stirred to alarm. He had her to himself. He *should* be imagining that she'd share his bed tonight.

And maybe he was, but what he seemed to care about right now was making her feel better. Taking away the hurt and the fear.

He almost groaned. Instead, he backed away, took a last look at her face and went to the kitchen.

She was asleep by the time he had the curry chicken in the oven. She lay on her side, her head on a throw pillow, her knees drawn up, one hand tucked under her cheek, the other curled neatly to her chest. She didn't abandon herself in sleep, lose inhibitions to sprawl. Instead, she looked sweet and young, not like a woman he should want as a lover.

There was no excuse whatsoever for the slam of desire that froze him in place. Why *now?* No answer, but he couldn't have moved if someone was kicking down the front door. He stared, and he ached.

The curve of her cheek, the way her lips were softly parted. Her throat. Her position plumped her breasts, emphasized a tiny waist and delicious curve of hip. If he'd been sleeping with her, he'd have been spooned behind her. His groin pressing against her lovely, firm, perfectly rounded bottom. He could wake her by nuzzling aside her hair and nibbling at her nape. Fill his hand with her breast. Enter her from behind.

He jerked, so powerful was the image.

She needed to sleep. Her face was the most relaxed it had been since he'd walked into her kitchen and seen terror so stark he'd gone on battle alert.

This is why you brought her here. Not *for sex.*

However desperately he wanted sex.

The muscles in his body gradually unclenched. He scrubbed a rough hand over his face, feeling dazed. At last he sank down onto the one easy chair in the room. Where he could watch her sleep, the hunger in him alive and well however hard he tried to repress it.

ROWAN WOKE DISORIENTED, then embarrassed. Niall had gently shaken her into consciousness.

"Head better?" he asked, smiling

"Yes. Thank goodness," she said, surprised to realize it was.

"Go splash some water on your face. I'm dishing up dinner."

She escaped to his bathroom, which was as clean and neat as the rest of the cottage. She was horrified by her own face staring back at her from the mirror, pallid, with awful bluish circles under her eyes. Her hair was stringy, her lips colorless.

"Ugh," she muttered. After following his advice and drying her face on one of the thick, dark brown towels that hung on the rack, she slid open the top drawer of the vanity and was relieved to find a comb. Fortunately her hair wasn't tangled; it was too fine to really tangle. She combed it and put it back into a tidy ponytail. The end result wasn't anything to brag about, but at least she looked less pathetic.

Dinner smelled amazing and she was starved. Her headache had already been coming on that morning, and it was invariably accompanied by queasiness. She'd had tea and one piece of toast for breakfast, and only picked at lunch. Niall dished up hefty portions for her and watched in seeming satisfaction as she ate.

"Mmm. It's so good to have something the kids would hate," she declared, then blushed. "I'm sorry. I didn't mean…"

He laughed. "I made something I figured wouldn't appeal to them. You must get tired of spaghetti, macaroni and cheese, hamburgers…"

"Hot dogs, pizza, ham and mashed potatoes." That pretty much summed up her weekly rotation of meals. She did make a couple of casseroles the kids liked only because they'd been eating them their entire lives. "This was nice of you, Niall. Thank you."

He studied her. "You've got some color in your face."

She set down her fork. "I've only been that shocked a few times in my life."

"Did some officers bring you the news about your husband?"

Rowan nodded. "Yes. That was one of the times. And I know this sounds dumb, but I was really blown away when my mother called to tell me she and Dad were separating. That he'd asked for a divorce. I mean, I'm an adult. It's not like when you're a little kid and the idea of your parents separating is unthinkable. When it erodes *your* sense of security." She remembered belatedly that having his mother walk out on her family the way she had must have done exactly that to him. "I'm sorry. Compared to what you went through…"

Niall took his head. "Maybe we're always little kids where our parents are concerned. I have this recurring fear—or maybe it's a fantasy, I don't know—that one of these days I'll be playing the bagpipe at something like the Highland Games and my dad will be there. Right there in front of me. When I imagine it, I feel like a kid. Con-

fused, not knowing if I hate him or love him."
He shrugged.

His understanding freed her. "It was only a
few weeks before Drew was killed. I needed
Mom and Dad but they weren't there anymore.
Or maybe they would have been if I asked, but
I was angry at them, too, so I didn't." Rowan
grimaced. "Donna and Glenn seemed so...solid.
There for me and the kids. I was so grateful."

He was watching her again, his eyes percep-
tive. "Do you have an attorney?"

Rowan shook her head. "We had one who did
our wills, but I wasn't that crazy about him." She
looked at him with sudden hope. "Can you recommend someone?"

"Yeah, actually. A woman named Elizabeth
Foster. I've seen her a couple of times in family
court, heard good things."

"Thank you."

His face was abruptly impassive. "If she thinks
I should, I'll move out."

"No," she said again. She was certain about
this. She didn't like the way he kept pulling back,
but when she or one of the kids had most needed
him, he'd been there, more than anyone in her
life ever had. And it was *wrong* to suggest that
she wasn't a good mother because she'd become
friends with the tenant of property she owned.

"We'll see."

Rowan glared at him. "Don't you dare."

He smiled. "Stubborn woman."

She didn't think of herself that way, but she supposed she could be. Certainly in defense of her children. Of the people she loved.

Heavens. She might as well have touched a bare, sizzling electrical wire. The shock ran through her.

I've fallen in love with him.

What a fool! Rowan didn't kid herself that he felt the same. That he'd *let* himself feel the same. The habit of guarding himself was too entrenched.

It was one too many shocks in a day. Rowan gathered herself. "Thank you for all of this, Niall. I think I'll go home now."

His eyes riveted her. "Don't. Stay, Rowan."

"Stay?" she whispered. Did he mean...?

"For now." His voice was thick. "Don't go yet."

If she was smart, she'd say, "I'm sorry," and insist on going home. Of course that wasn't what came out of her mouth.

"All right." She took a deep breath. "I can stay for a little while."

He pushed back his chair and stood up, then held out a hand to her. He'd done that so many times. She could hardly ever resist the temptation. It felt so right to put her hand in his.

She did this time, too, allowed him to pull her to her feet.

"I want to kiss you when I can see you," he murmured. "I never have, you know. I lift my head and wish I could see the expression on your face. During the day, the kids are always with you."

"You could have gotten me alone if you'd wanted. Invited me to go somewhere."

He winced, almost imperceptibly but not quite. "I should have."

There they stood, perhaps a foot separating them, her hand warmly clasped in his. Rowan let go of the hurt. Tonight…she didn't know what she'd have done without him. What if, after she read that horrible letter, he *hadn't* come bursting into her kitchen?

"Why did you come over earlier? I mean, you didn't know anything was wrong."

His eyes were shadowed. "No, I had no idea about the letter, but I did know something was wrong. I hurt your feelings again."

Pride should have had her laughing and telling him that of course he didn't. But with Niall, pride wasn't nearly as important as honesty. They'd been astonishingly honest with each other from the first.

She tilted her chin up. "You did."

The lines on his face deepened. "I...seem to be at war with myself."

"I can tell." She was afraid she knew which part of him would win. If she'd been single, if he could have eased into the idea of a family, maybe he could have handled a relationship with her.

Or maybe his attraction to her was *because* of the kids. She wasn't exactly the sexiest woman around. She cringed, remembering her last view of herself in the mirror.

Niall frowned at her. "I don't know what you're thinking, but I don't like it."

"I only wondered why you're wasting time with me. I can't be anything like the women you usually see."

"See." He laughed shortly. "No, you're not. Rowan, I don't have relationships. I have sex."

"Isn't that what you have in mind with me?" It had taken courage to ask.

He looked stunned. She saw his throat move. "Yes," he said after a minute. Then, "No. I want more. But I don't know if I can do it, Rowan." There was another of those laughs that hurt to hear. "Talk about a push-pull."

Her eyes burned. They stared at each other, for once with no guards up at all.

"I'm scared, too," Rowan admitted, voice barely audible.

Niall groaned and tugged her forward. "Let me kiss you."

There was no choice at all, was there?

"Yes. Please."

His head bent; she rose on tiptoe. They met in a storm of need and fear.

CHAPTER TWELVE

THE OTHER KISSES—there had been no chance of them going anywhere. Maybe that's what made this one so different. Or maybe it was that he'd confessed to feeling something for her. If not love, still something that frightened him.

Drew had claimed to love her.

The thought came and went in less than a heartbeat. She didn't want him here. *Niall is different,* Rowan thought fiercely, and was surprised at how certain she was.

His mouth was hungry but still gentle. *That was it,* she realized with a last flicker of consciousness. He never forgot to be careful with her. Except when he ran away, he'd been unselfish, always.

She kissed him back with all the passion in her. Clumsily, she knew; this felt startlingly new to her.

Niall sucked her tongue and let her suck his. They nuzzled and played and rubbed. At first his hands only pulled her close, set hers on his shoulders. He wrapped the back of her neck, splayed the other hand on her butt to lift her against him. But when she didn't resist, he began to explore: this curve, that dip, the weight of her breast, the hollows above and below her collarbone.

She wanted to do the same so desperately but was timid when she began. It was enough to test the thickness of the muscles that tied his neck to his shoulders, the power of his biceps, the flat, strong muscles in his chest. But her hands wanted bare skin, and apparently so did his. At the same moment his hands slid beneath the hem of her T-shirt, she found his neck, smooth and hot, and dove into his thick, wavy hair. Coarser than hers, it felt masculine between her fingers. She shivered and arched into him.

He muttered something under his breath and pulled her T-shirt up and over her head. She tugged at his and he shed it. Rowan had seen him shirtless a few times and had tried hard not to stare. Now she didn't have the chance, because he was kissing her again, voraciously but tenderly, if that wasn't a contradiction in terms. She'd seen him, though, the bright curls of dark copper against tanned, sleek flesh. The arrow of hair that led over his taut belly beneath the waistband of his jeans. The fire the sight lit in her was unfamiliar, but she wasn't naive enough not to recognize it. When she'd first met Drew, she'd felt something like this.

She'd sworn to ignore any such feelings if they ever came again.

But this was Niall.

He'd unclasped her bra so deftly she hadn't even noticed. He had pulled back enough to cup both breasts in his hands like offerings. His expression was rapt; a flush crept across his cheekbones. The sight of his eyes, darkened by passion, that color in his face, his hands, big and brown and so very capable of violence but now holding her most tender flesh with something like reverence—all of that melted her fear and her resistance.

Rowan heard herself making small, desperate sounds. Was she *begging?* Shocked, she thought she might be. But what for?

He knew, because he abruptly lifted her high and carried her into his bedroom. She didn't take in the surroundings, only felt herself sink onto the bed with him coming down atop her. That might have sparked fear, except he was talking.

"So beautiful," he muttered. "You don't know, do you? But you are, Rowan."

He pressed his face between her breasts; evening stubble was scratchy but also unbearably sensuous. And then he was kissing her breasts, his tongue encircling one of her nipples, and she wanted…she wanted…

His mouth closed over the peaked nipple and

drew it deep in his mouth. He suckled, pulling hard, and a surprised cry came from her throat. Her hips bucked, and now she wanted more. So much more.

Again without her noticing, he had unbuttoned and unzipped her pants. He moved to her other breast, dampened it and then drew it into his mouth in turn. Meantime, his hand slipped inside her panties, long fingers delving into the slick crevice. Her thighs clamped shut, wanting to hold his hand there, where it felt so extraordinary.

He laughed, a husky sound. "Patience, sweetheart. God, you feel good." He rose to his knees and shimmied her pants and underwear both down. She didn't object, even though she'd never made the conscious decision to let this happen. It was too late now; she *needed* him in a way that was entirely unfamiliar. Her stirrings of passion had never been stoked like this. Rowan knew in one way, and not at all in another, what was happening to her.

It occurred to her that she should have been embarrassed. She hadn't offered the least resistance. She was making all these strange little noises and grabbing at him and letting him do anything, but his groans and murmurs sounded satisfied and as hungry as she felt.

She discovered she was unzipping his jeans

and yanking them down, even though this was the part that really scared her. *Should* really scare her.

Niall growled something in his throat and rolled away from her long enough to strip. "Don't go anywhere," he said.

She felt bereft when he leaped from bed and disappeared. Where?

Oh. Her eyes widened. *She'd* never have thought of birth control. Wouldn't that have been a disaster?

Why didn't he keep condoms in his bedside drawer?

Because, of course, he didn't bring women home with him. She knew it was so with an instinct that wouldn't be denied. This was his sanctuary. Even Gran had said he hardly ever had visitors. Since Rowan had moved to Gran's house, the only people Niall had had over were his brother and his sister-in-law.

Was she the first woman he'd brought to this bed?

Pleasure ran through her. But she couldn't think about it, because he was back. He tossed several packets on the bedside table, tore one open and rolled the condom on. Then he came down beside her, pulling her to face him.

"You have no idea how much I want you." His voice was hoarse and somehow stark.

Please don't hurt me. Please. But she couldn't say that.

"I want you, too."

She thought he'd climb atop her then and push into her body whether she was ready or not, but he didn't. He kissed her, caressed her, touched her until she had gone mindless again and her hips lifted and her thighs spread and she wanted him there. Only then did he kneel between her legs and press forward into her. Carefully, slowly, filling her, and it didn't hurt, it didn't hurt *at all.* It was…glorious, and she was grabbing him again and trying to pull him deeper, to keep him from retreating even though when he did and surged back into her that felt incredible, too.

But eventually her body caught the rhythm and she rose and fell with him. Deep in her belly a knot of pleasure grew tighter and tighter and she had this animal need to let it loose but didn't know how.

He did. "Now, Rowan." His voice wasn't his. It was as desperate as she felt. *"Now."*

He did something—changed the angle, or pushed deeper. Something. All that agonizing tension inside her sprang loose, in a white-hot jolt of pleasure that spread and spread until it reached her fingertips and toes and cheeks. When it finally settled, she discovered her entire body had arched, lifting him, and her mouth was open in an astonished O.

He thrust a few more times, made a single, raw sound, and his body shuddered in and over hers. And finally, because he was Niall, he rolled immediately so he didn't crush her. But he didn't let go, not for a second. He arranged her against him, her head on his shoulder, one of her legs lying over his, and cradled her as if she was the most precious thing he'd ever held.

So now I know, Rowan thought, dazed. *This is why people do it.*

And wasn't it sad that she was twenty-nine years old before she discovered it?

Is sex always *like this?*

"No."

Now she blushed. "Did I say that out loud?"

"Yep." He lifted his head from the pillow and tipped it so he could see her face. Was it her imagination that he looked as shell-shocked as she felt? "You were married."

Her skin abruptly felt chilled. "Yes. But, um…"

"Sex wasn't good?"

"No." She hadn't thought she'd ever admit that to anyone. "It was… No."

"He wasn't the only guy you'd ever made love with, was he?"

"Yes. I was, I don't know, really shy in high

school." She was mumbling into his chest. She couldn't have talked about this at all if she'd had to look at him. "I dated some in college, but just never... Until I met Drew. And even then, we waited until we got married." The words seemed to rush from her, as if once she'd started she couldn't stop. "I hadn't been much of a church-goer, but he'd grown up in the church so I assumed that was why. Except I knew he wasn't a virgin. There'd been other women. So, well, maybe it was respect for me. Because he loved me." She squeezed her eyes shut on a hideous surge of embarrassment. "What am I doing? You can't possibly want to hear this. Especially now."

Niall's hand had been moving in gentle circles on her back, she realized. It didn't stop, but he was silent for a moment and she stiffened.

"I do," he said finally. "I can't pretend I like thinking about you with another guy, even if you were married to him. But I want to know."

"Know what?" Rowan asked cautiously.

"Why you've been so skittish with me. So surprised when something feels good. As if..." He stopped.

"As if what?" She couldn't do anything but whisper.

"As if you were totally inexperienced." He paused. "Or as if you've been abused."

Shame did, finally, crash over her. She tried to

pull away; her knees drew up as if her body instinctively wanted to curl into a fetal position.

But for the first time Niall compelled her. He held her firmly, rolling so that they were face-to-face and he was looking into her eyes.

"Tell me," he said.

HE HAD TO DRAG IT out of her, and he hated every twist and turn of her confession. It got worse as it went on.

First she admitted the husband hadn't much believed in foreplay. Sex had been quick and dirty. Probably worked for the guy but not for her. But then she started talking about how she thought maybe Drew had been ashamed of himself. Ashamed to want her at all, and of the way he treated her.

"He…hurt me," she whispered. "I think he liked it best when it did hurt." She'd gone back into hiding, her forehead resting against Niall's shoulder. "I got so I thought it always hurt for the woman. That we were being conned by books and movies."

He swore. "Tonight, it didn't hurt because your body was ready for mine. You wanted me."

Her head bobbed. "The first few times with Drew, I was, and… He couldn't." She peeked to see if Niall had understood this.

He nodded.

"After that it was always really fast and rough. He liked it if I struggled. A few times he asked me to…to bite him or claw him or…" Rowan shuddered. "I couldn't." Her body trembled again. "Are you sure you want to hear this?"

He closed his eyes and tried to contain his anger and pity. "I'm sure."

"I should have left him, but he was always sorry. I think he really was. And he was a nice man. You probably won't believe me, but he was. I got pregnant practically right away. And he was a good father."

He felt dampness on his skin and knew she was wiping away tears. His arms tightened. "Sweetheart." That's all he seemed able to say.

"He didn't want to talk about it." Her voice was small and shamed. "But he told me once he'd been molested, and he thought maybe that's why…"

"Did he say who?"

She shook her head. "He wouldn't. He said he never told anyone before. Knowing his parents, I can see why. He insisted it didn't matter anymore." Rowan was pressing tight to Niall now. She seemed to vibrate as she listened to her own words. "But it did. It did matter."

"Yes. I'm sorry. So sorry." His hands were moving, giving what comfort he could.

"Thank you. I mean, for tonight. For…for…"

Anger and shame of his own racked him. "Don't thank me," he said harshly. "This wasn't... God. I wasn't doing you a favor. This is what making love *should* be like."

"I've never had an orgasm," she said in a small, dry voice.

He closed his eyes on the rush of emotions and rubbed his cheek against the top of her head.

I've never had one before, either. Not like that. The awareness sliced into him. Scared him like nothing ever had. Formed a sick ball in his belly.

He rejected the very thought. What a stupid thing to even let cross his mind. Having Rowan had been good. Of course it was; he'd been waiting for her long enough. Anticipation always heightened sensation, right? With sex, he'd rarely had to do a lot of anticipating. Women didn't make him wait.

Easy explanation.

"Want another one?" he heard himself say.

She lifted her head and blinked at him with big, owl-like eyes. "Is it, um, possible? I mean, *can* I? And...and you?"

"Oh, yeah." He rolled her beneath him. Despite all the blasted emotions churning in him—the anger and fear and heart-wrenching regret for everything this gentle woman had experienced—he wanted her again. Fiercely. He couldn't possibly give voice to any part of what he felt, so he kissed her.

She gave herself up to him with a tiny, wordless cry.

He proved to her that she could. That he could. And then he proved it again.

HE WALKED HER BACK to the house in the morning and found the listing for the attorney he'd recommended in the phone book. He was beginning to ice over inside, but he made himself offer to go with her to pick up the kids.

Rowan gave him a single, devastatingly sharp look and shook her head. "Thanks, Niall, but I think it would be better if I went by myself. I need to get myself together. You know?"

He knew. How in hell was he going to get himself together? Was it even possible?

"Sure," he said, smiling and kissing her lightly. "Hey, Anna made it through the night."

Rowan's expression brightened. "She did, didn't she? It was her first sleepover, except at her grandparents' house." That dimmed her joy.

"Call your parents," he suggested. "Tell them what's going on."

"All right." There were shadows in her eyes, but determination, too. "You're right. They're going to be really mad."

"Having them backing you will help."

"Okay." She smiled again. "Thank you, in the nicest possible way, for last night. I know you weren't doing me a favor, but it was a gift. One of the best ones I've ever had."

She was making this so damned hard. He'd have sworn she was releasing him, letting him know she knew it was a one-off and that was okay, he shouldn't feel bad about it.

But Rowan wasn't the kind of woman who'd even consider meaningless sex.

That's what she was telling him, he realized with shock. That it hadn't been meaningless, but she didn't expect any more from him.

The realization outraged him on one level, and on another he was grateful. *You did hurt me,* she'd said. And she was trying now to be sure that he couldn't again.

Feeling sick, he couldn't blame her for her caution. He did retreat every time they got too close. He knew that he was going to this time, as well.

"I'll let you go get the kids," he said, backing away. He couldn't keep hanging around. He had to get out of there.

Niall went back to his cottage and donned his leathers, then got on his Harley. As he rode it out of the driveway and onto the street, he saw Rowan on the sidewalk. She must have heard the throaty roar, but she didn't turn.

He went the other way.

Beneath the hammer of guilt, panic clawed him. He could feel things for her that he'd never felt before.

Could? Maybe already did.

No! He'd vowed never to set a foot into that trap. It hadn't even occurred to him that the damn thing would yawn open in front of him. He remembered Duncan, when he'd first met Jane, asking Niall if he or Conall ever had real relationships with women. Niall had been surprised Duncan had to ask; of course none of the MacLachlan brothers would do anything that stupid. That risky. In the end, he'd accepted that his big brother had chosen to do so. But Duncan, Niall had always known, was different from his younger brothers. Mom had loved Duncan as much as she was able, stayed for him until she believed he no longer needed him.

But she had been wrong. Her decision had been the worst thing she could do to him right then, but Niall had also known for a long time that both of their parents had been utterly self-centered.

In that moment, he knew. *If, one of these days, I turn and Dad's there in front of me, I will walk away. No conflict. No question.* Niall didn't want to be like Rory MacLachlan. Wanted no ties.

He shuddered at the fear that, in rejecting Rowan and what she could offer, he was like

Rory. Untrustworthy. Unable to feel deeply enough to give anything more than fleeting pleasure to another person.

God, he thought in horror. *Am I like Dad? When all I've ever wanted is to measure up to Duncan?* Duncan, who when he loved, was unshakably reliable?

Niall wanted to talk to his brother, but he couldn't. Not now. Not yet.

Maybe never.

Once on the highway, he opened up, needing the speed and the power and the kind of risk he accepted.

WHAT SHE'D THOUGHT HURT before was nothing compared to this.

Rowan had expected it. She'd believed she was braced for Niall's withdrawal, but she'd been lying to herself.

It was all she could do to concentrate Wednesday, when she had her first in-service training for the school year. Or Thursday, when she worked half a day helping prepare the third-grade classroom for the opening of school.

It wasn't that Niall had disappeared, not this time. Not entirely, anyway. He was friendly when he saw them. When he heard that Desmond was to start soccer right after Labor Day, he began kicking the ball with him. He even took him down to the school one evening so they could practice on a real field. The kids didn't notice that anything was wrong. They had no reason to see the complete lack of expression in his eyes on the rare occasions when they met Rowan's. They weren't aware, on a cell-deep level, of the body language that said Keep Away.

Sunday night she'd gone out and sat on her glider, telling herself she only wanted the peace and the cooler air, but knowing she was giving him a chance.

She might be wrong. He might slip out of the darkness and sit on the step. He might talk to her, that deep husky voice expressing so much his face never did.

But she wasn't wrong. He didn't come, and she didn't go out again after that. The hurt was too deep.

He'd never said he loved her. It wasn't his fault that she had fallen in love with him.

He must know, she thought with anger she carefully fed with small handfuls of tinder.

But she always cycled back to the same point. Maybe he did, maybe he didn't, but *she'd* known that all he really wanted was sex. And now he'd had it, had *her.* She couldn't possibly have been very good at it, not with all her hang-ups. Why would he want a repeat? Rowan was nauseated to think of everything she'd told him. A man who only wanted a good time, and she'd told him all her misery with Drew. She couldn't even remember why, except maybe it was because she'd been so stunned to discover how much Drew had cheated them both out of.

She'd had her first appointment with the attorney on Thursday, after the morning she'd spent in the classroom. She'd been a little bit afraid, after hearing the admiration in Niall's voice, that Elizabeth Foster would turn out to be a former lover of his, but she was a woman in her fifties who wore a wedding ring and had several pictures on her desk of an entirely bald but rather handsome husband, two daughters in their twenties and her first grandbaby.

Rowan had to spend an hour raking up every twig of the past she could recall. Not her sex life, thank God, but everything she could remember about the Staleys and their relationship with Drew and with Desmond and Anna. And her.

"I don't know if they always disliked me. They probably didn't think I was good enough for Drew. What I'll never understand is why he made us all live under the weight of their disapproval," she said.

"I feel confident in saying their claim is ridiculous." The attorney shook her head. "They want their grandchildren, and yet they're willing to risk the possibility that you will refuse them further contact." She hesitated. "You don't seem to think Anna or Desmond will miss them too much."

Rowan shook her head.

"I believe, in fact, that if this makes it to court we need to demand they have no visitation. I don't see how, after this, you can be expected to maintain any kind of congenial relationship, or trust that they won't bad-mouth you to your kids."

"I tried so hard to believe they were good for Desmond and Anna," Rowan said. She was embarrassed of the way her voice shook. "But it's gotten worse since my grandmother died and left me the house. They saw the move as a threat, even though we aren't even a mile from them. It's not like I swept the kids up and left the state."

"I know Detective MacLachlan," the attorney said, in a seeming non sequitur.

Suddenly wary, Rowan tried to keep all expression from her face.

"The fact that he's gotten so involved with your family is…unusual for him."

"So I gather," she said stiffly. "It's probably involuntary. We share a carport and a yard. Desmond especially latched on to him right away. I've been fortunate that he's been kind about it."

"Yes."

Rowan was suddenly paralyzed by the certainty that Ms. Foster was going to say it would be a good idea if he moved out and she found another renter.

I'll refuse.

But the awful truth was, she knew that for her it might be best if he *did* go. This could be an excuse. Niall would understand. He'd already expressed his willingness. The ever-present knot of pain in her chest cramped. Was it possible that he'd be glad of this excuse? Was that what he'd been trying to tell her?

She might be able to start getting over him, if she didn't have to see him almost daily.

"His conduct as an officer of the law is above reproach," the attorney said unexpectedly. "The Staleys won't find a judge in this county who will believe he's an inappropriate person to have a relationship with your children." There was a small but significant pause. "Or with you, if that's the case." She shook her head when Rowan opened her mouth. "You don't need to tell me," she said. "It's entirely irrelevant, unless you've been holding drunken orgies at home when the kids were there." She smiled at Rowan's expression. "No, I didn't think so."

"You don't think it would be safer if Niall—if Detective MacLachlan—moved out?"

"No. Absolutely no. His moving at this point might look like an admission of wrongdoing.

And, frankly, you have no reason to make concessions to your parents-in-law."

Her relief was so huge, Rowan wasn't sure her legs would have held her if she'd had to stand. It made her angry at herself. He didn't love her, didn't want anything long-term with her. She had to figure out how to armor herself.

They agreed that Elizabeth would first respond to Donna and Glenn's legal counsel, then see where it went from there.

Home, Rowan thought wearily. Pay Jenny, the teenage babysitter Zeke's mother had recommended. Make dinner. Pretend she wasn't scared Glenn and Donna would somehow win anyway. That Niall hadn't devastated her.

Her mouth twisted into a small, painful smile. With some planning and luck, maybe she could get as good at dodging him as he'd been at dodging her.

CHAPTER THIRTEEN

ROWAN STOOD UNDER THE SHOWER, letting the hot water beat down on her. This was one morning when she really could have used the chance to sleep in. When she wasn't so tired, she was amused by the unlikelihood of her spawning two early birds. Even with summer and her letting them stay up late, neither kid ever slept past seven.

This morning, she'd talked them into going downstairs and watching cartoons while she showered and got dressed. Thank goodness Desmond was so responsible for his age. If she'd asked, he could have gotten out bowls and poured cereal and milk for himself and Anna, but Rowan had made a habit out of cooking a special breakfast on weekend days, so they were waiting. Probably, she realized, not so patiently.

Once she was out of the shower and dry, the towel wrapped around her head, she opened the bathroom door so she could hear the sound of the TV downstairs. For a moment she frowned. That sounded like a man's voice, but then a blare of silly sounds reassured her and she reached in a drawer for shorts.

She was dressed and starting down the stairs when she definitely heard a voice that didn't sound like either of the kids'. Anger fired in her. Had Niall come over? Running on fumes these days the way she was, Rowan didn't know how she'd keep up the front if he was here.

Then she heard Desmond. "But I want to say goodbye to Mommy!"

What?

Heartbeat accelerating, she bounded the rest of the way down. There were a couple of strange thumps and…was that the sound of her front door opening? She reached the arched entrance to the living room and saw, to her shock, that Donna was already out on the front porch carrying Anna. Glenn held Des and had a hand over his mouth. Her son was struggling. His sneaker-clad foot glanced off the wall.

"You set them down this minute!" Rowan yelled, racing forward.

Glenn's face was mottled with purplish-red. He gave Desmond a hard shake and glared at her. "We're taking our grandchildren for the weekend, as we're entitled to do."

Rowan reached them and grabbed for Des. Glenn swung away, his shoulder slamming into her and sending her falling backward. Her legs collided with an end table and she went down with a crash echoed by the lamp that went down, too. She was screaming something, she didn't know what, and Anna had begun to sob. Desmond fought like a demon.

"Enough!" Glenn roared. He let go of the six year old's mouth to smack a hand down hard on his rear end.

Furious, she scrambled to her feet just as Glenn slammed the front door in her face. She was tearing it open when she heard running footsteps and turned to see Niall.

"What's wrong?"

"Glenn and Donna are taking the kids."

He was through the door on her heels. He leaped down the porch steps and grabbed Glenn's shoulder, swinging him around.

"Release the children. *Now.*"

"This is none of your business!" Glenn snapped.

Niall's face was inches from Glenn's. "If you don't set that boy down in the next thirty seconds, I will place you under arrest," he said in a voice Rowan had never heard before.

Her father-in-law went still. Desmond, sobbing, threw himself toward Niall, who caught him. Rowan hurried past them and snatched Anna back from Donna, who seemed shocked.

"We have the right to see our grandchildren," Glenn snarled.

Niall looked at Rowan. "Did you agree to this visit?"

"No!" She clutched her sobbing daughter. "They didn't even ask. They sneaked into the house while I was upstairs getting dressed and tried to steal them. Both kids were protesting. I heard them."

"You left them alone," Glenn said with contempt. "Were you upstairs with lover boy here?"

Rowan saw the whole, horrific tableau with preternatural sharpness. The hate-filled face of Drew's father. Niall's, hard angles and planes, eyes Arctic cold. Desmond's, white and scared.

Still holding her son, Niall took a step closer to Glenn. "You're on thin ice. I can and will arrest you for trespass and custodial interference." His jaw flexed. "If not kidnapping."

"Kidnapping?" Glenn turned that furious face from Niall to Rowan. "We've done everything we could for this ungrateful—"

"Don't say it." Niall radiated danger.

"And then she tries to cut us out of the lives of our grandchildren. Our only family. Do you think that's what our son would have wanted?" His stare was all for Rowan now. Spittle flew from his mouth. "Drew wanted his children close to us. We knew you tried to get him to move away. He admitted it. And now he's not here to stop you, you think you can do anything you want. You don't deserve fine children like these."

Niall backed a step away. "They're fine children because she's a good mother. You're fools." He looked at her. "Shall I arrest them?"

She was shaking. She had never hated anyone before. But with Anna and Desmond here and terrified... "No. Not if they go and never come back."

"You heard the lady. She owns this property. These are her children. If you make contact with Anna or Desmond again without her explicit permission, I will have not the slightest hesitation at taking you in. Is that clear?"

From the color of his face, Rowan wouldn't have been shocked if Glenn had had a stroke. But he turned without another word and went to the car. He and his wife got in and he drove away.

Rowan let out a breath and sank to the grass. Anna gripped her with wiry arms and legs. Niall joined Rowan on the lawn and let Desmond tumble into his mother's arms, too.

Some neighbors had come out to gape. Rowan couldn't even acknowledge them. She buried her face in children, one on each side, breathing in their scent, holding them so hard it must hurt. Neither protested.

It was a long time before she could pull herself together enough to lift her head and look at

Niall. "Thank you," she whispered. "Thank you again."

He shook his head. "I'm glad I heard."

Desmond wiped his nose and wet cheeks on his mother and looked up, too. "Grandad knocked Mommy down."

Niall tensed. "He assaulted you?"

For her children's benefit, she tried to smile although she felt her lips tremble. "He bumped me. I, um, fell down."

The anger on his face warmed her. "Are you hurt?"

Rowan hadn't been conscious of anything but the fact that Glenn and Donna were trying to take her children. Now the shock and relief were so great, she had to think about his question.

"Um…maybe a bruise or two. I crashed into a table. And broke a lamp."

He bit off some word that was not suitable for the kids' ears.

"Why did they try to make us go with them?" Desmond asked.

Rowan's face contorted and she pressed her cheek against Anna's head again.

It was Niall who spoke. "You know they've been mad that you weren't spending as much time with them."

Desmond nodded. His eyes were huge, his face still tear-streaked.

"Maybe they only wanted to do fun things with you guys, but they thought your mom would say no." Niall paused. "She *is* going to say no now. Until she says so, you shouldn't talk to your grandma or grandad if they phone, you shouldn't answer the door even if you know it's them. You say no if they try to pick you up from school unless your mom has said yes. Unless *she's* the one who told you it was okay."

"Today Grandad told us Mommy knew they were coming and she musta forgot. He lied, didn't he?"

"Yes." Rowan hugged him. "Yes, he did. I would have said no if they'd asked. So they didn't ask."

"We didn't want to go with them," Anna whispered. "Grandad was *mean* when Des said we should wait to say goodbye to you."

Fury to match hers was in Niall's eyes when she met them over the heads of her children.

"Yes, he was," she said. "Grandad didn't want to wait until I came downstairs. Desmond was brave to insist on talking to me."

He straightened. She let her arm fall away. He snuffled, but held his head high. "I kicked and tried to yell."

"I know." She was about to fall apart. But she couldn't. Her children needed *her* to be brave. She had to reassure them, but make them believe she could protect them. "I came running the minute I heard." This smile for Niall was much more successful than her earlier attempt. "Niall came running because he heard us all yelling, too."

Her son looked sturdier by the minute. "Niall rescues us every time he hears us yell, doesn't he?"

"Yes." Damn it, her eyes were burning, but she refused to let tears fall. "So far, he has." She prayed they didn't hear the qualification.

Finally, she had enough of a grip on herself. "Are you two ready for breakfast?"

Anna nodded vigorously but didn't let go of her mom. Desmond said, "I want waffles. Can we have waffles?"

"You bet. Pumpkin," she said to Anna, "I'm going to have to set you down so I can stand up."

Niall stood in an easy movement. "I'll take her," he said.

Rowan didn't want to relinquish her daughter to him. She was angry at him, she realized; grateful and resenting the fact that she had to be. He had Desmond convinced he'd always be there for them, but she knew better. Why did he have to be so...so *noble?* It wasn't fair.

But after a hesitation she hoped he didn't notice, she let him take Anna, and even accepted his extended hand and allowed him to hoist her to her feet, too. Of course she had to invite him to breakfast, and the anger churned in her stomach.

"That sounds good. Although maybe I should get dressed first." He rasped a hand over his jaw. "And shave."

As they crossed the front porch, she noticed for the first time that he wore sacky sweatpants and a faded T-shirt. He was barefoot and unshaven.

"I used to watch Dad shave," Desmond piped up. "He said *I'd* have to someday, too."

"Yep. You will. Happens to all boys." He smiled down at Des. "The upside is, boys don't have to shave their underarms and legs like girls do."

"I don't hafta," Anna told him earnestly. "And I'm a girl."

"Most girls start shaving about the same age boys do," Rowan said. "When they're teenagers."

She wrinkled her nose. Obviously, that was unimaginably far away.

But Des still had his eye on Niall. "Can I watch you shave?"

"No!" They all looked startled at Rowan's vehemence. She made herself take a slow breath. "Sorry, sweetie. You can help me mix the waffle batter instead."

His agreement was reluctant, she could tell. Something had changed on Niall's face, too.

She'd begun to recognize his subtle withdrawal. This time, it was her fault, but she didn't care. He'd pull away no matter what, so it might as well be sooner rather than later.

The kids scrambled onto chairs in the kitchen. Niall lowered his voice enough they couldn't hear. "Would you rather I didn't come back for breakfast?"

"No, of course not," she managed to say, completely polite. "You know we like having you here."

A nerve jumped beneath his eye. After a moment, he nodded. "All right. See you in a few minutes."

But they wouldn't have, she knew, if he hadn't once again felt compelled to come to their aid. He was a cop; he'd never fail to do his job. Rowan felt quite sure, however, that Niall would have managed to be busy all weekend if he hadn't heard the screaming and yelling.

I'm done, she thought, watching him go out the back door. Why this awful scene would have made her feel strong enough to make that decision, Rowan had no idea, but in a weird way she was grateful. She wasn't going to wait anymore for the yo-yo of his attention to swing her way again.

She'd keep being polite. He *had* been a good

tenant. Nice to the kids, since the one wretched week when he'd hurt Des's feelings so much. Their hero when they needed him. She would even allow herself to feel grateful that he'd showed her she didn't have to be afraid of a relationship with a man.

But it wouldn't be with him, however much she wished it. And she was strong enough to survive.

Rowan plugged in the waffle maker and got down a big mixing bowl from the cupboard. Smiling at her children, she asked, "Who wants to help stir?"

NIALL WATCHED ROWAN over breakfast, admiring the way she juggled conversation, cutting up Anna's waffle, gentle reminders to use good table manners, and an occasional bite herself. She must be feeling some major turmoil, but kept it from showing for the kids' sake. He compared her to his mother, most often angry and distracted.

Why had she stayed so long? Why hadn't she left Dad years before she did? He'd been too young then to speculate, too closed since to analyze. Now he did.

She hadn't stayed for her boys, he knew that instinctively. She might have told herself that she was doing the best thing for them, but it wasn't her main motivation, nor was it true. They'd have been better off if she'd taken them and left. Made a home, however poor, that wasn't imbued with unhappiness.

Maybe she'd liked the money Dad brought home when he'd slid off the straight and narrow and was dealing drugs. Yes, thought Niall, probably. But Dad hadn't made them rich.

Hell, she could have truly loved Rory Mac-Lachlan.

Niall knew Duncan had family pictures stashed somewhere. Would he get them out to show Jane now that they were expecting a baby? So they could both say, oh, he has your father's eyes or your great-aunt's chin?

Niall had only the vaguest memory of his grandparents, the ones on his mother's side. His grandfather had died of a heart attack, his grandmother of some kind of cancer, he thought. Mom had disappeared for three or four months to nurse her mother. Niall had been…maybe eleven, which would have made Conall eight. Dad wasn't much use. They'd all run wild.

He didn't remember his mom's sister very well, either. She hadn't liked Rory, Niall knew that, and she had refused to visit. Mom went to see her now and again. That's where she'd gone when she upped and left for good, Duncan said.

Rory's charm and lightness of spirit had passed

his two older sons by entirely. Only Conall had caught hold of it, probably useful in undercover work.

Rory had been changed by his first lengthy stint in prison. Niall remember his shock when Dad came home, thinner, his hair graying. He'd seemed smaller, maybe only because Niall had grown in his father's three-year absence. He'd shied at shadows, and yet been ebullient with relief at having his freedom and his family. Full of promises, too, ones Mom listened to at first with caution but must have let herself come to believe in.

Promises as shallow as Dad's character.

I don't want to be like him. Not in any way.

Desmond asked him a question and Niall snapped his attention back to the breakfast table and a family so different from his own he sometimes felt as if he'd teleported into another dimension. Anna and Desmond were so damn *trusting* it hurt to see. And now not only the Peeping Tom but their own grandparents were doing their damnedest to erode that trust.

Over my dead body. The vow came easily.

Des wanted to talk about shaving again. His daddy made himself bleed sometimes. And then he'd stick these little bits of toilet paper to his face, and sometimes he left for work and he'd forget to take them off.

"Do you ever cut yourself?" the bloodthirsty kid asked avidly.

Niall smiled. "Yeah, I do when I'm not paying enough attention. I use an electric shaver, though, and they're designed to keep from cutting skin. I have to be careful around this..." He fingered the mole on one side of his jaw. "Upper lips are tricky, too."

Desmond stretched his mouth so that he looked like a chimpanzee. "Daddy used to do this."

Niall laughed. "We all do."

Rowan was smiling, but her gaze was cool when it glanced off his. He sensed she would once again cut off any attempt on Des's part to coax Niall into letting him watch. Why? She let Niall take the kid to the school or the swimming pool.

Jarred, he wondered if she still would. Even running scared, he'd tried not to behave badly this past week, but knew he hadn't entirely succeeded. Was she reacting to that? Or only to this morning's turmoil?

When the kids got restless, she informed them that she'd take them swimming at the community pool later, but right now they could play outside as long as they promised not to leave the backyard.

"Mo-om." Desmond looked at her in astonishment. "We know that."

"I'm too short to open the gate," Anna informed them.

Rowan laughed. "So you are." She wiped sticky fingers.

Niall got up and poured himself a second cup of coffee to give himself an excuse to linger. He could feel her gaze on him as he demonstrated how at home here he felt by opening the refrigerator, adding a splash of milk to his coffee, then sitting back down.

The door banged as the kids rushed out.

"Have another cup of coffee," he suggested. "I'll help you clean up afterward."

Rowan hesitated, then did refill her mug and sit down, as well. There was an uncomfortable silence.

"I do appreciate…" she began.

At the same instant he said, "Rowan."

"I can't believe they did that," she said then. "It's even stranger than the threat to file for custody."

"Yes, it is. I really could have arrested them for kidnapping. It was an unbelievably stupid thing to do."

"Should I have let you?" Her eyes met his, her expression troubled.

"I don't know. It depends on whether they really did intend only to take the kids for the weekend."

She shivered. "They wouldn't have gotten away with keeping them. Not unless they planned to go on the run, and I can't imagine."

Niall grunted agreement. "Did you get the feeling Glenn was the driving force?"

"I think he's *always* the driving force. Donna is... I don't know. I think she means well. She loves to cook, and mostly she was really nice to the kids. She's hard to like, but I trusted her." She cradled the mug in her hands as if they were chilled despite the fact that the day was already promising heat. "You know, it didn't occur to me earlier, but they couldn't possibly have come over this morning planning to grab the kids the way they did. I mean, what were the odds they'd have the chance?"

Niall nodded. "I thought about that, too. They probably intended to bully you, make it so awkward in front of Anna and Desmond that you'd agree to let them go for the weekend."

"After that awful letter?" She took a gulp of coffee. "I don't think so."

"It was supposed to intimidate you," he said gently. "Bring you back in line. 'Give us what we want or else.'"

"You're right," she realized. "I'll bet that's exactly what they had in mind. Only it misfired, big-time."

"They misfired this morning, too."

"Boy, did they." A good case of anger sparked on her face. "I saw Elizabeth Foster this week. She's going to do a lot more than scare them. I'm going to cut off all visitation."

"You'll want to call her and tell her about the tussle this morning."

"Tussle." Rowan gave a broken laugh. "Thank goodness you were here."

This morning, Niall had discovered something. He hated the idea of Rowan Staley or her children ever facing any kind of crisis without him there to provide backup.

Ever was a word that edged right into *forever.*

Forever wasn't in his vocabulary.

I'm a man who won't buy a house. Who is staggered by the idea of being an uncle. What if something happens to Duncan? God help us both, what if the kid ever really needs *me?*

So what the hell was he thinking here? Was he deluding himself to think he was capable of a real commitment to Rowan?

If he was…did he want to make it?

Familiar panic swirled with a far less familiar ache of need and something else. It felt somewhat like the protectiveness that was an intrinsic part of him, one of the qualities that made him a good cop. But this was different, too, because it was so intensely focused on this woman. Her kids, too, sure, but mostly her.

Man, he was in over his head.

"Quit thanking me," he said gruffly.

"When you quit doing things that deserve thanks."

"You'd have coped this morning. Worse come to worst, you could have called 9-1-1 and reported an abduction before they'd gotten a block away."

She shuddered. "Do you have any idea how petrified I would've been if they'd actually taken the kids? I'd have been tearing down the middle of the street chasing them and screaming."

"Did that bastard knock you down on purpose?"

Rowan looked wary, and he guessed his eyes had chilled. He couldn't help it, not when he thought about anyone hurting her.

Like you've been doing?

"I don't know. He hit me with his shoulder. Des was struggling, and Glenn was trying to keep me from being able to grab him. All he meant was to knock me aside, but he was so enraged I don't think he cared whether I got injured."

"I should have arrested him."

"No." She reached out and laid a hand over his. "You gave me the choice. I appreciate that. And maybe I was wrong to say no, but…they were good to me and the kids, in their own way. Maybe I *am* ungrateful…."

"No."

"Yes." She looked down and seemed to notice that she was touching him. She snatched her hand back, curling it out of sight under the table. "The thing is, I hated having to feel grateful all the time. Even the kids never felt at home with them. We were guests for a year. I'd ask if I could help with dinner and be assigned a small chore. Clean the bathroom only to be chided because I hadn't put the toilet paper on the roll properly, or informed that, in the better households, dear, towels aren't just *slung* over the racks, this is how they're folded, and really shouldn't Anna change clothes before we went out? People would wonder what kind of mother I was if they saw her wearing an outfit like that." She took a breath. "It seemed like an eternity."

He nodded, imagining it. Yeah, it would be hell, in its own way. *Enid,* he thought, *you did a good thing. I wonder if you saw how desperate your granddaughter was.*

Probably she had.

He braced himself. "I've been wanting to talk to you."

Her eyes flashed to his. "Have you," she said flatly.

The anger he'd seen her struggling with wasn't all aimed at her in-laws. He couldn't blame her.

"The night with you was—" *the best of my life* "—amazing."

She laughed, and it wasn't a real warm sound. "I'll bet. A woman scared to death of having sex, who then proceeds to tell you all about why she feels that way. I'll bet that was your dream date."

He was hammered by the realization that's exactly what it had been. She'd given him everything, including her trust. He was drawn to her for countless reasons, starting with her air of innocence, the generous passion she offered him and only him, her sweetness and gritty determination, the way she was with her kids.... In that one night, he'd gone down for the count, if he hadn't already long before that.

He discovered that he was sweating. His relaxed posture was a pose for her benefit. A fight or flight reflex had kicked in. *I love her,* he thought with incredulity.

How could that be?

Don't do anything stupid. Be sure.

That was good advice. He set down his coffee cup and surreptitiously wiped his hand on his denim-clad thigh.

He'd made a few vows in his life, a couple of which were in danger right this minute of being broken. But the most serious was that he'd keep what promises he made. Which meant he rarely made them.

He realized he'd let the silence go on too long. She'd withdrawn, her expression closing and even her body retreating so that her back must be pressed hard to the chair.

"You underestimate yourself," he said, voice hoarse. "You make me feel things I never have before."

She scrutinized him from that still, quiet face. He felt as if he'd just crawled out from under a rock.

"And it's taken you a week to tell me that? Niall, you've made it plain that you're not interested in any kind of committed relationship. That's okay. But the truth is, I'm not interested in any other kind. I let myself be tempted, and I'm not sorry. You...opened me to possibilities. I already said that. I didn't think I could ever let anything start with a man, but now I know I can."

He unclenched his teeth. "The hell you can."

"Yes." He heard pure steel. "I can. I'm telling you that I'm through with whatever it was we were playing at. I hope for the kids' sake we can keep being friendly. That's all it's going to be."

"I've been trying to say that I'm sorry. That... that I want to try." *Oh, yeah. That was guaranteed to sweep a woman away.* He winced.

Pain flashed on her face, and she pushed back her chair and stood up. "Your apology is accepted. But no. Please keep your distance, Niall."

He sat there stunned despite his guilt over how little he'd offered her. She'd said no. He had finally realized what he felt for her, and she told him to get lost.

He blundered to his feet. "Give me another chance."

Her knuckles were white on the top rung of the chair. "I can't. I can't keep doing this. Don't ask me to." She swallowed. "Please go, Niall."

He couldn't remember hurting like this since… No. He didn't want to think about that.

After a moment he dipped his head and went.

He wanted to crawl back into the hole that was his life. But he couldn't yet, because the kids were waiting outside to pounce on him, and they deserved better of him.

He was careful not to let the screen door slam.

CHAPTER FOURTEEN

THAT NIGHT, NIALL CAME ABOUT as close as he ever did to getting drunk, then felt like crap Sunday. Hoping his churning belly would allow him to keep down the painkillers for his headache, he thought about what would have happened if Desmond had screamed last night.

I'd have slept through it.

All week he was irritable at work. Tuesday he nearly lost it when a guy he was arresting for beating the shit out of his wife slammed an elbow into his gut and made a run for it. For everyone's sake, he had to let a fellow detective cuff the bastard and wrestle him into the back of the car.

He called Conall, something he rarely did, but his brother's cell phone was turned off.

"It's Niall," he said to voice mail. "Nothing important. I was, uh, thinking about some things. That's all." He hung up feeling like an idiot. Great message.

Some of the worst times were when he was with Rowan and the kids. They'd be going back to school next week, after Labor Day. He suspected he'd see less of them then. Des would have homework, soccer practices. Rowan would be tired. As it was she never came out on the porch at night anymore. He looked, hoping. When he joined her, Des and Anna in the yard in the still-hot early evenings, she was friendly but distant. She did let him take Desmond to the school to practice soccer, which was something.

But not enough.

The Peeping Tom made no reported appearances that week, increasing Niall's frustration.

As his mood got darker, he thought about talking to Duncan. Once upon a time, he would have dropped in on his big brother. They'd have had a beer together, and when he had to he could have left. But things were different now. Jane would be there. Even when he was invited, she'd be there, and he didn't want to talk to her.

Duncan did still drop in on him sometimes. He'd wait.

Friday evening of Labor Day weekend, Niall and Desmond had the entire soccer field at the school to themselves. Plenty of families went away for Labor Day. Camping was popular. Niall wondered where Rowan's family was. Had she called her parents? Didn't they know she needed them?

Des was starting to move the ball down the field pretty well, and Niall could see him becoming a goalie. He threw himself on the ball with real enthusiasm.

As they walked home, dusk catching up with them, Niall asked if he'd ever watched the bigger kids play soccer.

"Nuh-uh. I coulda played last year, but Grandma Staley thought five was too little."

Niall looked down at him. "Do you mind not seeing your grandparents?"

Des stared down at his feet, scuffing the first leaves that had fallen from an old maple tree. "Not really," he mumbled.

"It's okay if you do. Even when we're mad at someone, we can love that person, too."

The boy lifted his head, his eyes like his mom's trained on Niall's face. "Did you ever feel that way?"

Niall's fingers twitched. He'd have been drumming a table or the arm of a chair if he'd had the chance. "Yeah," he said. "I told you about my mom leaving us kids."

Desmond nodded.

"I was mad and hurt, but I guess I kept loving her anyway."

"Do you still?"

He had to think about that one for a minute. "No. She never came back. It was like she wiped us out of her life," he said finally.

He could see on the kid's face how unimaginable that was. Even now, Niall found it stunning that his mother could do that.

He didn't say, *I've been thinking about her more lately,* because he wouldn't have wanted to explain why. He didn't miss her anymore; he didn't love her. But he did wonder.

Desmond hopped over a few cracks in the sidewalk. "Sometimes Grandma was real nice," he offered.

"Not Grandad?"

Des's steps dragged. He grabbed Niall's hand when they reached a corner, which he always did. Mom said he had to, he'd explained.

"He said I'm like Dad." The kid sounded worried, lacking his usual animation. "Real special. He liked to hug me and stuff."

Niall felt like a cartoon character with a lightbulb blinking on over his head. Dark corners were suddenly, hideously illuminated.

He kept his voice casual. "You don't like it when he hugs you?"

Desmond cast an anxious glance at Niall. "He likes me to sit on his lap and he doesn't let go when I want him to. Grandma just says, 'What are you fussing about?' But... I don't know." He was quiet for half a block. "He said he liked to cuddle Daddy, too, when he was a little boy."

I bet he did. Grimly lining all the ducks up in a row, Niall felt dense for not suspecting sooner.

Andrew Staley had been sexually molested as a boy. As an adult, he had a clearly dysfunctional relationship with his parents. A push-pull, Rowan said. Resenting them, and needing them. He was incapable of a normal, healthy sexual relationship with a woman, even the one he loved and had married.

Desmond's grandfather liked to hold the boy on his lap. His "hugging" made the six-year-old uneasy, although he clearly didn't understand why.

A man had been peeking in the bedroom windows hoping to see naked boys all about Desmond's age.

He'd taken the greater risk of climbing onto the carport roof to look into Desmond's window. Desmond was his one target that was a little bit outside his usual geographic range.

He had been desperate enough to try to abduct his grandson and granddaughter.

It fit. It all fit so well, Niall thought he'd have seen it sooner if his thinking hadn't been muddled by all this unfamiliar emotional crap.

When they reached home, they found the backyard empty. Rowan and Anna had already gone in. The back door stood open, the screen door keeping out bugs. Niall followed Des inside.

"Mom, where are you?"

Niall cringed. The kid really knew how to bellow.

"I'm upstairs," Rowan called. "Giving Anna a bath. She's almost done and it'll be your turn."

Des gave an exaggerated groan. "Do I hafta?"

"Yes, you 'hafta,'" his mother said firmly.

"Niall's here."

Silence.

Niall raised his voice. "Rowan, can you come down when you get a minute? I want to ask you something."

Another silence.

"Give me a minute."

Niall handed over the soccer ball he'd been carrying under one arm. "You'd better get going, buddy. She sounds like she means it."

Des groaned. "I'll get dirty tomorrow. Why do I have to take a bath?"

Niall grinned. "I have no idea."

The boy sighed and started trudging up the stairs. Halfway he stopped. "It was fun playing soccer."

"Yeah, it was." Niall smiled at him. "I'll probably see you tomorrow."

He waited in the kitchen, too restless to sit. He might as well have had a shot of adrenaline. He liked this feeling, the knowing he was closing in on some scumbag. Some cops got their highs kicking in doors; he liked solving mysteries. His mind raced, his skin tingled and he paced her kitchen, a lot roomier than his own.

"What is it you wanted?" she said behind him.

He swung around, startled. How had she gotten down the stairs without him hearing?

She was barefoot, that was how, her long legs exposed by denim cut-offs. Bath water had splashed onto her thin cotton shirt, the wet patches clinging to her stomach and breasts. Niall's body reacted predictably, but he tried to keep his gaze on her face.

"Where do your in-laws live?"

Her astonishment showing, she pushed a damp tendril of hair off her forehead. Her ponytail was giving up the battle, as it often did. "I told you they're not that far from here. Why do you want to know?"

"Rowan, tell me."

"You could have looked them up in the phone book."

"You lived with them for a year. Did Glenn make a habit of taking evening walks?"

"What?" She stared at him.

Niall waited, and saw slow, horrified comprehension awaken in her eyes. Her mouth opened, closed, opened again. She gave a small, anguished cry. "You're saying... Oh, God! Desmond."

Niall stepped forward and gripped her upper

arms. "No. I'm pretty sure nothing has happened, Rowan. I talked to him tonight. That's what got me thinking. He doesn't like the way his grandfather hugged him and insisted he sit on his lap, but I think mostly he was confused and uneasy. He wasn't afraid or holding back."

"Dear God." Her teeth chattered, and she whirled and hurried to the foot of the stairs. "Des?"

His voice floated down. "I'm washing my hair, Mom."

"Okay," Rowan called, then turned back to Niall. "It doesn't make sense. Why would Drew have stayed in contact with his parents if…" She couldn't even say it.

"Because kids who are abused or molested get really messed up about their parents. You said yourself his relationship with them was strange."

"Yes, but…" She had a death grip on the bannister. "He loved Desmond. How could he put him at risk?"

"Did he ever let you leave him alone with his father?"

She was dazed, so scared and shocked she didn't protest when Niall led her a few feet into the living room and seated her on the couch.

He sat on the coffee table close enough to touch her.

"I never thought about it." She was thinking now, though, and her eyes widened. "No." It came out as barely a puff of sound. "No. It never occurred to me, but there were times…"

Niall nodded.

"Why didn't he *tell* me?"

"Maybe because he'd have had to admit what happened to him. You'd have asked him the same questions you're asking me, and he didn't understand himself why he still wanted his father to love him." Niall spoke harsher than he should have. "And, Rowan, it could be I'm barking up the wrong tree entirely and getting you upset for nothing."

Her eyes, unguarded and distressed, met his. "But it makes sense, doesn't it?"

"I'm afraid so."

"What can we do?"

He warmed to the sound of that *we*. "Tell me where they live."

"1390 Cedar Street."

He visualized the town grid, and felt the tingle of certainty again. That placed Glenn Staley within the handful of blocks where Niall had guessed the Peeping Tom lived.

"You think it was *him* looking in Des's window." Rowan bent forward, her hand pressed to her mouth. "His own grandfather."

From upstairs, Des called, "Mom, I got out."

Somehow, she pulled herself together enough

to tell him to get ready for bed. Then she looked at Niall. "What will you do?"

At least she had enough faith in him to be leaving it in his hands.

"An old-fashioned stakeout," he said. "*Does* he take evening walks?"

"Yes." She bent forward again as if she was nauseated or her stomach hurt. "This is unbelievable. Yes. Yes, he does."

"Then he's going to have company the next time he goes for one." He hesitated. "Unless he admits it, we won't be able to prove he molested your husband…."

"I don't want that." She shook her head. "Drew didn't want anyone to know. This will be horrible enough."

Des yelled again from upstairs.

"You need to go tuck him in," Niall said. "Are you all right, Rowan? Do you want me to stay?"

She straightened, pulling her dignity around herself as if it were a warm afghan she used to ward off a chill. "Of course I'm all right. I'm shocked, that's all. And so grateful I moved out of their house. I would never have forgiven myself…"

He couldn't help himself. He had to touch her, whether she welcomed it or not. Niall took her hands in his. "If his grandfather had tried anything, it wouldn't have gone very far. Des would have talked to you, Rowan. And you'd have listened. It wouldn't have been the same as it was for your husband when he was a little boy."

"You're saying he tried to tell his mother." She shivered. "Of course he would have. But Donna wouldn't have believed him, would she? No, I can imagine it. She supports Glenn, no matter what."

"If a woman let herself believe such a thing," he said quietly, "it would devastate her, undermine everything she thinks she knows about her husband and how he feels about her. I'm not defending her, but I can see how she might convince herself it can't possibly be true."

Rowan shook her head and kept shaking it as if she didn't know how to stop. "But her own son."

"It might not turn out to be true," Niall reminded her. "I shouldn't have said as much as I did."

Her eyes pinned his. They were as dark as he'd ever seen them. "You'll tell me as soon as…as…"

"You know I will." He stood and drew her to her feet, cocking his head at the sound of Des calling.

She raised her voice. "I'll be there in a minute."

"You said that last time," he complained.

Niall chuckled. "Not so patient, is he?"

"Were you, when you were six?"

"Probably not."

Somehow she'd come to be standing several

feet away, holding herself stiffly. She wanted him to go away. There wasn't any softening, any suggestion she would let him hold her or, God forbid, kiss her good night.

He heard her saying, *I'm through,* and saw again that she meant it. His heart clenched.

Niall inclined his head. "Good night, Rowan."

She followed him to the kitchen and said goodnight. The minute he was out the door, he heard her locking it behind him.

THE NEXT NIGHT WAS a bust. Donna had decided to accompany her husband on his evening walk.

An unhappy hunter deprived of his prey, Niall followed them for a few blocks. He caught enough snatches of conversation to know that Glenn hadn't welcomed the company.

"Why did you insist on coming if all you wanted to do was dawdle along like this?" he grumbled. "You know this is how I get my exercise."

She complained in turn about how there was nothing on TV but reruns, and she thought it would be nice to look at the neighbors' yards. Why couldn't they walk earlier while it was still light?

"It *is* still light," he snapped, but she was closer to right than he was. It was dusk, time for predators to come out.

Irritable, Niall went home.

The following night, Glenn didn't go out at all. Niall heard some crying and then some shouting from the house. He imagined they'd heard from Rowan's attorney via their attorney.

Each day when Rowan looked at him, Niall shook his head. *Not yet.* The strain showed on her face.

On night number three, Glenn went out by himself, Niall a ghost behind him. Sure enough, not two blocks from home the creep melted into the darkness and made his way along the side of a house. Niall couldn't see even a shred of light around tightly pulled blinds, and Glenn didn't linger. He tried several other houses with no more results. Niall would have been justified in arresting him for trying to peek in windows, but Glenn might have come up with a believable excuse. No, better to wait. Eventually Glenn gave up for the night.

His tension must be ratcheting up, Niall thought with satisfaction.

Half a block from home, he saw a big, dark SUV sitting in front of Rowan's house and tensed himself before he recognized it and the man who sat on the bumper.

"You could have been more comfortable on my porch," Niall pointed out when he was close enough.

His brother straightened. "I didn't want to alarm Rowan if she spotted me."

Niall nodded. "Still have time for a beer?"

"Coffee, maybe."

Sam met them joyously inside the gate and accompanied them to Niall's door. He let the dog in, as he'd taken sometimes to doing. Duncan raised his eyebrows at that, but didn't comment.

"You abandoned Jane," Niall observed.

"She conked out at least an hour ago. She's tired all the time."

He sounded worried rather than disgruntled, but still Niall grinned. Jane had barely gotten over being sick all the time, and now this. "You're going to forget you ever had a sex life."

A smile that was both lighthearted and smug changed Duncan into another man. "Now, I wouldn't say that."

Well, damn. Duncan had gotten some *before* his wife conked out. Niall was painfully jealous.

"Is there a reason for this visit?" he asked.

His brother shrugged. "Haven't talked to you in a while. I almost left, thinking you were at Rowan's, but I could hear her and the kids and not you."

"I'm conducting a stakeout." Niall hesitated, but finally chose to explain.

"Son of a bitch," Duncan muttered.

"Brace yourself. The shit is going to hit the

fan. He's a banker with Northwest Federal. I don't intend to let him go quietly."

"He targeted the wrong kid."

"Yes, he did."

His brother's gaze on him was thoughtful, but he only nodded. "Consider me braced."

Niall poured coffee for both of them and pulled out a chair.

"Things okay with you?" The question was casual, the sharp look not. Duncan must have heard something.

Even though a part of him had wanted to have this talk, Niall's reflex was to say, *Sure, why wouldn't it be?*

A soft grunt escaped him. "No."

The furrows on his brother's forehead deepened, but he only waited.

"It's… Oh, hell." His fingers bit into his thighs. "I'm, uh…" Why couldn't he say it? He looked helplessly at Duncan, pissed to see a trace of amusement in his eyes. "You think this is funny?" he bit off.

"Honestly? Yeah. Assuming you're beating your way around to saying what I think you are."

His sigh was closer to a groan. "I'm in love with her."

"And that's bad why?"

"You have to ask me that? God. I never intended to do this. I couldn't *imagine* doing this."

"Plenty of people who have worthless parents fall in love and get married," Duncan observed.

"I don't…connect with people."

"You're my best friend," was the quiet response.

Niall had to laugh at that. "Sad to say, you're my best friend, too. Do you know how little actual time we spend together?"

"More than we used to. We're…learning how to be family." Duncan frowned. "I never knew if you'd forgive me."

"What for?" Niall asked, astounded.

Now his big brother's face went slack with surprise. "The car. For being such a hard-ass."

"I could think of some more explicit ways to put it."

They shared a grin.

Niall shook his head. "There wasn't anything to forgive. It didn't take me long to realize you didn't have any choice. The car thing hit Conall harder than it did me even though it wasn't his."

"It wasn't only the car."

Niall reflected on that. "No." He never had totally figured out Con's problems, but knew they went deep.

"I love you."

Niall was embarrassingly aware that his mouth had dropped open. Duncan was moving his shoulders a little uneasily, but he let the bald words lie right where they were.

There was only one answer. Niall cleared his throat. "I've always loved you, too. You know that, right?"

"Maybe not always, but…for a long time." Was that satisfaction on his brother's face? "So you admit you know how to love someone. Why the heartburn over Rowan?"

He blew out air like a winded horse. "She's got a house. Kids."

"I've had the impression you love those kids, too."

That almost made it worse. He bowed forward and bumped his forehead on the table.

Duncan whacked him affectionately between the shoulder blades. "Yeah, I thought so."

He made himself straighten and look his brother in the eye. "Every time I get close to her, I freak."

"She know that?"

"Yeah. This last time, she pretty much told me to get lost." Honesty had him adding, "Not pretty much. She said she was done."

"You're accepting that?"

"No, but…" This was what it really came down to, wasn't it? "She's been hurt once. What if I make a commitment to her and can't keep it?"

"Can't?" Duncan repeated the word as if it were in a language he didn't understand.

"What if I'm like Mom or Dad?"

His brother looked gravely back at him. "Are you?"

He was closer to squirming than he'd been since he was about twelve years old and in trouble. "No," he said finally, huskily. "I don't think so."

"I don't think you are, either."

Something settled in Niall. Gave a soft sigh, circled around and found a comfy spot to stay. It was a weird and unsettling sensation. In some astonishment he thought, *I am not like either of my parents.* It wasn't a surprise. Maybe he'd never bought a house or had a long-term girlfriend, but he'd gone to college, worked damned hard and graduated with excellent grades. He was dogged on the job. He considered his integrity rock solid. He would have done anything in the world for either of his brothers.

"I don't know if she'll ever trust me," he heard himself say.

"You've given her plenty of reasons to trust you," Duncan pointed out, his tone gentle. "With herself… That's always harder."

She hadn't evicted him, or even suggested he think about moving. She wasn't trying to edge him out of the kids' lives. Which meant, unless things changed, he had time to prove himself capable of constancy.

He could do that, Niall decided on a swell of what felt like optimism. Another new emotion to pin up on the bulletin board of his life.

"You're really happy?" he asked, as if he hadn't before. "I mean, with Jane?"

"Yeah." Duncan's hard face softened. "She's got a built-in panic button I have a way of pushing, but we're getting better at compromise." His grin flashed. "I'll bet you didn't know I could."

Niall laughed.

"She has bruises inside. I think they're healing, though. I've said this before, but it's true. We make each other happy." His laugh held more embarrassment than amusement. "Listen to me. Captain MacLachlan, writing greeting cards." He pushed himself to his feet.

Niall did the same. "You have changed."

"So have you." Duncan reached out and gave Niall's upper arm one quick squeeze. "Good night."

After a glance at Rowan's dark house, Niall stood on his small porch, watching his brother make his way to the gate. Sam was happy to accompany him out of the reach of the porchlight. Niall heard one muffled curse; the dog did like to get underfoot.

He was still smiling when he went back inside,

trying to remember the last time anyone had said those words to him.

I love you.

Or when he'd said them himself.

Maybe when he was a little boy. There must have been a time, but it was lost in the confusion of his childhood. A few times, Duncan had said, "I'm proud of you," which was almost as good. Maybe it was even code for "I love you," which wasn't something men said to each other. But hearing it, admitting it, that was important.

If he ever had kids of his own—and Niall was including Des and Anna—they would never doubt that he loved them. His *wife* would never doubt he loved her.

He thought the words might get easier to say with practice.

CHAPTER FIFTEEN

DES BURST INTO THE KITCHEN. "Can Niall and me go play soccer?" He hopped from foot to foot with eagerness.

"Can Niall and *I* go play soccer," Rowan corrected automatically.

"That's what I said!"

She felt Niall's presence before she saw him, standing on the other side of the screen door, his gaze on her. He'd already changed after work, from rumpled dress shirt and slacks to faded jeans, T-shirt and athletic shoes. The wariness on his face made her ache.

She'd put that expression there.

"Sure," she said cheerfully. "I was going to put dinner on in a few minutes, though. Can you be back in an hour?"

"Yeah! I gotta get my soccer ball," her son told Niall, and bolted for the stairs.

"Use the bathroom," Rowan called after him, then said to Niall, "You're welcome to come in, you know."

After a momentary hesitation, he opened the

screen door and stepped into the kitchen. His gaze went to Anna, sitting at the kitchen table drumming her heels on the chair legs and coloring.

"Hey, Anna Banana."

"Can I come?" she asked. "I want to play soccer, too."

Smiling, he shook his head. "Next year is soon enough for you, kiddo." He looked over her shoulder. "Nice job there."

How was it he always knew the right thing to say to both the kids? And what did he mean, next year? Was he implying that he'd still be around?

Dear heavens, Rowan thought, *I won't survive a year of him being around all the time but not really here.*

His gaze going to her, he leaned a shoulder against the refrigerator and crossed his arms. "You talked to your parents?"

She nodded. "Mom is mad I didn't tell her what was going on earlier. She wanted to come roaring up here, but I put her off. With school starting, the last thing I need is a house guest."

"Tomorrow, isn't it?"

"Yes, thank goodness. They're both hyper."

His smile was quick and amused. "I noticed."

"Thank you for distracting Des tonight."

"He can hardly wait for soccer practice to start. He's worried because he's sure all the other boys played last year and will be way better than he is."

Rowan rolled her eyes. "I seriously doubt that."

"You'll let me know if you need help getting him to practice or picking him up."

This was killing her. Why was he doing this?

"Niall, you can't possibly want to get sucked into chauffeuring duties," she said.

"You're wrong." Voice and eyes were both quiet but steady. "I do."

Rowan didn't see anything but him. Leaning there, so casual, so big and male and determined. Her ribcage felt as if it had shrunk a size or two à la Dr. Seuss.

The thunder of feet on the stairs brought her head around. "Be careful..."

Grin wide, Des raced into the kitchen. He threw the ball at Niall, who snagged it one-handed out of the air.

"Desmond Staley, we don't throw balls in the house."

"Oh, yeah." His chagrin didn't last long. "I knew Niall would catch it."

"We're supposed to be kicking it and heading it anyway, not throwing it." Niall ruffled Des's hair. "Let's get moving, buddy."

The screen door slammed and they were gone. Rowan moved to the kitchen window where she could see them briefly before they disappeared toward the gate. The sight gave her heart another wrench. Des's face was tilted up and he was obviously chattering a mile a minute. Niall was listening with a lopsided smile, his hand resting on her son's shoulder as if it belonged there.

She wanted so much for it to belong there. To know that Niall wasn't going anywhere.

She heard him say, *I want to try.* His voice halting, imbued with emotion she hadn't let herself hear. Regret and hope.

How could she trust him not to run away again and hurt not only her feelings, but the kids'? She couldn't risk them. She couldn't.

A small voice whispered, *Is it really them you're afraid for?* Rowan couldn't answer.

She summoned indignation. What was it he wanted to "try" anyway? He'd never even invited her out, not her alone. He'd insinuated himself into her family, he'd talked to her, he'd kissed her. He'd made love to her.

After which she'd become a distant acquaintance, if she was lucky enough for his gaze to glance off her at all.

Yes, but she'd known that was an act. She knew fear when she saw it; she'd felt it often enough. He'd given them all so much. A young, single guy, a police detective, he was finding time almost every day to spend with Des, who was blossoming under the male attention.

"Look, Mommy," Anna said. "I colored the horse blue."

Rowan pulled her attention back to the here and now. "It's beautiful." She kissed her daughter's head.

He could decide any day to move out. Maybe she was more of a coward than Niall was, but *I want to try* wasn't enough of a declaration to justify the risk she would be taking. With her own heart, *and* Desmond's and Anna's.

HE'D SECRETLY HOPED for a dinner invitation. But Rowan barely glanced at Niall when he brought Desmond back.

"Go wash your hands," she ordered him.

"I get to start school tomorrow," Anna told Niall.

He smiled. "I know. I'll look forward to hearing about it." Then he offered a general "Good night" and went home to his cottage, where he nuked a frozen burrito that didn't smell half as good as the casserole Rowan had been setting on a trivet on the table.

He wouldn't have had time to linger anyway, he reminded himself. Thin clouds hazed the sky. There might be rain tomorrow. Glenn would go out tonight, and Niall intended to be right behind him.

My quest. He had a moment of rueful amusement. He wasn't so sure bringing her a trophy on his bloody lance would get him what he wanted, but he intended to do it anyway. For Des, if not for her.

He drove to within a couple of blocks of the Staleys' and walked the rest of the way. After a two-minute wait behind a large rhododendron in the next-door neighbor's yard, Glenn appeared on cue.

This was the kind of neighborhood where kids could play out in their yards and the street until dusk or even night fell. With the first day of school being tomorrow, though, the younger children had been called in earlier than usual and even the older ones were being summoned to take baths and lay out their clothes for morning. Niall heard complaints. Kids called goodbye to friends; garage doors rolled down.

Niall of all people knew the town wasn't as innocent as it appeared, or as safe. Domestic abuse happened behind some of these doors. There were parents who were drunks. A few of these good folks had committed petty theft or had embezzled from an employer. Marriages were breaking up, affairs were happening. But mostly these were decent people.

Drifting behind Glenn, Niall felt intense anger at the threat to this peaceful community. This anger was personal, different than it usually was

JANICE KAY JOHNSON

327

when he worked the street or pursued a case. Somewhere along the way, he'd started to feel more like a father than a cop when he thought about a pedophile targeting kids in his own neighborhood.

In the deeper shadow of some shrubbery, Glenn veered off the sidewalk. Niall walked faster. Staley had stopped at this same house last night and been thwarted.

He was tonight, too.

Ditto the second house. Sticking close to him now, Niall slid silently from one bit of cover to another. The moon was behind clouds tonight, but Glenn passed briefly under the yellow light of a streetlamp. He strolled like anyone taking a walk; even lifted a hand to a man who was wheeling his kid's bike into the garage.

Niall didn't let anyone at all see him.

Another patch of darkness, and once again Glenn cut across a lawn. It helped that this time Niall knew where he was going. The son of a bitch had a route. Maybe several, but with no luck last night on this one, he'd decided on a rerun.

Not quite like the ones Donna was watching at home.

Tonight, the boy's window was a golden square. Nobody had pulled blinds or curtains yet.

Crouched by the foundation, Niall felt shrubbery quiver as Glenn pushed behind it.

A woman's voice within rose. "Eddie, are you ready for bed yet?"

"Almost."

There was a faint scratching sound. Recognizing it and repelled—the creep had pulled down his zipper—Niall lifted the digital camera he'd been wearing around his neck. He thumbed the On button. Yeah, he was going to enjoy scaring this bastard.

He stepped closer until he was on the edge of the square of light. Practically on top of Glenn. Glad he couldn't see him. The next sounds were bad enough, soft, but he recognized them, too.

Still Niall waited. He was going for complete humiliation. Pants down, wet semen.

It didn't take Glenn long. A rush of air, a grunt, and Niall moved. He flipped on his flashlight, snapped a photo, shoved aside the stiff, spiny branches of some foundation planting, and pressed his elbow and forearm between Glenn's shoulder blades.

"Police," Niall said loudly. "You're under arrest."

He convulsed and started to spin, but Niall shoved him against the house. "Hands on the wall," he ordered, applying more pressure against the bastard's spine. Slowly, Glenn complied.

Inside the boy squeaked, "Mommy! There's someone out there!"

A woman appeared in the window.

"Police," Niall repeated. "Ma'am, open the window."

She wrestled the old-fashioned wooden sash window up. "Who are you?"

"Ma'am, please call 9-1-1. Tell the dispatcher Detective MacLachlan requests immediate uniformed backup at this address."

She was staring at Glenn, highlighted in the flashlight. "He was looking in the window?" she whispered. "Oh, my Lord." She abruptly disappeared.

"You?" Glenn blustered. "Listen to me. She puts on a good act, that daughter-in-law of mine, but she's a slut. Think with your head. I heard a noise over here and thought there might be a hurt animal. I'm an important man in this town—"

"You shouldn't insult a nice lady. The mother of your grandkids." Cuffing him was a pleasure, although Niall was careful to confine his touch to Glenn's forearms and wrists. He didn't like knowing where those hands had been.

Pulled away from the house, Staley couldn't keep his pants from dropping. He hobbled a few steps; they went down around his ankles. Niall was glad the boxer shorts stayed up. The additional photo he took now was plenty effective anyway.

To kill the time, Niall recited him his rights, but he'd have the arriving officers Mirandize him again. This slimy bastard wasn't getting any wriggle room.

A man came thundering out of the house carrying a flashlight of his own in one hand and a baseball bat in the other. Glenn turned his face away from the harsh light, groaned and fell to his knees, head bowed and hands cuffed behind his back.

"What in the hell is going on?" the man asked roughly.

Niall had holstered his weapon. Now he held out his shield. "Detective MacLachlan. Had you heard that we had a Peeping Tom in the area?"

"Yes, but—" The man looked toward his son's window and swore. "He was looking at my boy?"

As the man's voice rose to a roar, Niall stepped in front of Staley to prevent any trouble. "I'm afraid I can't let you lay hands on him, sir." Tempting though it was to let him.

A siren cut through the quiet of the night. Within moments a squad car pulled to the curb, lights flashing rhythmically.

"Over here," Niall called, and looked down at his quarry, who was hunched over, weeping. His legs looked skinny and shockingly white.

Niall felt no pity at all.

ROWAN POUNCED ON THE PHONE when it rang. Most people didn't call this late. Her heart drummed when she saw Niall's cell number.

"Yes?" she blurted. "I mean, hello?"

"I promised to let you know as soon as I made the arrest," he said, sounding calm. "It's done. We're at the station right now booking him."

Dizzy, she fumbled her way to the nearest chair and sank onto it. "It was really him? Glenn?"

"Yes."

"You caught him looking in some little boy's bedroom window." The idea was still horrific, unthinkable.

"I caught him doing more than that," Niall said grimly. "He was masturbating, Rowan. His pants were around his ankles when I cuffed him. There's not an excuse in the world that he can come up with to get himself out of this one."

She closed her eyes. "Poor Donna. Poor Drew. I wish he'd told me."

"Drew wasn't the only victim." His voice was hard, all cop. "And Donna must have willfully blinded herself to what this SOB was doing. Don't feel sorry for her."

"Have you told her yet?"

"I'm heading over there next."

She asked what would happen; he said once

the paperwork was done Glenn would be trans-
ported to the county jail.

"He'll doubtless be out by morning, but his life
is never going to be the same. I'm guessing he'll
lose his job."

"They'll move," she said. "I can't imagine
they'll stay here in Stimson."

"No. I'll be keeping tabs on them, though.
Wherever they go, I'll call the local police department. I'd rather see his ass in prison. Inmates
aren't real fond of child molesters. But first of-
fense, getting off by peeking in a window, he's
going to slide by without any time." Disgust un-
derlay every word. "His attorney will bargain for
counseling."

"I wonder if Donna will leave him."

"Think how much she'd have to admit to herself if she did that. Is she capable of it?"

Rowan was shaking her head before he fin-
ished. "No. No. She'll convince herself that
he was…I don't know. Concerned because he
thought he saw someone else looking in the
window? Or that you set him up? But something.
Whatever he tells her, because that's what she
does."

"Yeah, that's my take, too." His voice changed,
became gentle. "You don't have to worry about
them anymore, Rowan. They're out of your life.
Out of the kids' lives."

She was shivering, she realized with astonishment. Shock. A part of her had believed that Glenn and Donna had no grounds to take her children from her, but she'd been more frightened than she'd known. She was so flooded with emotion she wasn't sure she could speak. It wasn't only relief, either. She was angry, so angry. Mostly for Drew, but she couldn't help wondering what he would think if he was here. How he'd react. Had he, too, become so steeped in denial he'd defend his father? What would the shame have done to him? He might have wanted to move *his* family, too.

Right now she wished her name wasn't Staley, but she would hold her head high. It was lucky the kids were so young. Their classmates wouldn't know anything about this.

"Thank you," she said. "Niall…" She had to swallow.

"I was doing my job." He sounded brusque. "I told you. I don't want your thanks." She heard muffled voices. "I have to go. Good luck with tomorrow."

Tomorrow? Setting down the phone, she had trouble recalling what made tomorrow any different from today.

School. The first day, of course, for Anna, Desmond *and* her. She'd be helping in a third-grade classroom this year. It was a fun age and she'd been looking forward to it. Lately she'd begun to dream about going back to college to get her teaching certificate, but it would have to wait until the kids were older, more independent.

Was Donna already wondering why her husband wasn't yet back from his evening walk? Was she getting a little bit scared? Rowan took a long, shuddering breath. Despite everything, she did feel sorry for her.

WHAT LITTLE SLEEP ROWAN had wasn't restful. She woke in the morning unable to hold on to her dream, but knowing it had been unpleasant. Anna and Desmond were both subdued at breakfast and during the drive to school. Anna clung to her as they walked Des to his classroom. He wasn't scared, not like last year when she'd dropped him off for the first day of kindergarten. After all, he already had friends, including Zeke, in this class. The fact that he was quiet told her he was nervous, though.

Outside the cheerfully decorated door, he stopped. "You'll be here when school lets out, right?"

They'd gone over this already, but Rowan had expected it. "Right. Remember, I have bus duty, so you need to walk down to Mrs. Sanchez's classroom and wait for me there. Okay?"

"Okay." He knew where that was. His thin

chest expanded. "Don't forget we have soccer practice today."

She smiled and gave him a hug. "I won't."

He returned the hug but then he backed away hastily. Already he was getting to the age when guys didn't want their friends to see them doing mushy stuff with their moms. Then he turned and walked into his classroom, with his brand-new backpack and his cowlick sticking up.

"Well." Dumb to feel teary. "Let's get you to your school, kiddo."

"I wish you were staying, Mommy." Anna's eyes were big and scared. "Can't you stay, just today?"

"You know I can't, but I'm only a block away. See, there's my classroom right there." They stopped for Anna to take another look. The buses hadn't yet arrived, but a few kids had filtered in and the teacher Rowan assisted, Mrs. Sanchez, was greeting each at the door.

"Anna," she said, beaming. "Isn't this exciting? I can hardly wait until you're in my class."

The preschool was in an old house down the street from the elementary school. It was rather gaudy, painted turquoise with a bright red front door. There were two classrooms, one for the three-year-olds, one for four-year-olds like Anna. The fenced backyard held an array of climbers and forts as well as picnic tables for outside activities. Rowan greeted Anna's teacher. Conscious of the ticking clock, still she lingered while her daughter shyly joined the group.

Once she'd made it to work, a day she'd looked forward to now felt interminable. Rowan felt as if her mind had split into several screens, too many for the monitor to display at once.

Please let Anna be making friends. Rowan had the semihysterical thought that it was lucky she'd enrolled her; what if she'd been counting on Donna to babysit this year, like last year?

Rowan had heard good things about Des's teacher, but that didn't mean he'd be right for her son. Desmond was so bright and confident, he didn't always wait his turn to speak and he didn't think twice about arguing even with adults if he thought he was right. Some teachers would squelch him.

Was Glenn already home, or had he had to appear in a courtroom downtown? Did they take a mug shot of him? Did he feel any shame at all?

Niall had sounded so distant at the end of their conversation last night. Her fault. She'd been distant with him when he brought Desmond home. She should have asked him to dinner.

What if *he* decided he was done with *her?* What if that's what his distant tone had meant? What if it was too late for her to change her mind?

"Mrs. Staley." An arm in the air waved insistently. "Mrs. Staley, I have to sharpen my pencil."

"Didn't Mrs. Sanchez ask that you make sure you have at least three pencils sharpened so you don't have to get up during an assignment?"

The girl had a winning smile and a whine Rowan suspected would wear on her nerves by the end of the year. "Yes, but I didn't know that until today, so I only had one. And see?" She held up her pencil with the tip snapped off.

Rowan sighed and let her go to the sharpener.

At lunch, she spotted Des in the cafeteria, sitting at a table between Zeke and a boy who'd been in his class last year. He was eating his fruit leather and the three were wrestling in that way boys seemed to do, like puppies. He wasn't even looking for her. Reassured, Rowan dismissed the Desmond screen and wondered how Anna's day was going. At least there hadn't yet been a desperate call from the preschool.

Bus duty was a nightmare, as it was every year on the first day of school. Even some of the older kids were confused over which bus they were supposed to ride. Rowan helped her third graders, then pitched in with the teachers and aides trying to get the littlest kids on the right buses.

Both Anna and Des were hyper on the way home, eager to tell her *everything*.

"And then Zeke said…"

"Mommy, I can read! I read all the colors on the board…"

"I got a big bruise on my knee during recess." Des sounded satisfied rather than distressed. "It doesn't really hurt, though."

"I don't wanna go to Des's soccer practice. It's *boring*."

Rowan almost groaned. She didn't wanna go, either. Could she drop him and leave?

Not for the first practice. He'd be hurt if she didn't stay and watch. Then dinner, cleaning the kitchen, supervising homework—Des was sure to have some. Baths.

The neverending day.

She imagined a time when she could drop her son off at soccer practice and count on Niall to pick him up. When he'd kiss her hello the moment he walked in the door, his eyes warm on her face. When he'd be there to help referee dinner table conversation, baths, tucking kids in. When she could look forward to talking to him after Des and Anna were asleep.

Going to bed with him.

Her heart cramped with longing.

So easy to dream only because he'd said, *I want to try?* Because he'd offered to pick Des up from practice sometimes?

Yes.

It was nearly six o'clock when they got home.

Rowan's disappointment was acute at seeing the empty space where Niall's car should have been parked.

It wasn't as if she'd planned to invite him to dinner, she told herself sturdily. She wasn't sure the leftover lasagna would have stretched that far even if she'd wanted to.

They'd barely walked in the door when the phone rang.

"Put your stuff away," Rowan told the kids. "Dinner won't take long." Then she picked up the phone. "Hello?"

"How could you do this to us?"

So much pain and fury filled the voice, Rowan took a few seconds to recognize it.

"Donna."

"Was this the price you charged to get that man in your bed?" The accusation had to have come from Glenn. "All you ever wanted was to take our grandchildren away from us."

Rowan felt sick. "That's not true."

"Don't you have any shame? Our son loved you."

Her stomach roiled, but a banked coal of anger in her chest ignited. "Yes, he did. He loved me enough to tell me he'd been sexually molested as a boy. He loved *you* too much to ever try to bring his own father to justice, but I know the last thing in the world Drew would have wanted was to see you and Glenn raising Desmond. If there's any shame here, it's Glenn who should be feeling it." *Oh, God, I never meant to say that.* "Please don't call here again, Donna," she said, voice shaking, and hung up the phone.

And then she heard a noise and whirled to see her son standing in the kitchen doorway staring at her.

"Was that...was that Grandma?"

Desperately she wondered how much he'd heard.

"Yes." She hesitated, then went to the table and sat down. "Is Anna still upstairs?"

He hadn't moved. "Uh-huh."

"Come here, honey." He rushed to her, and she lifted him, still so slight, her little boy, not that grown-up yet, into her arms. She hugged him hard. "I told you that you wouldn't be seeing Grandma and Grandad anymore."

He drew back slightly. "Yes, but...*why?*"

Niall, where are you when I need you?

How much dared she tell a six-year-old? Surely he didn't need to know that it was his own grandfather looking in his bedroom window?

"I made a mistake moving in with your grandparents," she said, almost steadily. "Your daddy loved them, but he was angry with Grandad about things that happened a long time ago. I know he didn't want you to spend much time with Grandad."

"What kind of things?" Trust Des not to accept vague allusions.

"Things you're not old enough to understand," Rowan said firmly. She tried never to lie to her children, but this was a truth he didn't need to learn until he was much older. Perhaps never.

He thought about that. "Does Niall know?"

"Yes. But he isn't going to tell you, either."

He gusted a sigh, but his body had relaxed. "Will you tell me someday?"

Absurdly, she found herself smiling. "Maybe."

"Okay." He squirmed out of her lap. "I'm awful hungry."

"And I haven't even started dinner. I'll hurry," she promised. "Did you wash your hands? If you have, you can help."

He feigned reluctance but agreed. Rowan reheated the lasagna in the microwave, then the garlic bread, too. Settled for frozen peas, quickly warmed on the stove, as the token vegetable. She kept listening for Niall's car, but not until she was tucking the kids in did she hear it.

"Niall's home," Des said sleepily.

She kissed him. "Sounds like it," she agreed, as if she didn't care at all. But she did.

The promised rain had held off, but when she stepped out onto the back porch, she saw that it was now drizzling. She shivered a little, but sat down on the glider anyway. Tonight she left her porch light on, hoping he'd see her. Knowing that even if he did, he probably wouldn't come over.

Rowan was chilled and about ready to give up when Niall came out of his cottage and crossed the yard.

"You're cold," he said, frowning at her when he climbed the steps.

"Only a little."

He couldn't sit on his step, which was already wet. Instead, he came all the way onto the porch and leaned one broad shoulder against a post. That placed him only a few feet away, looming over her.

"Was this an invitation?"

"Yes. I wondered what happened."

"Pretty much what I predicted." His voice was expressionless. "He was out by midday. Furious, trying like hell to explain why it looked like he'd been jacking off in front of a kid's bedroom window, but stumbling over the fact that we had digital photos."

"Donna called."

Without looking up, she knew he'd straightened and taken a step closer. "What did she say?"

Rowan crossed her arms, more because of the chill inside her than the one outside. "She said all I ever wanted was to take their grandchildren away from them. She thought I should be ashamed of myself."

He crouched in front of her, but didn't touch her. "You know better."

"Yes." She made herself look at him. "Niall, I think she knew. Even though she'll never admit it."

"Probably."

"Desmond heard part of what I said."

Niall swore.

She told him what she'd said, and ached because she loved his smile.

"So he thought he'd bypass you and get the answers from me."

"Kids do that. Play one par..." Aghast, she stopped. They stared at each other.

"Play one parent off against the other," he said softly.

"I didn't mean..."

"Same principle."

"He's...grown very attached to you."

"I have to him, too."

"You've done it again. Rescued us."

He made an inarticulate sound and rose to his feet.

She tilted her head back. "Were you just doing your job?"

Niall's eyes looked almost black. She had no

idea what he was thinking. The seconds hung heavy as she waited.

"No," he said finally.

She waited. That was it. *No.*

"Then…why?" she whispered.

Again Niall hesitated. At last, one side of his mouth tilted up in an almost smile. "Because I'm in love with you, Rowan." His voice was gravelly. Rueful. "I love you. You and your kids. Keeping you safe matters to me."

Her ability to speak seemed to have seized up. She wasn't even sure she could breathe.

His face again became impassive. "Think about it. That's all I can ask of you."

Before she could manage a word, he nodded and left her. While she still sat there frozen, he crossed the lawn, went into his cottage and turned off the porch light.

Rowan let the glider come to a stop.

He loves me.

He'd said it and walked away.

How could she be both elated and terrified at the same time?

CHAPTER SIXTEEN

MIDMORNING, DUNCAN stopped by Niall's desk. "Good work."

"Thank you." Niall felt damn good about this arrest, better than he did about closing many murder investigations. Sad to say, he could respect the motives of some killers more than he could Glenn Staley's.

"You mentioned what the fan would be wafting my way."

Niall raised his eyebrows.

"The bank president has already called." Duncan smiled. "Unfortunately for Staley, Mr. Seversen has a five-year-old grandson."

"Good. Did he fire the scumbag?"

"Apparently it wasn't necessary. Staley resigned."

"Good," he said again.

"Rowan okay?"

"Yes. Her mother-in-law called to accuse her of framing Glenn, but Rowan dealt with it."

"Had she really convinced herself?"

"Rowan thinks she knows, but she's too entrenched in her life and the decisions she's made to do anything but stay committed to her husband."

"At least you'll have your evenings to yourself again," Duncan said before leaving.

Niall didn't want his evenings to himself. Hunting the Peeping Tom had given him a focus. He no longer looked forward to solitary hours in the cottage, once his refuge. Now he was more likely to be hovering by the window, hoping Rowan or one of the kids would come outside, wondering what they were doing if they stayed in.

He wished he had the slightest idea what she felt about his declaration. The way she'd gaped hadn't given him a clue. Did she believe him? Believe him but not trust him?

If she didn't want him to love her, if she didn't feel anything like that for him, he'd probably embarrassed her. Niall hadn't meant to tell her like that, or to tell her at all yet. He should probably have said something like "I care about you and the kids." That was more in line with what he'd intended, which was to hang around for weeks, maybe months, steady and faithful, not flinching from emotional intimacies. If any happened.

Now... Hell. He had no idea what to expect. And his instinct was to avoid her. Put off dealing with any repercussions.

He winced.

He was daunted by what he felt and, more, by what it meant. Heart-pounding, night sweats scared. But he had begun to believe he could do this. That loving Rowan, being worthy of her trust, was powerful enough to keep him on a path he'd never intended to walk.

The irony didn't escape him that he hadn't ever expected to trust a woman enough to commit to her, but what it had come down to in the end was proving himself worthy of *her* trust.

IF YESTERDAY HAD BEEN interminable, today was worse. Unending? But it wasn't really; bells did ring, recesses and lunch came and went, and eventually Rowan had collected both her children, and they were driving home.

"Can we have pizza tonight?" Desmond begged. "Or go to McDonald's?"

No soccer practice, thank goodness.

She wanted to see Niall. "Maybe," she said. "Let's go home, you can do your homework, Des, and let me think about it. Okay?"

"Okay. Maybe Niall can come."

Out for cheeseburgers. With a four-year-old and a six-year-old. Not quite the venue she'd imagined for her next meeting with him.

"He probably won't be home."

Astonishingly, he was. Or maybe he'd come

home long enough to get his motorcycle. No, it was there, too. Her heart thudded.

Desmond had already unhooked his seat belt and was scrambling out. "I bet he'd go play soccer with me."

Doubts assailed her. Niall's "I love you" didn't necessarily mean what she wanted it to mean. Why would he want to take on two kids who weren't his? Did he realize how all-consuming a family was? She pictured him the way he so often was—aloof, guarded—and couldn't imagine. But then she remembered how he was with the kids and hoped. These ups and downs were worse than a roller coaster. The one time she'd ridden on one, she'd screamed on the downward swoops, but sat frozen with fear, hands clenched on the bar, as the cars clank, clank, clanked their way skyward. Her knees had been so wobbly when she stumbled off at the end of the ride, she'd sworn she would never get on a ride like that again.

She'd sworn she would never get involved with a man again, too, but look at her.

She was still helping Anna extract herself from the car seat when the gate opened, Sam burst out barking and Niall came behind him to greet Desmond, who immediately launched into telling his hero about the first two days of school and soccer practice.

"Coach said I'm a really good goalie. He said if I want to I can play goalie in games. Did you know goalies wear pads and a different color shirt than everyone else?"

Laughing, Niall answered Des's questions, but his gaze met hers over her son's head. She was breathless when she grabbed her purse and Anna's pack.

He was here. What did that mean?

"You're home early," she said oh, so casually, as she dodged one of Super Sam's happy lunges.

"Yeah, I was hoping to make it to one of Desmond's practices, but he says it's tomorrow."

"Can you come tomorrow instead?" Des's disappointment was plain. "I'd really like it if you were there."

Niall gave his shoulder a squeeze. "I'll try. You know I'm a police officer. If someone commits a crime, I can't always leave work when I want to."

"Like if somebody gets killed," her son said with relish. "'Cuz you're a detective and that's what detectives do, right?"

"Yeah, or if someone robs a bank or steals a whole lot of money or…" He was obviously sifting through the possibilities for ones suitable for a child's ears. Rape wasn't, and maybe not kidnapping, after what had happened with Glenn and Donna. "Big crimes," he concluded. "I don't give tickets for speeding or arrest teenagers for shoplifting a candy bar." He grinned. "I'm too important for that."

"Yeah!" Desmond bounced. "Can we go play soccer?"

"Homework…" Rowan began.

Her son looked aghast. "But I can do *that* when it's dark."

Niall waited. The expression in his eyes was patient and tender and hungry, all at the same time. Or it was all in her head, and she didn't want to believe that?

"Fine," she said, and smiled at Anna. "What say we go to the playground instead, pumpkin?"

"Yeah!"

Desmond danced toward the house to get his soccer ball, but turned part way. "Mom said maybe we'd go out to dinner. Anna and me want McDonald's, right, Anna? But Mom said maybe pizza. And she said you probably wouldn't be home, but you are, so do you want to come?"

Niall looked at her.

"We'd love to have you come." Like she could have said anything else.

"Would you?" he murmured, and she knew he was really asking.

It took some courage to answer. "Yes," she said firmly.

He smiled. "It's a date."

A weird one, she thought half an hour later as she pushed her daughter on the merry-go-round. Niall had gone off to the school with Desmond, while she and Anna walked the other direction to the small city park.

Once she got the merry-go-round spinning so fast Anna was chortling, she leaped on and clung herself, quickly becoming dizzy.

He'd come home early to spend time with her and her kids. Not for the first time, she realized. Giddy, laughing as she and Anna spun, Rowan knew she'd made her decision.

The two of them got home first, time for her to think about changing clothes and realize that, no, she couldn't without occasioning comment from her ever-inquisitive son.

When Des and Niall arrived, she learned she'd been out-voted. Burgers it was.

"I suppose you eat fast food a lot," she said to Niall while they waited in line.

He shrugged. "More when I was a patrol officer. Now I try for something better. I even take my lunch when I expect to be at my desk most of the day."

"You brown-bag it."

He flashed a grin. "Yep. Peanut butter and jelly sometimes."

"And a juice box?"

"You kidding? I'd have to make the straw poke through that tiny hole."

"And you know this…how?"

"Because Anna made me do it for her one day. I came closer to failing than I want to admit."

Rowan was laughing when they stepped up to order. How long had it been since she felt so happy? *Please let him mean what he seems to be promising.*

As usual, the kids dominated the conversation while they ate, but Niall didn't seem to mind. He also carefully removed the pickles from Anna's cheeseburger for her. And he managed to look as if he was having a good time. Was it possible?

They'd taken her car because of the child seats. He didn't seem to mind being a passenger. "I admit I'm not usually a good one. Most cops aren't. But you're a careful driver. I haven't slammed my foot to the floorboard yet," Niall said when she asked him about that.

She accelerated just to scare him and he laughed.

At home she said, "Homework now for you, Des, and, Anna, you get the first bath."

"Mo-om," they both whined, pro forma.

Niall grabbed Anna to steady her when Sam launched an assault. "I'm going to be taking my shower right now, too, Anna Banana," he said.

She frowned. "I don't like showers, 'cuz I don't like water in my face."

"Hey." His face brightened. "You haven't gotten sick since they took out your tonsils, have you?"

Rowan smiled. "Nope."

"Which means we can teach you to swim pretty soon, and then you won't be scared to have your face in the water anymore."

We. Such a tiny word to promise so much.

Rowan had never hated so much for an evening to end. She knew she'd never have the nerve to go sit out later on her glider unless he said something.

"Say good-night to Niall," she ordered the kids, shutting the gate behind them.

"Good night!" They both raced for the house, Sam at their heels.

"Rowan." Niall's gravelly soft voice stopped her.

She turned, and there was that expression again, the one that made her pulse skip.

"Will you come out later?"

"If...if you want."

"I want," he said, low and forceful.

"I do, too," she whispered, and saw his face change.

"Damn it, Rowan..."

She gave him a cheeky grin and hurried after

her children. So much was going on inside her, but most amazing was to feel *playful*. She hadn't in…forever. Not like this.

Rowan supervised homework, baths and bedtime, then lurked until she felt confident both kids were asleep. When she finally slipped outside, night had already fallen and she discovered a first: Niall was waiting for her.

He pulled her into his arms before the screen door had closed behind her. "I thought you'd never get here," he groaned, and his mouth came down on hers.

They kissed deeply, intensely, straining together. She felt his arousal, but sensed as well that, right this minute, his need for her wasn't all sexual any more than hers for him was.

When he finally lifted his head, his eyes were dark as they searched hers. "Does this mean you'll give me another chance?"

"Yes. Of course it does." She swallowed. "Only…" How could she not ask? "A chance at what?" Her cheeks heated. "I mean, I'm not sure what you have in mind besides…you know."

His laugh was husky, the hands that framed her face gentle. "Lots of 'you know.' Rowan." He shook his head. "I told you I love your kids, too. Did you think I was hoping you'd sneak out every night for hot sex?"

"You saw tonight what my life is like. It's not

very exciting or…or romantic. You're…you could probably have any woman you wanted," she said, even more embarrassed.

That earned her another laugh. "What gave you that idea? But I'm glad you think so, because it means you find me irresistible."

She bit her lip. "Yes."

"Good," he whispered against her ear. He nibbled on her lobe. "Rowan, I won't push you. I haven't given you any reason to trust me."

"What?" She pushed away. "You've been here, right here, every single time we've needed you."

"Except when I was freaking out because falling in love wasn't in my life plan."

"Except then. But you've changed your mind. Right? Oh, heavens." She buried her hot face against Niall's chest. "I sound exactly like Desmond."

"Yes, you do. And the answer is…right. Rowan." He waited until she lifted her face. "I can't swear I won't screw up. I'm scared. I can't lie to you. It might take me a long time to get over being scared."

"Scared of what?"

He hesitated. "Can we sit down?"

She nodded, took his hand and led him to the glider. Another first: he'd never sat with her, holding her hand, letting her set the pace. It was as if he'd made a conscious decision to eliminate all the distance between them.

She let him take his time. "You know my background," he said finally. "Parents that fought a lot, who were so absorbed in their own troubles they couldn't spare any energy for us kids. Did I ever tell you I stole a car once? I was in and out of juvie half a dozen times. It took me a long time to realize that Conall and I were lucky Mom decided to ditch us. If she hadn't, we'd have kept getting in trouble. Worse and worse trouble."

"I can't believe that of you."

"Believe it." For a moment, his voice was harsh. His fingers tightened on hers, then relaxed. "Duncan, he was our saviour. But I didn't see it that way then. Mom walking out on us... I guess she left me thinking I couldn't trust anyone, and I wasn't big on trust even before that. Duncan had to be tough on me to get me to turn my life around. We'd been close when we were younger, but when he became the authority figure, that changed."

"What about your younger brother?"

"Conall has never been close to anyone. I'm not sure he knows how to be."

It chilled her that this man, who had so much trouble himself with intimacy, saw his brother as incapable of any meaningful relationship. Was that true?

He moved his shoulders in that way Rowan knew meant he was uneasy. "Duncan told me the other day that he loved me. I can't remember anyone ever saying those words to me before."

"Oh, Niall." She turned and reached for him. Holding hands suddenly wasn't enough. She wanted to hold *him*.

He didn't wait for her to say, "I love you." Instead, he went on, cheek pressed to the top of her head. "I told him I loved him, too. It was unbelievably awkward. Guys don't say that."

"You did to me."

"But you're a woman." Was he smiling? She thought she could hear it in his voice. "That's different. We don't say it to each other."

"Okay," she said doubtfully. "I'll take your word for it. I don't have brothers."

"Trust me. But here's what I'm working my way around to. I realized how far Duncan and I have come. We're friends again. It happened so gradually I didn't really notice. The big change was when he met Jane. I don't think he'd ever imagined getting married, having kids, the whole deal, either. Only there he was doing it, and damned if he wasn't happy." He still sounded bemused at the idea. "It made him more—I don't know—open."

"Vulnerable."

There was a pause. Another word guys didn't use?

"Yeah," he finally said. "Anyway, when things changed for him, they changed for me, too. And then I met you."

She pulled back from him, wanting to see his face. "I'm pretty ordinary-looking."

Smiling, if crookedly, Niall shook his head. "Not to my eyes. But it isn't only looks, you know. It's…your gentleness and patience, your smile. It's the fact that you're a great mother, that you worry about other people, that you're fierce in defense of Desmond and Anna."

The emotions were so sharp, she wasn't sure she could speak, but she did, her voice husky but audible. "I'll be fierce in defense of you, too. I love you, Niall. I do."

"God," he whispered. "When you said you'd had enough…" He stopped, the tension in his body speaking for him.

"I was scared, too."

"I know this isn't easy for you. I meant it when I said I wouldn't push. I don't blame you if you need time to believe in me. Time for the kids to get used to the idea, too."

That made her laugh, a miracle when her eyes were damp and her chest squeezed with love. "Get used to the idea?" She lifted her head.

"Niall, they're crazy in love with you, too. Haven't you noticed? All I hear is Niall this, Niall that. Des wants you to go to soccer practices and games with him so bad."

"He misses his dad."

"Yes, but that's not it entirely. Drew did love him, but Desmond was still a preschooler. It wasn't the same. Now he's a boy, and he sees the other boys have dads. He picked you, pretty much on sight."

Niall had relaxed again. His hands moved up and down her back, lingering to explore here and there. "So I've been targeted." He sounded amused.

"Definitely." She nuzzled his throat, expecting him to drop the conversation and kiss her again. But he didn't.

Instead, he rubbed his cheek against her head. Beside her, his thigh muscle bunched as he pushed to set the glider into motion again. Setting the pace.

"What about you?" he said finally, voice a little deeper. "Do you need time?"

Did she? Rowan struggled to be honest with herself. Was she afraid that he'd hurt her physically?

The answer was a resounding no.

What if she threw herself headlong into this, and then she said or did something that struck too deep and left Niall feeling too vulnerable? What if he went all distant on her? Did she believe he'd get over it? That he did love her, even if there would be moments he might not be able to fight his need to retreat to some state of self-sufficiency?

She made a little sound and his arms tightened.

Yes. Oh, yes. No matter what, he'd been there when she needed him. Home and marriage and family might not be easy for him, but she did believe he would always be there when she needed him. As she wanted to be there for him.

"No. I don't need time."

He kissed her again. "I've been living for moments like this. Do you know how pathetic I felt, lurking behind the window hoping I'd see you out here? Or one of the kids would give me an excuse to come out? I don't want to be out here waiting anymore. I want to be in there with you."

Now tears did burn her eyes, but she smiled, too. "I want you there, too."

"Will you marry me?"

She grinned at him. "What do you think?"

"I think we should put flowers on Enid's grave every Sunday for the rest of our lives."

WEDDINGS WERE FOR WOMEN. Everyone knew that. Guys showed up, stood where ordered, spoke their lines and hoped they weren't screwing up in some way their wife would remember and throw at them for the rest of their lives.

Niall was embarrassed by how amazing he felt on his wedding day. How much he wanted this.

It wasn't a huge, formal occasion, although they did get married in the church. A surprisingly large percent of the Stimson police force had come. Duncan was at Niall's side, Jane looking seriously pregnant in the front pew. She beamed at him as if she'd had something to do with him being up here.

Maybe she had, in a cosmic sense.

Desmond was at his side, too, cute in a brand-new suit bought for the occasion. He had the rings, a responsibility he was taking seriously.

Anna was the flower girl, wearing a peach-colored dress with a puffy skirt, carrying a basket of rose petals she strewed unevenly down the aisle. She ran out of petals before she got to the end and stopped dead, looking confused.

"Come *on,* Anna," Des whispered loudly. Accompanied by laughs she scurried the rest of the way to join them.

They'd decided to keep this wedding in the family, so Rowan's mom was her attendant, and she was letting her dad walk her down the aisle. Dad, Niall was thankful to see, had had enough sense not to bring a girlfriend.

His knees almost buckled when his bride appeared, her eyes on him. No veil, but she wore a long white dress and glowed. He heard a low chuckle at his side.

"Breathe," his brother murmured for his ears only.

He couldn't look away from her. She was his. A woman who made him laugh, who fired his blood, who trusted him with herself and her kids. He was still stunned at how sure *he* was that he could trust her, too.

He looked away from her only once, after she'd taken his hand and stepped to his side. Before they turned to face the pastor.

He'd thought Conall would come. He felt disappointment, but there was a spark of anger there, too, that his little brother hadn't been willing to overcome his issues enough to show.

Shaking off those useless emotions, Niall turned his back on the lost hope and focused on the future.

"Do you, Niall Alan MacLachlan, take this woman…"

Oh, yeah. He definitely did.

* * * * *

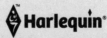